Wolves Aren't White

THE AUTHOR

I. K. Watson was born into a military family in 1947 and grew up in a succession of military quarters, being educated at St George's in Hong Kong, and St John's in Singapore. Prior to becoming a full-time writer, he worked as Head of Quality Administration for British Aerospace. In the early 1980s, he was editor of the infamous *Pin Green Chess Magazine*. He lives in Hertfordshire with his wife, Alexandra, and their two children. His first crime novel, *Manor*, was published by Allison & Busby in 1994.

Wolves Aren't White

I. K. Watson

a&b

First published in Great Britain in 1995 by
Allison & Busby
an imprint of Wilson & Day Ltd
179 King's Cross Road
London WC1X 9BZ

A catalogue record for this book is available from
the British Library.

ISBN 0 74900 256 5

Designed and typeset by N-J Design Associates
Romsey, Hampshire
Printed and bound in Great Britain by
Redwood Books, Trowbridge, Wiltshire

For Christie and Tom

ACKNOWLEDGEMENTS

I am indebted to Sue Read for permission to use some of
the background from her harrowing autobiography *Only
for a Fortnight* which, as an indictment of the state of
Britain's secure units, should be required reading for
anyone in the business of 'institutionalizing' our young
people. The shocking account of her incarceration is
soon to be a major film. Most of the good lines in
Chapter 11 come from it.

I must also thank Dr R Dugdale who provided invaluable
advice, along with copious notes and corrections, about
medical matters. Any errors that might remain are
down to me.

Finally, my daughter, Christie, gave me the jazz.
Without her this wouldn't have happened.

ONE

It wasn't raining.

If Ted Lewis were still alive you could go and tell him that it wasn't raining. He was the author of the book on which the sixties film *Get Carter* starring Michael Caine was based. It was the film that made me realize that there were gangsters in this country. Until then I thought they all lived in the States and looked like Rod Steiger. Mind you, I was only about ten years old then. My brother, Richard, ran a small cinema club in Notting Hill, and ran the X films for me and my mates. He used to let us watch the films starring Brigitte Bardot twice. I remember his surprise when I asked him to play *Get Carter* a second time. He thought it was Britt Ekland playing with herself I wanted to see again, but he was wrong. It was the violence that intrigued me. I'd never seen anything like it. It was real. People really hurt. I sat there and watched it on my own and thought that when I grew up I was going to be just like Michael Caine.

But Michael Caine couldn't play the part of Paddy Delaney. Not now. He might have done at the time he played Jack Carter but now he was too old. Delaney wasn't much more than forty. He just looked older.

It wasn't raining.

The splashes were flicking off Joe Gabriel's forehead. He was our clarinet. It was a long time since we'd seen him give his left shoulder such stick. On the long mellow breves his neck almost disappeared. Mike on the drums caught my look of appreciation and nodded in agreement.

While we finished the number, Delaney and his party were being led across the room to the best table, just about twenty yards from our platform. As far as I knew, it was the first time he had been to the club; in the old days, before he disappeared in South America, he sent one of his men around to look after the collection. I wondered if he'd come back to reclaim his crown.

I wondered what the going rate was now that he was back, just how much Peter Selvey had to cough up to stay in business. He was the owner of the club that had once been on Delaney's West End manor. A tricky little place, a couple of dozen tables, subdued lighting, smart décor – almost art nouveau, one of the top French chefs and some of the best acoustics in town. If you needed to ask the prices, you couldn't afford it. Peter himself was a jazz nut. Most nights he booked someone a bit tasty. Last night it was Scott Hamilton. Tonight you had to put up with his resident band.

To get in here you had to book at least a week in advance, even on our nights. Unless, that is, your name is Paddy Delaney. Then you get special treatment. You get Peter running around wetting himself, pulling out your chairs; you get the best champagne tinkling against ice in the silver buckets; you get the head waiter and the wine waiter lined up to serve you at the best table while everyone else waited.

And it was all on the house.

Paddy Delaney – his face was pretty well known. He had become something of a celebrity. Over the years the tabloids had carried photographs of him and we had watched him grow towards middle-age. When the public grew bored with pictures of Ronnie Biggs the Sunday supplement snappers chased after Paddy Delaney. He had always been on the fringe of showbusiness, pictured next to up-and-coming actresses, sharing meals with flaky MPs, even some from the front benches. He always looked the part, well groomed, well dressed, totally photogenic.

Then came the gold bullion robbery from a south London security depot, just about the biggest blag this country had ever known, and then just after a police surveillance officer from C-eleven was found with more holes in him than Wentworth and the search for the missing millions reached its climax, Paddy Delaney disappeared.

He surfaced in South America. Police sent out special units to interview him but without success. Extradition proceedings proved equally fruitless.

Now he was back. About two months ago he had marched through Heathrow terminal like a king returning from exile. Half of Fleet Street was there to greet him. But no kozzers. No Flying

Squad officers waiting for touch down. No plain-clothes police going aboard to lead him off in handcuffs. No overnight stay in a twelve-by-twelve in an East End nick with just a mattress and toilet bowl for company. No van laid on for the morning to rush him to Bow Street Magistrates where he would sit in the line of petty offenders and skagheads.

"Of course I'll help the police," he said, his eyes glinting in the flashbulbs. "I've got nothing to hide. I've come to spend some time and Christmas with my sister." His enigmatic smile filled the front pages of the *Mirror* under the heading 'London Mob Back in Business'.

He was back, confidence oozing, making the most of the festive season while he waited for the police to arrange the interviews. Other people, some of his old colleagues and friends, were getting a little bit nervous. We finished the number. No one listened because they were too busy watching Delaney's party settling down and getting the special treatment. There was a ripple of applause because the silence was recognized.

We called Joe Gabriel 'Clarinet'. As far as we were concerned that was his name. He spoke into the microphone.

"We're going to take a short break now. Be back in about half an hour." His voice was like a good port, tinged with smoke. He did a few vocals during the evening to give me a break, but he preferred the blow job.

The lights went off us as he turned off the amp and in the shadows we stored our kit before heading out the back, and then, unobtrusively, to the bar.

There were six of us: black suits, black ties, white shirts. I was the youngest. All the others had played around, some of them in top bands, but they were getting on now. Joe, our clarinet, you've met: pushing mid-sixty, fat, a wide friendly face, a real musician. Not so long ago he was backing up the likes of Jimmy Conway. He had survived our piss-taking after completing 'A Day In The Life Of' in *The Sunday Times* and 'The Questionnaire' in the *Guardian*. He had been interviewed on the radio by Brian Hayes on *Midweek* and been the subject of a half-hour documentary during BBC2's jazz week. Our drummer, Mike, was about ten years younger. He had come to jazz late and we had to straighten him out. He was, what some people call, a middle-aged rocker and, until he joined us, he played like one. Alan and Keith, guitar and double-bass, came from the same band so they were in tune. Cell, a skinny little man who looked like a black Frank Sinatra, played the trumpet. They'd all been put out to grass until Clarinet found me and needed some noise. Then, having got it together, they did their own gigging in various spots throughout Europe and I joined them on a regular basis.

Drinks were waiting on the bar. Clarinet lit a cigar, the rest of us cigarettes. Mike slipped a couple of Es in his rum and mixed it with a straw. The black bits of his eyes started to expand before he even raised the drink to his lips. Later, just before we went back on, he would excuse himself for a quick stone, a ten-minute high. Sometimes a dig. Cell occasionally went with him. Alan and Keith shared the odd roll of weed, Caribbean black, probably in bed, but as far as I knew Clarinet didn't use the stuff. Neither did I.

There was only one subject tonight.

"Never thought we'd see him again," Alan said. "Last I heard he was fighting off extradition. How long's he been back?"

"Not long, that's for sure." Clarinet.

"Who's Paddy Delaney?" Mike.

"A son of a bitch. He likes to hurt people. Not for money, not for anything. He just enjoys it." Clarinet. "You musta heard of him."

"Well, he's certainly got Peter running around. Peter's certainly impressed." Keith. "He's goin' to be in a right fuckin' mood tomorrow when he works out how much it's all cost."

"The cost ain't relevant when it comes to keepin' Delaney sweet." Clarinet.

"Well, how is it I've never heard of him then?" Mike asked.

Clarinet growled. "If you'da read a paper in the last ten years, maybe you woulda done. If your head wasn't so full of dope every night, maybe you woulda done."

"Oh man," Mike looked hurt. "A few bergers for the buzz, that's all."

"Yeah, them things is spiced with skag. No wonder you've been playin' like a headbanger lately."

"Listen to me, these things get your feet tappin', what's wrong with that? The smack is just like the icing on the cake."

4

Clarinet nodded thoughtfully.

"Who's the girl?" I asked.

"The girl?" He turned for another look at Delaney's table as though he hadn't noticed. "He's got a sister. Maybe that's her. He don't have girlfriends. Not unless he's changed."

"His sister? Out of bounds then, eh?"

"Not fucking much!" Clarinet said. "Even Moses couldn't part her legs, man. Not when her brother's in the same country!"

"Shame," I said and stole another glance. "How come he's back here, out in the open?"

"Who knows? Maybe he's paid somebody off."

"She's a bit tasty, though."

Clarinet grunted his disapproval. "You don' want nothin' to do with her, man," he said.

Mike said, "Cool, man," for no reason then wandered off to join the others at an empty table. I lit another cigarette from the stub of the first.

"What's he into, Delaney?"

"Was. I dunno about now. But just about everythin', I'd say. You name it, Lenny, he was into it."

"The girl?"

"His sister?"

"Married?"

"I don' know. Don' know much about her. She's always been in the background. But don' even think about it. I've heard of people gettin' stamped on for simply sayin' good mornin' to that man."

Peter Selvey appeared. He was flustered. His little pop-eyes were slipping around the room. Eventually they hung on to us, to Clarinet. He caressed his own cheek.

"Boys," he said, shaking his head. "Something special tonight, pleeease!"

"We're always special," Clarinet growled. "Just because you don't appreciate us . . . "

"No! No!" His hand left his cheek, joined his other and spread out in front of him like a butterfly. "It's his sister's fuckin' birthday. He wants you to play 'Happy Birthday'."

"He can fuck himself!" Clarinet said. "We're not a fuckin' showband, Peter. Whaddaya think this is?"

"Pleeease, boys. Just this once, indulge me. For me. I'll make it up to you."

"You mean you'll start payin' us?"

"Please? Look at me, I'm grovelling."

Clarinet smiled. "Yeah, and it's makin' me feel ill."

Peter Selvey was a skinflint. If he had been born female, he would have rolled his own Lil-lets.

"Pleeease?" he repeated.

"OK. If it's goin' to save you messing yourself, just this once."

"You can play it," I said. "I'm fucked if I'll sing it."

"If I'm goin' to play it, sonny," Clarinet said seriously. "Then you're goin' to fuckin' sing it."

He didn't have to be that serious. I would have done just about anything for him. And he knew it. His big worn boat spread into a black grin. He had found me ten years earlier, working a bar in Tottenham.

"You gotta dark brown voice, sonny," he had said to me. "Like Daddy's sauce."

I looked at him now as his grin widened to a full set, including two gold fillings.

"Yeah," I said and turned to Peter. "What's her name?"

"Eh?"

"For the 'Happy Birthday to-'"

"Oh, right. Julie. Julie Delaney."

"I'll leave out the Delaney."

Peter frowned.

The break was half an hour, enough time for three cigarettes, two pints and a short. Mine was a Scotch and one sixth of a gill didn't come in to it. Nor did twenty-five millilitres, or whatever the new measure was. The others drank white rum, maybe because they came from the tropics – or their ancestors did. I didn't. I was white. Whiter than white. I hadn't seen the sun for weeks. By the time I surfaced the sun was already slipping. The only thing that coloured my skin was the nicotine and an occasional doze under a sun lamp.

We were back on, tapping mikes. Clarinet ran through some scalar warm-ups, hitting some of the regulars right in the gut. You could see them, glasses suspended below their lips, mouths slightly open. Alan and Keith joined in with some chords. It was all to do with street cred. Before the lights came on I had a closer look at Delaney's camp.

There were eight of them around the table. It was obvious the way the others looked and listened that Delaney was in charge. In his evening suit he cut quite a figure, almost cultured, certainly not one of the Smoke's heaviest noises. His hair was cut short but styled, black and grey. His features were on the sharp side, sharp nose and jaw line, prominent cheek bones. His eyes were dark and engaging. He could have been a banker, or a Tory politician, except he had a better tan than most of them and, from where I was standing, there was no dandruff on his shoulders. The other three men were a cross section, just faces, maybe businessmen he was courting. They didn't look like villains. But who did?

The women with the businessmen seemed a little intimidated. For much of the time they remained silent, concentrating on their food. Their ages ranged from thirty to sixty but they were out of the same mould: slightly overdressed, albeit in beautiful clothes, slightly too much make-up, slightly too deliberate in their manner. They were not at ease and wanted to stay in the background.

Julie Delaney was in her mid-twenties, five eight or nine, willowy but with full hips below a tight waist. She was very pretty with a pale complexion and delicate features capped by short black wavy hair. There were definite traces of Delaney: high cheek bones, brown eyes that sometimes narrowed and questioned, and a wide mouth. Her only make-up was a touch of eyeshadow and the blood red on her lips. She wore a long white mohair dress with a side split that went on for ever and white chiselled shoes with slightly raised heels. Her jewellery consisted of hanging gold earrings and a gold bracelet. Simple style in designer labels, the sort of simplicity that costs a fortune to put together. It called you over from a hundred yards, never mind twenty.

We were ready. Clarinet gave Peter the nod.

Peter Selvey, greased black hair swept back from a polished forehead, introduced us in high pitch.

"Here they are, fresh from a successful tour of Europe where in Copenhagen they teamed up with the legendary, sadly late,

Kenny Drew." Peter swept his arm out towards us. "Pleeease welcome Joe Clarinet Gabriel and Wolves Aren't White!"

Clarinet leaned into the microphone and pointed across to me.

"That one is!" he shouted and the spotlight slid my way.

It was banter, expected, and some of the regulars applauded. It was party time.

As he spoke into the mike, Clarinet sounded like a bag of chipped gravel being run over by a Merc.

"We're gonna get rollin' with a little number from Hot Lips Page, 'Just Another Woman'," he said, and started blowing.

I took two steps to the front of the small platform, exhaled some smoke and came in a bit late. I still sounded pretty good; I knew that much. Everybody looked up, including Delaney's sister. Eye-contact was important; the women loved it. The singer could be a dog, but while he was up there, and if he had an OK voice, he was a celeb, something to be looked at.

She was staring. Her eyes were right through me. Dark Delaney eyes. They weren't appreciative, they were too narrow for that.

Clarinet went straight into Christie Watson's 'NHS'. It had a long intro and I stood back while he scored on another breve, eight after eights that had most of the people in the room holding their breath. When he paused on another D you could hear the tinkle of ice in a glass of malt. His little quiver reminded me of an early Ornette Coleman.

I came in low with a thirty-a-day throat.

"We're fighting disease and politicians . . . This isn't what Nye Bevan had in mind . . . "

We made eye contact. It lasted about two seconds longer than it should have done.

"Are you fuckin' mad?" Clarinet said once the number was finished.

"Me?"

"Yeah, can you see anyone else in here who's certifiable?"

"What are you talking about?"

"Don't fuck with me, sonny. You were givin' her the come on, man. I saw it and your back was to me."

I put up my palms.

"Don't mess with him, I'm tellin' you."

"It was just a bit of fun."

"He hasn't got a sense of humour. Believe me."

"I believe you. It's over. Shortest affair I've ever had. OK?"

"I'm warning you, sonny, for your own good. She don't exist. Don't even look at her."

"OK, OK, you've made your point."

I lit another JPS and we went into the next number and I looked everywhere and anywhere but not at the top table. It wasn't easy. On the periphery of everywhere I looked, her eyes were on me and, more than that, they were like a magnet, drawing me toward them.

Smoke lying in layers, alcohol smoothing the edges, stinging eyes and long Ds that soothed like a mouth full of menthol, something you drew in that was deep and satisfying; something dizzy about the notes, addictive almost, and you had to be made of stone if your foot didn't tap or your head didn't nod. Delaney wasn't moving; he just sat there looking dark and bored; but some of his guests were tapping and nodding and his sister was too. But then, she must have been about ten years younger than him and she probably didn't have his – what was it Clarinet had said? Son of a bitch? That'll do. She probably didn't have his son of a bitch streak.

Clarinet went into his favourite Benny Goodman and tried his 'Shirt Tail Stomp'. His tone was a bit reedy but he made it with timing. I knew he would. I retreated into the shadows and stood behind Mike.

Delaney's sister was on her feet. I could look now; out of the spots it would take infrared to find me.

She danced by herself. She moved with a feline grace, as though her body were made of rubber. As she swayed, an undulatory continuous movement, her dress clung tightly and the side split flashed acres of thigh. She watched the band in a knowing half-smile from beneath her dark fringe. It was intimate; she was a seductress. She danced well, her slender frame captured a smooth, rhythmic wave motion, as sexy as anything I'd seen in ages. Perhaps the booze had heightened my sense of exhilaration but I thought not. She was making the

9

same impression on most men in the room. Not Delaney. He didn't seem too impressed. The others at the table were smiling and swaying with her. Alcohol and the atmosphere had relaxed them. We went into 'Happy Birthday'. Most of the room joined in. When it was over we went into another break.

As I came down the two wooden steps from the stage Peter grabbed my arm.

"He wants to see you," he said earnestly.

"I'm going for a drink. It's my break."

"Pleeease," he curled up and held his hands in front of him. "For me." He looked nervously over his shoulder. Delaney was watching us. "I can't say no, can I?"

"In that case, nor can I then, Peter."

He stepped aside, relieved, and I weaved my way across to the top table. Delaney watched my approach. The others at his table hadn't noticed. The two guys sitting just behind him had. They looked like they were wearing shoulder-pads, but you knew they weren't. They were smiling at me but not humorously.

As I stepped up the conversation stopped and everyone turned my way.

"You wanted to see me, Mr Delaney," I said.

He nodded slowly. A cufflink holding together three inches of silk slid from beneath the sleeve of his hand-stitched black jacket and sparkled. His manicured hand toyed with a crystal glass. He studied me for a moment then said calmly: "If you fuck my sister, I'll tear your fuckin' throat out!"

Some people say things they don't really mean. You can tell by something in their voice. Delaney was deadly serious and I believed him. His eyes had dulled. His gaze was unyielding. At that moment I felt myself shrink about six inches and my dick disappeared altogether.

I glanced at his sister. Incredibly she remained expressionless, almost as though she hadn't heard him.

I cleared my throat to find my voice and said, "I get your drift, Mr Delaney. I wouldn't dream of hurtin' your sister, or anybody else's sister, come to think of it."

People at the closer tables turned our way. They could hear every word. I was glad of the subdued lighting and hoped it covered my embarrassment.

Slowly he lifted his drink. The cufflink glinted again, like ice.

"Who said anything about hurtin' her? I was talkin' about fuckin' her!"

The women at the table sat open-mouthed. One of them had her fork suspended between mouth and plate. It quivered. A flake of salmon fell to the plate; sauce flicked on to her white blouse, just below some pearls.

"I was talkin' about you gettin' between her legs and stickin' your dick up her hole. Fuckin'. Understand? Somethin' like you were doin' a minute ago when you were singin' 'Happy Birthday'. But for real. You looked like you were comin' and I'm sure she was too."

He turned to his sister. She remained expressionless, her lips slightly parted, her eyes on me, unblinking, not frightened, not even embarrassed. It was almost a stoned look. Maybe that was it. But I was embarrassed enough for both of us.

"I'm talkin' to you," Delaney nudged her. "As well as about you. He wants to know if you were coming? He wants to know if your cunt is wet?"

I shook my head. "I don't, really," I said. It came out nervous.

"Don't tell me what you fuckin' want, son. I'll tell you what you want around here." He turned back and glared at her. His face had flushed bringing a red rash to his cheeks. "Well? Well?"

Her tongue flicked out and turned her lips to a darker shade.

"Please don't do this," she said in almost a whisper, but it was all too natural. She didn't seem that upset.

Delaney thumped the table. Glasses jumped. The woman next to him jumped. Her fork and the rest of the salmon fell to her plate. Her white blouse was splattered with yellow sauce.

"There! What did I fuckin' tell you? I know my sister. When she doesn't answer, it means I'm fuckin' right!"

He wagged a finger. The gold ring on it was the size of a knuckle-duster.

"Fuck her and you're dead. Now, piss off back there and sing some more. That's what you're gettin' paid for!"

That extra Scotch grabbed hold of my legs and stopped them running. When I didn't move he frowned.

"You know, Mr Delaney," I said, surprised at the level tone of my own voice. "You should show your sister a little more respect.

11

And come to think of it, the other ladies around here deserve it too!" It was Michael Caine speaking through the Scotch, not me. And I knew he was making a mistake.

Now it was Delaney's turn to look open-mouthed. Eventually he nodded. "I'm going to put it down to your age, son, and pretend I was hearin' things."

"I'm an England cricket fan," I said.

"That explains it. Now, piss off before I lose my temper."

This time I was on my way.

I had a couple more Scotches during the break. I was angry, still shaking, partly through embarrassment, but loathing came into it somewhere too. Forget me for the moment. The way he had treated his sister was humiliating and disgraceful. Two or three couples close by had already left; the others who remained were suitably disgusted. Even the people at his own table were stony-faced, trying to hide their shame.

When we got back on stage and Peter had gone through his Wolves Aren't White routine and handed over to Clarinet I moved forward to meet the spot and spoke into the mike.

"Mr Delaney over there has just threatened to tear my throat out. Some of you heard him. So if my voice isn't quite up to it tomorrow night you can blame him."

They applauded, all except the top table. Delaney wasn't applauding. He wasn't even smiling. Even the girl was giving me a look that had come straight out of a bottle of Sarson's.

And Clarinet? He was cringing so much his neck had disappeared.

During the session Delaney disappeared for ten minutes. While the band went through some Charlie Parker numbers, Peter caught me at the back of the stage.

"Lenny, Lenny, what have you done to me?" He wrung his hands, laced his nervous fingers, made circular patterns in front of him. "If he tells me to sack you, Lenny, then you're history. You're outa here. Understand? It ain't personal. It's your own fault. Now, pleeease, go and apologize. Grovel a little. For me. Pleeease."

He almost pushed me toward the steps.

I reached the table just as Delaney had settled himself. I stood

12

braced, waiting for more obscenities.

"I've been told to come and apologize to you. Apparently I was out of order. I'm sorry." I looked from him to his sister. The others at the table seemed to hold their breath as they waited for a response.

Delaney took a deep breath and half stood up. His features seem to relax and I thought he was going to shake my hand. Instead, his hand swung round and he smacked his sister in the face. Her head snapped back. The surprise on her face turned to horror. Her move back continued. The chair teetered and she went over. There was a rustle of nylon and a flash of stocking tops, white legs, suspenders and blue underwear. The tablecloth dragged glasses, ashtrays and a silver candelabra with three lit candles after it.

I was too stunned to react.

Delaney shook, his face flushed to explode, his fists clenched tightly in front of him. His mouth opened and a horrible strangled sound came from deep down. He wheezed, his tongue came out like a piece of black sponge, and then the phlegm came with a cough. Black phlegm. It oozed from his mouth and dripped over his chin on to his shirt.

The woman with the salmon sauce stains fainted. Her head lolled forward and smashed a glass on the table. Her blood ran down on to the tablecloth.

Delaney reached out toward me but I stepped backwards and he crumpled and fell sideways from the chair. His two minders shoved me aside. One of them turned my way and pointed a threatening finger before he kneeled beside his friend to help his boss.

I made a speedy retreat. At the back of the stage Clarinet said, "That's what the snow does for you man!"

Mike scoffed at the idea. "Man, that wasn't snow. Listen to me. His lungs are busted open, turned to coke. He's freebasin' man. What you're seein' there is long-term crack! That reminds me . . . " He reached into his jacket and handed me an envelope. "This is for Roger. You know what I mean, man?"

I nodded and slipped it into my pocket.

"There's a monkey in there. I want my stash back for that."

"I'll tell him."

13

Peter rushed up. "What the hell did you say to him?" He poked me in the chest with a thin delicate finger.

"I apologized. What else? That's what you asked me to do, isn't it?"

We looked back. Delaney was still on the floor. The soles of his shoes faced our way. His goons were still bent over him, gently smacking his face and damping his forehead with a wet napkin. His sister was being comforted by the other guests. She held her cheek. Tears had washed mascara down both sides of her nose. Her eyes were on her brother. She seemed more concerned than hurt or angry.

"Oh Jesus!" Peter said, turning this way and that, beginning to panic.

Clarinet said, "Well I'm calling it a fuckin' night. We're not a showband, Peter. We didn't ask you to put on a fuckin' cabaret!"

TWO

I lived on my own in a second-floor flat in Bruce Grove. On match days, if the wind were coming from the west, it carried the roar from White Hart Lane. At one in the morning it took about twenty minutes to motor from the West End. I had bought the flat at two-thirds of its market value: it had been a repossession. My good fortune had come from someone else's grief. Thank you, Maggie. Whoever had lived there had obviously loved the place. None of your paint on paint. Each door frame and window, every length of skirting, had been sanded to perfection. It consisted of a large lounge, dining-room, two bedrooms, kitchen and a bathroom that you had to see to believe. A large corner bath was sunk, all the china was avocado, and the fittings gold plated.

The lounge was a mix of ideas. I didn't go for colour match or themes. Wives do that and I didn't have one anymore. I was still enjoying the freedom of being single again. That's what I kept telling myself. I was more into comfort. To hell with the looks. Some of the furniture was chintzy; some, like the coffee table, late-Georgian, and some of the stuff on the walls was borderline exotic. On the shelf above a real gas fire were two nine-inch porcelain figures of Marilyn Monroe, one with her dress blown to her waist, the other of her leaning forward in a low-cut number. I'd picked the pair up along with a nude statue of Suetonius on a stall on the Portobello. Not that I'd paid anything less than the market price; in that part of town the day of the bargain had long since disappeared. The Roman governor was now a toothbrush holder on the bathroom windowsill. The end of the brush slotted neatly into the hole vacated by his baton. Opposite the fireplace was the music stack, a combination of Japanese and German, and a small fortune tied up in recordings. The cost was really immaterial. Some of the collection was irreplaceable. There was one photograph on the sideboard: my kids, taken last year.

I had been home ten minutes and was making some coffee in the small kitchen when my front door burst open. Part of the frame cracked and flew on to the carpet. The brass Yale lock hung from the door as three screws fell to the floor. The door crashed against the hall wall as two men saw my stunned look through the open kitchen door and smiled.

I recognized them instantly. They were the two gorillas who had sat behind Delaney, the two that had moved to help him. The older of the two led the way towards me. He'd been the one who had pointed a threatening finger in the club.

Inviting them to stay for coffee wasn't on my mind. Call me unsociable. They got the kettle instead. It wasn't boiling, but it wasn't far off. The plug snapped out as I hurled it toward them. The man in front lifted his arm instinctively and the kettle glanced off his elbow. The lid flew off and the kettle, followed by a shower of hot water, hit the man behind.

"Shit!" he shouted as he tried to hold his steaming wet jacket and shirt away from his chest. The first guy caught me just as I was pulling open the door to the dining-room and about twenty stone of solid muscle pulled me back. He let go of me in the front room. The man with the water stains on his jacket had cooled down sufficiently to say: "You shouldn't have done that, Lenny. It could have given me a nasty burn!"

I saw his massive fist coming but there was nothing I could do about it. It hammered into my side and sent me right over the Georgian coffee table. One of the spindle legs snapped. The side of my head smacked against the sharp edge of a chair leg and immediately my vision misted over. Everything turned red. I thought my ribs had broken. The pain exploded into my lung so that I could barely draw a breath. For a moment I thought I would pass out.

I stayed put, on my back. Not that I could have moved had I wanted to. The older of the two men – he was about forty-five – stood over me. His voice was surprisingly calm and clear. This was just a job, nothing more than that. It wasn't personal.

"Lenny, Lenny," he said and smiled sympathetically. "In public you gotta show respect. Understand? In private it's different, eh? There you gotta show even more respect. He told us not to touch your throat, or anything that could mess with your

16

singin'. He obviously likes you!"

I tried to nod but my head banged the floor.

"You young guys have gotta remember to stay in check. You gotta remember who pays the bills, eh?"

He aimed a foot. He was wearing shiny black slip-ons, lightweight, man-made uppers. I was grateful they weren't Doc Martens, or steel toe-cap jobs. Nevertheless, he caught me just under the balls and as far as I was concerned that was the end of life. I could move to Arabia, sing in some Muslim harem. I had never known pain quite like it. It made the blow in the chest feel like a caress from Anna Ford. Not that I knew what that felt like. But she was the only one I could think of who made bad news sexy. I threw up. Three or four beers, two or three Scotches and six, seven and fourteen of a Chinese take-away created a Salvador Dali on the plain grey wall-to-wall.

"Now don't forget," the man said. "You gotta learn by your mistakes. You gotta show respect to your elders."

"I'm learnin'," I said. My voice was shaky and wet; my throat was still having trouble with the residue of some sweet and sour.

"OK then, that's the end of this lesson."

The other guy stood the other side of me. "The second lesson, Lenny," he said. "Is that you shouldn't throw kettles at me."

He smiled and let me have his boot. He was wearing Doc Marten's leather uppers.

My ex-wife's name is Donna. Her father, John Gresty, had brought his family over from the West Indies in the early sixties. Donna had been three years old and had been carried into this country in a hold-all. We had twins, one of each, who were now six years old. Four years ago we split up and two years ago she married Roger, one of the few black policemen in the Met. He was a Detective Inspector and treated my kids like his own. Three months ago Donna had her third baby, another girl. They named her Kate after Roger's mother. The new baby and her second marriage seemed to suit Donna very well. She hadn't lost all the weight she had built up during her pregnancy and had taken up a number of slimming and keep-fit classes. In my book the few added pounds looked well on her. I missed her. I still dreamed about her.

They lived in a three-bedroomed semi in a small leafy avenue in Bruce Castle, next to the park, walking distance from my flat. From the back bedroom windows they could see the massive oak tree in the centre of the green. Four years ago their house had been my home. I had dug the garden and planted some of the bushes that were now well established.

Except for her doorbell, the avenue was silent. I had been ringing it for over a minute. She turned on the porch light and drew back the hall curtain to check me out before opening the door.

She looked horrified and ushered me in.

I held a handkerchief to my forehead.

"I was right out of plasters," I said and shrugged. "Don't worry. It looks worse than it is."

I hobbled into the hall, bow-legged, stiff. Normally I wouldn't have minded stiffening up in the place it hurt the most, but this wasn't one of those times. I followed her into a bright kitchen and sat down at a pine table.

"If it didn't, you'd be in a box and some vicar who never knew you would be telling us what a wonderful husband and father you were, and from the front pew we'd all be thinking what a load of old bollocks that was!"

"That bad, eh?"

"It's bad, Lenny. What's happened to you, man?"

"I didn't know where else to come. I still think of this place as home."

"Well, it's about time you didn't. Roger's on duty. He won't be happy when I tell him what time you knocked me up."

"I bet he won't!"

She punched my arm.

She sponged my face. The smell of her drifted across, her breath, her perfume, the sprinkling of Johnson's Baby Powder. Suddenly I felt empty. The feeling intensified the pain shooting up from my side.

"The kids?"

"They're asleep. Christ, Lenny, it's after two!"

"Yeah, I'm sorry."

She spread a Band-Aid across the side of my left eye. I inhaled her hot breath again. She stood back and shook her head.

"Make me some coffee, girl, and I'll be on my way."

While she made it I went quietly up the stairs to look in on the twins. The landing light was on for comfort, their door slightly open. I opened the door silently and gazed into the gloom. It was warm and secure. Jack was asleep; his breath was calm and deep. Laura whispered: "Daddy".

"Ssshush, baby," I whispered back.

"Night, Daddy."

I left the door open a crack and negotiated the stairs again. Going down was more difficult. By the time I made the bottom I was flinching from the pain.

"Oh, Lenny," she said. She looked sad, worried, mildly disappointed. "Where else did they hurt you?"

I rubbed my side.

"You ought to get around to casualty and have it X-rayed. Your ribs might be cracked."

"It's not that bad," I said. "I've had worse than this before."

She shook her head in dismay. There was some truth in what I'd said. Clubland was a dangerous place: booze and dope was an unhealthy mix; jealousy often got in the way of reason. If some piss-artist didn't like the way his girlfriend looked at you, or thought you were singling her out for special treatment, then you relied on a bouncer to get you out of trouble. Unfortunately, with Peter's cost-cutting, we didn't have one. Not that it would have made much difference last night. Even bouncers don't see you home.

"I wanted to see Roger. But thanks for the First Aid. How is he?"

"Not so good. Ever since they gave him a desk job at the Yard his friends have been callin' him Yardie. That's an insult."

The Yardies were a gang of thugs who had arrived from the West Indies along with their gun culture.

"It's not funny, Lenny. A tag like that could have repercussions in that place." She shrugged away a moment's anger and said, "Anyway, who did this to you?"

"There was a bit of bother at the club. A couple of 'em followed me home."

She nodded. The club! Further explanations were unnecessary. If there had been one thing that had driven us apart then it was the club. But things weren't that simple. They never were.

"You think Roger can help you? Why didn't you call the police?"

"I don't want to make it official, Donna. You know how much I hate fillin' in forms."

"What forms, man?"

"Well, anyway, signing my name on a statement for a starter."

"I'll tell him. He can pop over tomorrow."

She pushed coffee toward me. "There's gonna be a school concert next Friday night. Laura's gonna be Mary, Jack's one of the kings. Seven o'clock."

I looked doubtful. Outside of Saturday, Friday was the busiest night of the week.

"Oh sod you, Lenny Webb, it's only your kids' first concert, that's all!"

Her rebuke stung me. I felt the blood rise.

"I'll be there. What time did you say?"

"Seven o'clock, man. I'll tell them, so don't you go and let them down."

I finished my coffee and stood up. She saw me grimace and clutch my chest and concern touched her face again. She drew her dressing-gown together and tightened the cord around her thickened waist. She reached forward and dusted the shoulder of my black leather jacket.

"You're getting too old for leather jackets, or pony-tails in your hair," she said. "It's about time you got yourself a proper job. Then you wouldn't get hurt. You wouldn't be knocking me up at two in the morning."

"Like joining the police?"

"Well at least you wouldn't have to call a policeman if you did that."

I smiled. "Mention it to Roger, sweetheart. I'll see you on Friday."

She followed me to the door. "I'll tell him all right. You'll be in in the mornin'?"

"I'll be sleeping late."

"I should think so too. You're looking terrible. You're not sleeping, or eating properly. No wonder."

I grinned and kissed her cheek. "You're still as beautiful as ever, you know that?"

"Get out of here. Go and get into a cold shower!"

The door swung shut on her pretty smile.

20

THREE

The morning arrived. Air clanked in the central heating pipes. The windows swam in condensation. I had left one of them open but it made no difference. Salmon could have leapt up the glass. Parts of the curtain net were stitched into patches of ice that hadn't yet melted. I thought about double-glazing. Then about the cost. Then I remembered my dream.

I pictured the perfect curve of Donna's behind and remembered the wonderful warm feel of her. The memory produced a reaction and the pain started and I forgot her quickly. I swept back the quilt and examined myself. Delaney's gorillas should have played for England. At least they knew how to kick a ball. Mine were swollen and a nasty colour of blue. Looking at them made me wince. There was another darker bruise just below my rib-cage on the left. I should see a doctor, I told myself, but I made do with a shower and four aspirin.

I threw on some jeans and a sweatshirt, put John Coltrane's 'Ascension' on the stack and made some coffee. I was just pouring it when Roger came in. He glanced at the door-frame. I had put it back together with three nails and longer screws on the lock. Unfortunately they protruded from the back of the door.

I filled an extra mug.

He was tall, athletic and good-looking. He had a wide clean face beneath Afro hair.

"Man, Donna told me you'd been in the wars." He grinned. Roger came originally from the Brick Lane area. His family had moved out when the Bengalis moved in.

I pushed the mug towards him and sat down at the breakfast bar. He perched on a stool opposite and bunched his shoulders over his drink.

"What's happening?" he asked.

"Paddy Delaney happened."

He raised his straight eyebrows and puckered his lips. "That ain't so healthy."

"Tell me about it."

He grinned again. "What happened?"

I told him.

"I didn't know he had a sister."

"Ask around for me, will you?"

"I know enough without askin' to tell you to be careful. The man's got a bad name. I didn't even know he was back in the country."

I didn't buy that. It had been all over the papers and, I imagine, the police canteens. His response was crap and I narrowed my eyes.

He caught my scepticism and shrugged it away before continuing, "Our people have been breakin' their necks tryin' to get him back. Fuck knows. But I'll ask the question. Meanwhile, you better take it easy. Keep out of his way."

There was something in his voice, an uncharacteristic reserve. I wondered if he was on Delaney's payroll.

I nodded. "You didn't have to say that."

I took Mike's envelope that was standing up against a bowl of bruised fruit and slid it across the bar.

"That's from Mike," I said.

He felt its thickness without opening it.

"Is it all there?"

"Five hundred. He's hoping he'll get his stash back for that."

"He's kidding, right?"

"It's more than the fine."

"Man, he would have gone down this time. What is it, his sixth attempt?"

"I think so."

"So what is he, a fucking comedian, or what? You tell him to give up the drums and take up comedy."

"I'll do that."

"Seriously, though, he better watch his step. There's some grass out there that needs mowin', man. It's got his number." He pulled a face at the coffee, put his mug down and got up to go.

"Donna asked me to remind you about Friday."

"The kids. I hadn't forgotten."

"You better not, man. You know Donna."

"Yeah. Will you be there?"

He shook his head. "Nights," he muttered. He closed the door behind him. I tipped away his coffee.

I went down to Joe's Café for a late breakfast of saturates and cholesterol and spent the afternoon pottering around the flat and generally feeling sorry for myself. I ironed the fronts of some shirts, the bits that showed, and thought about cleaning the cooker. I compromised and did some hoovering instead. At least that was one up on dusting. I made the club just after seven. Clarinet wanted to run through a couple of numbers before the place opened.

Beneath some flashing blue neon the doorman, Herman, growled a good evening. He was ex-army, a Royal Fusilier sergeant, and he didn't like long hair, especially when it was tied back in a pony-tail. His hot breath snorted into the cold air. He hid a cigarette in his cupped hand.

"It's all right for you," he muttered.

"Yeah, I suppose it is," I said as I swung by and pushed open the gleaming glass door.

Peter was in his office sulking about the cost of last night. He didn't acknowledge me as I tapped on his door.

"Did you give Delaney's thugs my address last night, Peter?"

Eventually he looked up over his thick reading spectacles, slowly nodded, and gave me a nervous self-conscious little laugh. He raised both hands in an apologetic gesture.

"That was really good of you," I said.

He remained hunched up over a stack of invoices. Ash from his limp cigarette fell on the top sheet. He looked down and studied it before brushing it away with his hand. It left a smudge.

"Now look what you've made me do," he said and gave me a sad resigned look. The look of a sick man, one who knew he was beaten.

In the bar Clarinet saw the bruises that showed around the edge of the plaster and grimaced.

"It's your own fault, man. You was warned!"

"Yeah, yeah."

"Skirt's goin' be the death of you."

"Peter's still upset?"

"He's had a whole heap of complaints. Some of his regulars

23

said they won't be back. Didn't like Delaney's outbursts at all. Know what I mean?" He dismissed the idea with a wave of his hand. "Come on, let's get on with it." He turned to make sure the band was ready.

Mike was giving me a questioning eye. He wanted to know what had happened to his monkey and whether he was off the hook. Mike was a small-time dealer but they didn't call it dealing anymore.

"You juggling today?" they ask.

"It's cool," he tells them.

He juggles in weed or solid, Rocky or Scunk, Soap, Compressed Leb that fluffs up to multiply, Red Seal, or Squidgy Black with its distinctive taste. You name it, he has it, but only the good gear.

It works this way. Someone sells it to someone who passes it to Mike. It comes in eighths. There's eight eighths in an ounce. Every quarter that he sells he can have an eighth to himself. Fifteen notes buys an eighth and that makes about thirty weak joints. Nowadays they're called spliffs. Next year it'll be something else. Most of it is grown in window boxes and allotments. In every wedge you find a few seeds, maybe half a dozen or more. Not a lot of people know it but if you flatten the seeds to get rid of the gas then you can smoke them as well. Unless you've got brains. Then you plant them out in your window box. But it's all small-time. My guess is he makes just about enough to cater for his more expensive habits. The habits that are going to give him Parkinson's and destroy his brain cells.

The club filled up into a regular evening: there were no histrionics; the mood was subdued. There were half-a-dozen tables of four or more, the rest just couples, some of them courting and therefore not interested.

Clarinet tried me on a couple of numbers before throwing up his hands in despair.

"You better take the rest of the night off, sonny, and get yourself together."

I rubbed my chest and pulled a face.

"It probably sounds worse than it looks," he muttered and glanced my way. "No," he growled. "Maybe it don't!"

During the break I gave Mike Roger's message that he ought to take up comedy and that one of his friends was being less than friendly.

"All this grassing," he said despondently. "Brother against brother. What's happened to the days of the plentiful yam when British Rail suckled our brothers and sisters from her soot-coated tit? Now everything is electrical and one hundred miles an hour. Even your tickets are swallowed by machine. I ask you, what good is a ticket without a punch hole?" He paused and narrowed his hot eyes. "What use is a machine that can't give you false directions and get you on to the wrong train?"

I smiled. Liking him was easy.

It took an hour for some more pain-killers to work and I tried again, this time with more success. Clarinet smiled and flashed some teeth.

She arrived at about eleven. I had just finished 'Bye Bye Blues', trying a Cab Calloway that received applause from some of the more knowledgeable punters. She stood at the bar facing me. Her elbows were raised to the bar surface and bunched her shoulders. She wore a black neck body and a flared silk skirt, a suede belt and hand-stitched Italian high heels. There was a thin black ribbon tied around her neck. The light from the bar glinted in amber drop earrings.

I searched the room for Delaney's face and, when I didn't find it, I looked for one of his heavies.

Clarinet nudged me."D'ya see who I see?"

"Yeah," I breathed. "In all the gin joints in all the towns in all the world she has to walk in here. Can I get out the back way?"

He chuckled and said, "Go and breathe some smoke on her. Ask her if she wants me to play it again?"

I waved the mike at him. "He never said that. Don't you watch Barry Norman for Chrissakes?"

Clarinet shook his head. His lips turned serious. "Never. That man reckons *The Searchers* is John Wayne's best film, and everyone knows it ain't, man. When they made *Rio Bravo*, they coulda stopped makin' Westerns."

"I never knew you were a Wayne fan?"

"Well, man, it's not somethin' you spread around, is it?"

I grinned.

"Fuck you," he said. He sashayed into the next number, easy, moving with a style that we honkeys can only dream about.

When we broke she waved me over.

"You stay away from me," I said and held up both hands.

"Please," she said. "Can we talk?"

"I raised the drink that was waiting on the bar. "That might not be a good idea," I said.

She looked away, her quick eyes took in the other faces.

I said, "Do you know—?"

She interrupted: "You sound just like Michael Caine."

"No?"

"Yes, really. What were you going to say?"

"There's a place in the Pacific, an island, where if a man makes eye-contact with a woman it means come to bed. So they don't look at each other. You see, they haven't got time to court, wine and dine, go through the ritual of the chat-up. They probably can't afford it anyway. So, making eye-contact in a flippant way, or with a woman who's already got a man, is considered an insult."

Unblinking she held my gaze while she lifted her drink.

"Not a lot of people know that," I said.

She laughed out loud and touched my sleeve.

"Come on, let's go and sit in there." She indicated a small annex to the bar where the light wasn't skidding across the walls. "It's quieter." She moved skittishly toward the door, swaying in time with the music. She turned back. "Are you coming?"

I picked up our drinks and followed her. I knew it was a mistake right from the off, but I didn't regret it. My bruises regretted it. The pain every time I walked regretted it, but I took no notice.

"I don't know if I should be talking to you," I said as we crossed to an empty table. "There's danger written all over those big brown eyes of yours. I'm still suffering from our first meeting."

"I heard. I'm sorry. Occasionally Paddy gets these ideas into his head. It's like a seizure, almost. In the morning he can't remember anything about it. He genuinely regrets it. I think it's a combination of alcohol and coke. He should leave off both. He doesn't realize the power he has and that his instructions are followed to the letter."

"How often does it happen?"

"Once in a blue moon. I wouldn't put up with it happening more than that. It's an illness. He goes to a clinic in Switzerland to dry out. But that doesn't help at the time. It doesn't help people like you who get in the way."

"Or you, I imagine."

"I'm OK. I can handle it. It's best just to keep quiet and do whatever he says. I owe him, in a way. Our parents died while we were pretty young . . . "

"But he hits–"

She interrupted: "That's mostly for show. Have you seen any bruises on me? When he slapped me last night he held back. I barely felt a thing. People who saw it thought he had knocked out my teeth but it was only a push."

"I thought he had."

She opened her mouth. Her teeth were perfect. "There's your answer," she said. "It's all for show. When he trips he has to prove how hard he is and I become his obsession."

"It sounds bloody dangerous."

"The doctors say it's not. They say he would do anything for me and that apart from those few hours when he loses control, my welfare is all that concerns him. He takes care of me. He'll get me anything I want."

"Don't you get a clue before it happens?"

"Sometimes you can see the pressure build, you can see his mood darkening over a few hours. That's easy. When that happens you just get out of his way, disappear for a few hours then go back and pick up the pieces. Other times, they're the dangerous times, then he can turn in just a instant. Snap. Something said or seen, sometimes something quite innocuous. Like last night. Then you have to put up with it."

"What started it?"

"That was the silly part. That's why we came here in the first place. They were financiers, bankers . . . " She smiled. "Jazz buffs, traditionalists – that's why he chose Peter's instead of Ronnie's. He wanted to make an impression. Ronnie had some experimental thing going–"

"Tell me about it," I sniggered.

"Doesn't he always? Anyway, the evening was important to him. He was on pins all afternoon. I should have seen the signs.

But . . . I was getting myself ready. He was trying to get his capital transferred to this country and he needed help. I don't know much about it. He never talks to me about business. He blew it, of course. They were quite disgusted with his antics. He spent all day in an awful mood. You'd have thought it was the end of the world. He was crying, the whole business. A doctor came and settled him down with something and lectured him on drink and drugs. He apologized to me a thousand times. He's talking about going back to Switzerland. He'll probably stay about a week. It usually takes that long. I told him that I would move out unless he did. He asked me to find you and apologize."

A frown gripped my forehead and I had to shake it away. I was hardly believing my ears. It seemed impossible that this fragile, waif-like woman could dictate terms to a man like Delaney.

"When will he go?"

"I don't know. He's got some urgent business to sort out. But it won't be long. He knows that I mean it." She sighed. "He is really sorry," she said. "He wants me to sort out your door and pay for any damage. Compensation. If you won't take cash he suggests we buy you something."

"I was really frightened back there. Those two gorillas of his meant business. They hurt me." I fingered the plaster on my forehead.

"I know."

"I don't want his money. I just don't want to see him again, ever."

"I'll tell him. Does that include me?"

"No, that doesn't include you. Just that gangster brother of yours."

Her face fell. "Gangster?"

"He is a gangster. A pretty powerful one."

"Don't believe everything people say, Lenny."

"I don't, but I know he was hiding in the South American jungles for years. I know the police in this country were doing their level best to get him back–"

She interrupted, "Well he's back now and they're not showing too much interest. It was newspaper talk–"

"I believe those two gorillas would have killed me if he had told them to."

"You're right. But he didn't tell them to. I don't deny that some of his business dealings are a touch on the shady side but he doesn't go around hurting people. Not when he's in control. And he's getting better. The seizures now, well, they aren't nearly as regular as they used to be. You do believe me, don't you?"

I gave her a searching look. Her eyes widened fractionally. She looked worried, as though my believing her meant a lot.

I nodded. "I believe you. Why shouldn't I?"

She seemed suddenly flighty and nervous. "Let's change the subject. I've given you his apology and that's that. You accept it or not. What about you, are you attached?"

"Only to my plastic."

She gave a sharp affected smile. "Come off it, you must be attached."

"No."

She reached for her glass. Her fingers were long and narrow, her nails manicured. The quivering liquid betrayed her.

"You're wearing a wedding ring," she said.

I looked at it and smiled wistfully.

"I stopped being married four years ago."

"Ah!" She tossed me a sad smile. She glanced about. Her eyes were seldom still. A tiny shiver worked its way up her body and she bunched her shoulders. She relaxed again and said, "I guessed there was something."

"Well you're wrong. There's nothing now."

"No regrets?"

"None."

"What was she like?"

"She was very pretty. Still is. But she couldn't stand me being out most nights. She worked for Social Services at the time, a Children's and Families' department. Can you believe that? Me getting mixed up with a social worker. I think she needed someone at home to share some of the stress. You know, offload some of the pressure? And when I went on tour . . . "

"I understand."

"Do you? She comes from Jamaica, Kingston. Her skin is darker than your eyes."

"So what? Is that supposed to surprise me?"

"No. I don't even know why I told you."

"Is that what caused the split?"

"No, there was never a culture clash. If anything that's what kept us together for so long. We were fighting against that instead of realizing it was just a battle of the sexes, that we couldn't live together. We're still mates. I still care for her very deeply. More than when we were together. It sounds silly, but the day-to-day niggles seemed to get in the way of caring. You lose sight of friendship. Does that make sense?"

She nodded. "I think so. Were there any children?"

"Two, twins, boy and girl. They're six now." I glanced up and caught her gaze. When her eyes actually stayed still they were quite beautiful. "What about you? Are you attached?"

Her brow creased and her eyes dropped. She hesitated before shaking her head.

I said: "Well, now we know all about each other."

She looked up. "No," she said simply. "No we don't."

She stood up and picked up her Chanel bag. She was suddenly strung out tighter than Alan's guitar. Again her eyes flashed nervously around the room. "I must go now."

I watched her walk away, a slim streak of woman, her hips swinging gently, her movements paradoxically relaxed and easy. I watched her all the way out.

FOUR

On Friday I met Donna just before seven in the reception area of the Grove Infants' School. The twins had gone off for a final run through of their lines. Donna's smile when she saw me was more out of relief than anything else but there was affection there too, the sort that you couldn't get rid of even when you tried.

"Everything OK?"

"Jack's nervous. He's trying hard not to show it. Laura's just Laura. She's loving every minute of it. She wanted to use Kate instead of the doll."

I grinned and asked, "Where is Kate?"

"With Hazel next door. She was sleeping when I left."

Donna slipped out of her raincoat and folded it across her arm. She wore a navy-blue waistcoat over a plain white shirt and a plumwatch tartan pleated skirt, black tights and low-heeled shoes. She looked trim and very pretty. Her exercise classes were working wonders. For a moment I was stung, gutless, running my hands over every inch of her again.

"It looks like it might snow," she said. "We might have a white Christmas after all."

We followed a stream of mums and dads into the hall and sat on small uncomfortable red plastic seats. One of the teachers sat at the piano and began to play 'While Shepherds Watch', badly, and the curtains drew back on the Nativity. The kids stood wide-eyed, searching the crowd for their parents, waiting for their cue. Laura sat beside the crib playing with the front of her shawl. Jack stood beside her fidgeting with the band on his head-dress. As the shepherds made their way to the crib he saw us, beamed a huge toothy smile and waved. One of the three kings leaned forward and tried to stroke the baby but Laura snatched the jar of frankincense from his hands and pushed him aside. His head-dress fell forward and covered his face. The audience laughed and the few people who knew Donna turned to smile sympathetically.

It was all over inside an hour and the twins found us in the hall.

"You were wonderful, both of you," Donna said. "You're definitely going to be on the television."

I gave them some money for Coke and crisps and they went off with a group of friends to the tea-bar.

When Donna turned to me her expression was on the serious side. "We're going to Roger's parents for Christmas . . . "

I nodded.

"Do you mind?"

"It would have been nice to see them."

"I know," she said gently. "They've been askin' for two years runnin'. Roger feels really bad about it. He even suggested you come down there."

"Portsmouth? I don't think so. When will you go?"

"He gets off at eight in the morning, Christmas Eve. He'll sleep a few hours and then, maybe, just after lunch."

"When will you come back?"

"He's on duty again Boxin' Day. We'll have to come back that afternoon."

"I'll come and see them Christmas Eve, then. In the morning."

"I'm sorry, Lenny."

"Don't worry about it, Babe. It's one of the joys of divorcehood. It had to happen sooner or later. I bet your dad feels the same way, not seein' them on Christmas Day. It'll be the first time he's missed out too."

"He was a bit upset. Somethin' else he can blame Roger for."

"I'm sure he doesn't blame Roger, sweetheart. He's just sad about the whole business. Him coming from such a big, close-knit family. He still dreams about the old days in Kingston, everyone gathered around the family cooking-pot. He forgets about all the arguments along with the mosquitoes. If the truth were known, he probably blames himself for our break-up."

"What do you mean?"

"Well, that he gave us such a hard time in the beginning."

She frowned then instantly dismissed the idea. "I don't believe that," she said.

"No," I agreed and threw her a stray, knowledgable smile.

"Nor do I."

I drove them home. In the car she remained sullen. The twins were in the back, still full of it.

I said, "We need to get together sometime. You'll need to give me some idea on . . . " I hesitated, checked in the mirror to make certain the twins weren't listening and then whispered: "Presents."

She nodded. "Do you want to come in for coffee?"

"I can't. I'm late enough as it is."

She sighed heavily.

I asked: "Are you all right?"

"I don't know. I've just been a bit down. Maybe it's the thought of Christmas shopping."

I pulled up outside the house. She turned to face me. Her eyes seemed dark, sad.

"What is it?"

She shrugged, touched my hand and opened the door. "Come on kids, say goodbye to daddy."

I received two wet kisses, one on each side of the neck. They scrambled out and slammed the door. I watched them for a few moments as they went up the path, then drove away. I wasn't their dad anymore. I was just this guy they saw occasionally. Leaving them had become a way of life.

Christmas was still over a fortnight away but the fever was starting to show. The shops had been hammering the message ever since Bonfire Night. London was decorated like a kitschy cocktail: coloured lights, tinsel and baubles, white trees and Jingle Bells. Shop windows glittered with panicky messages while gloomy shopkeepers studied their till receipts and Santas sat in grottoes in every mall breathing bad breath and alcoholic fumes on to the wide-eyed kids. Rejoice! The whole crappy rigmarole is here again! Late-night shoppers thronged the pavements lugging their colourful parcels and bags.

The prospect of not seeing the kids unwrap their presents, a first for me, seemed to dull the afternoon. Ever since we had split and even after she had married Roger, Donna had always insisted on their seeing me, just for an hour or so, on one occasion for lunch at their place. But it was more than that. Laura and Jack were important, but the thought of not seeing Donna depressed me even more. Perhaps, finally, she was leaving me behind. It was a ludicrous thought. The only thing we had in common now were the kids and the odd memory; the day she married Roger all else had finished. I had spent a year or so kidding myself, wearing my guts on my sleeve. I shook away the thoughts as I climbed the green veined marble steps past Herman.

He blew a mixture of Senior Service and hot air into the early frost and hid his cigarette in a cupped hand behind the back of his blue uniform. The neon winked and turned our faces blue.

"It's freezing out here," he muttered. "I'd sooner be in there."

"You should learn to play the trumpet, or something. Maybe the mouth-organ."

"Maybe I will," he said and stamped his feet.

The tables were fully booked. Clarinet was in one of his benevolent moods, not with Mike, but with his audience. He accepted every request, even some blues, in good humour. His charity didn't extend to our drummer who had got hold of some very trippy tangerine dreams. Whatever he was doing he wasn't playing with the rest of us. He was surging, shifting tempo, all but falling off his drum chair. He needed a seat-belt.

His cymbals fizzed with caressing beats then suddenly took off into nowhere, his thin frame jerked and swerved about, surges of accents petered out, his flat snare-drum became a nervous pulse. It was all there. It just needed putting together. And of course, he had to remember that we were there too.

At one stage Clarinet turned on him: "You're playing like a fuckin' twat, man. If you're not careful they'll start throwing spunk at you!"

"Cool, man," Mike said and gave him a moronic grin. To keep his buzz longer Mike puffed the weed. He produced some more smoke and repeated himself, "Cool, man." They were his favourite words. They were his answer to almost every question. To some that were never even asked.

Alan hit a series of discords as he joined in on Keith's guffaw. For two or three minutes no one could play a note and Clarinet decided on an early break.

We sat at our normal places at the bar. Clarinet still seethed. It was unusual for him to get quite so upset. I wondered whether there was more to it than Mike's buzz.

"Well man, how many times do I have to tell him? A bit of puff is OK, a few lines now an' again, a bit of weed won't do you any harm, but acid and Es, they eat the brain away. You should tell him, Sonny. Maybe he'll listen to you."

I shook my head. "He isn't going to listen to anyone, let alone me."

He shrugged his thick shoulders and let his jowls sag in worry. He worried about his boys, Mike included.

Let me tell you something about this main man, Joe Clarinet Gabriel. He's a hero. He grew up in New York at the time Ornette Coleman was getting his head stamped on further south for trying some bebob in a jump-blues dive. New York at that time breathed jazz. In a funny sort of mainstream way it still does. The music comes out of the sidewalk with the steam, street corners and subways around Times Square stir with the clear sad sounds of Coltrane and Parker, the Hudson River echoes with the silent sax and the gut feel of the trumpet. Something orgasmic; like coming on a lonely night. The place, more than anything else, stamped his future. In the mid-sixties he followed Coleman to Copenhagen and played with him, Kenny Drew and Pedersen at the Montmartre, at that time just about the most impressive club in Europe. Eventually, when Coleman started on his classical stuff, Clarinet got on a boat to England. A face at the Ministry of Labour received a tiny bung and he was allowed to stay, and perform. He had been here ever since, sometimes making a good living, sometimes scraping by, but always doing his own thing with block chords and bluesy styles. When I once asked him what his greatest regret was he had said, "That Dinah hadn't lived long enough to crack real soul". That said just about everything.

I had just finished my first drink when my shoulder was nudged.

Delaney's gorilla, the big guy with the soft-shoe shuffle, the one who should have played for England, stood just behind me. He smiled and winked.

"I didn't whistle," I said. "So why did you come?"

I heard Clarinet's gulp. Some of his drink ran down his chin. Mike's eyes popped. Clarinet used a handkerchief then gave the gorilla his questioning, what-the-hell-do-you-want glare.

"My name's Nick," he said. He lifted a thick finger and prodded me gently in the chest. "You've been invited to a party. You've been given your own personal friendly chauffeur."

"I'm workin' a night shift here," I said.

Clarinet nodded. "That's true, man, an' he ain't leavin' early."

Nick turned slowly to face Clarinet. "What happens if he gets sick? You'd let him off early then, wouldn't you?" He prodded Clarinet's chest. "Or better still, what happens if you get fuckin' sick? It would all get called off then, wouldn't it?"

Clarinet pushed out his fat chest. "Not tonight. Christmas is comin'. We's busy," he said defiantly, but it came out shaky.

"Anyway, I'm not in the party mood."

"That is a shame," Nick said. "She will be disappointed."

"She?" Clarinet asked.

"Well, Delaney too. But Julie in particular."

"So Delaney's still in town, is he?"

"I believe he's goin' tomorrow."

"Have I got a choice?" I asked.

Slowly the gorilla shook his massive head.

"There's a lot of us in here," Clarinet put in. Mike had mustered the others and they stood close by.

"Cool, man," Mike said.

Nick glanced their way, studied Mike's odd grin for a moment, then looked coldly at Clarinet. "There's not enough of you," he said.

I believed him. Ever since Clint Eastwood got a taste for pasta and the Wild Bunch took out half of Mexico, the bad guys were in charge.

Nick turned back to me and shrugged his shoulder-pads and said. "You'll be all right."

"No, I don't think I will."

"But you'll come anyway?"

I turned to Clarinet.

"Don't go, sonny," he said. "You know what the man is like."

Nick moved something heavy in his jacket pocket. Clarinet didn't see it. I was certain that within seconds the old guy was going to be lying on the floor covered in his own blood.

"OK, I'll come after the next session. Give me the address and I'll make my own way."

Nick chuckled. My suggestion really tickled him. "I'll wait," he said. "I'd like to hear your music anyway." He nodded. "I'll wait and have a drink."

We played a complete session of Satchmo. Cell came into his own, his trumpet glittered, gave the period a fresh feel and produced a superbly controlled sixteen bars. Clarinet joined me for the final number, 'Ole Rockin' Chair', and we left the room buzzing with applause. Pops never failed.

Nick sat at the bar with his polished foot tapping out a devil dance. He seemed to enjoy the session. Away from his boss he was more at ease. Almost human. As I approached him he smiled genuinely and nodded.

"I could get into that stuff," he said. "Not bad, not bad." He stood from the high stool. "You ready?"

The prospect made my gut flutter.

He noticed my nerves. "I told you not to worry," he said. "He can be quite a gentleman when he tries."

"Tell me about it."

Nick grunted and led me to the door. I turned back to Clarinet who was watching anxiously from the bar. I gave him a resigned shrug and followed the gorilla out into the foyer.

FIVE

They lived somewhere beyond Mill Hill East. There was a pond and a Pilgrim Father's mission and then a right turn off the Ridgeway. The road led through a couple of fields and a small wooded area. We pulled up in a white Rolls on the drive of a large, detached two-storey building. A line of cars that filled the drive included two more Rollers, a Bentley and at least half-a-dozen Jags. Light flooded from the latticed windows and from twin spots above the porch and bounced across the polish and chrome. Nick let me out and closed the door gently behind me. From the house the strains of Police with 'Every Little Thing She Does Is Magic' cut across the drive. Through the lower windows I could see two rooms filled with people, some of them dancing, some of them in small groups holding drinks and plates of food. There were a lot of dark suits and evening dresses, one or two bow-ties. There were some beautiful people, and quite a few Delaney's age, and older.

From the side of the drive, Nick's side-kick, the one with the Doc Marten's, crunched on the gravel.

"What took you?" he asked Nick. "The boss has been askin' after you?"

"He had to finish the gig," Nick said matter-of-factly, not worried at all. He turned to me and pointed to the door. "There you are, Lenny, delivered safe and sound. You can find your own way from here, can't you?"

"I'm going to feel slightly underdressed," I said, brushing down my working clothes.

"Black suit, ain't it? You look fine to me."

"Yeah, but it was off the peg."

"Don't worry." The lights caught his wide grin. "Hide the tag."

I made my way to the door while the two big men watched me from the shadows of the driveway. The door opened just as I got to it. A couple stood aside to let me in. A large hall, dominated by a staircase, was bright and airy. The walls were covered in watercolours, landscapes and seascapes. A massive Christmas tree, perhaps twelve feet high and covered in glittering gold by Harrods, stood on one corner of the parquet floor. A dozen people stood in groups. One or two people glanced my way. Double doors were thrown open to the next room. In there the lighting was subdued, people danced.

Julie's face lit up as she recognized me. She came forward with her arms outstretched. "Lenny," she murmured. "You came!"

She took me by surprise. She wore a black off-the-shoulder number with three pearl buttons down the front. It clung to her and emphasized her tiny waist.

"I didn't have a lot of choice," I said.

She punched my arm. "Of course you did." She caught hold of my hand. "Come on, let's get some drinks."

She led me into another room where a buffet extended along the length of one wall. Mousses and pate, raw vegetables in circular patterns, a whole mess of *hors d'oeuvres*, were scattered around the remains of three huge salmon. She led me to the bar and splashed good whisky into two glasses.

She handed me a glass and said: "You look gorgeous."

"That should be my line."

"I got fed up waiting for you to say it." She smiled brightly. "What's all this in aid of?"

"It's our Christmas party. It's really a welcome home for Paddy so he could see all his old friends again. Some of his business colleagues are here too."

I glanced around. "Business must be doing well."

"Evidently it is," she said and shot me a quick look. "I'm sorry I left so abruptly the other night. I began to feel uncomfortable."

She put her arm around my waist. It seemed to fit. "Come on. Come and say hello to him."

"Do I have to?"

She gazed into my eyes and nodded. "Yes," she said.

She led me to another door and pushed it open on to a snooker room.

Delaney leaned across the table. His slicked back hair caught the overhead light. His jawline was tight, his eyes trained on the end of his cue. They flicked up for an instant as we entered, then returned to the table.

The other man in the room looked much younger than Delaney, perhaps in his late-twenties, but he bore a striking resemblance. He just had to be family.

As Julie entered he raised his hand in a little nervous wave. He saw me and instantly dropped it. He seemed mildly surprised to see me and just a tiny bit hostile.

Delaney potted a red and stood up. He looked faintly smug as he lifted a champagne glass to his lips.

"Hello, Kid," he said to me. "I'm glad you could come."

He leaned across the table again, rushed a blue and missed. He shrugged and turned back to me.

I said, "Thanks for the invitation."

"No sweat."

We watched the other man make his shot. His thumb waved in the air. You just knew it was hopeless from the start. The reds split, the one he had targeted missed the pocket by a foot. He stood up and smiled and seemed quite pleased with himself.

I marked him down as slightly dim-witted.

Julie introduced him. "This is our cousin, Anthony."

I smiled and nodded. The colouring was different, there was no grey, but there was an amazing likeness in the shape of the nose and jaw.

His smile spread and showed us his chipped teeth.

Delaney cleared his throat and asked, "Is this your game?"

"Only in fair weather," I said.

"We might give it a crack later," he said. He turned to his sister at my side. "Look after him, show him the sights."

They shared an affectionate smile.

"Go and enjoy yourself," he said to me. "The food is terrific."

I could barely believe that it was the same man who had caused such chaos at the club. I watched him for a moment as he bent and potted an easy red to finish on a good position on the black, then I followed Julie into the other room. She closed the door behind us.

"I told you there was nothing to worry about," she said.

We sat at the bar. She watched me chew on a couple of hot olives and her eyes glittered and kicked me in the bollocks.

* * *

Her hair brushed my face; she smelled of Coco. My hand fluttered on the small of her back. The track finished and left people in uncertain embraces but she didn't move to break away. Instead she held me firmer.

"Mmmmmn," she whispered. "You're a very sexy mover."

She pressed into me. I'm sure she felt me stir against her. Even sleeping she would have felt me. I was surging like a dog with two dicks. I'm sure my tongue was hanging out. Any moment I was going to run around in circles not knowing whether to sniff arse or cock a leg. Excited isn't the word. She put her head on my shoulder as the music began again. I felt her every tiny movement, her thighs, her breasts, her nipples poking through, her hands that stroked me. Her touch was almost electric, overwhelming. It was a long time since I had felt anything even remotely like it. I wondered whether anyone had noticed how intimate it was. In the dim light the other couples were just slowly moving shadows, oblivious to us and to the rest of the world.

Four tracks later she was quite content to press up against my expanding interest, holding me just as closely, moving in a mild gyratory fashion. Her hand dropped to my behind and she arched her shoulders back so that she could look into my eyes.

"Mmmmmn," she said.

A tiny smile lingered on her lips. She moved the lower half of her body a little harder against me. Suddenly she reached up, put her slender hands either side of my face and planted a kiss on my mouth. Her lips parted fractionally and her tongue made an exploratory flick against mine. She tasted of vermouth, sweet and clean.

When we broke I said, "We're being watched".

She turned her head and saw cousin Anthony's face in the shadows. For a moment she seemed to stiffen, perhaps at the idea of being watched.

"It's Anthony," she whispered. "We grew up together, Paddy, Anthony and me. Looking at him you wouldn't think that he's the same age as Paddy, would you? He looks so much younger." She sighed and went on, "Now that we're adults it's a bit sad really. When he was a baby he had meningitis and it made him a bit withdrawn. At the time, when we were kids, it didn't matter."

I wondered whether Delaney had sent him out to keep an eye on us. But surely not. If anyone were going to do that, it would be one of his gorillas.

She pulled away. "I need another drink. My throat has gone kind of dry."

She broke free, caught hold of my hand and led me toward the bar. While she poured the drinks a couple weaved their way from the buffet table.

The woman said, "You've been neglecting us, Julie – but I can see why."

"Lizzy, this is Lenny Webb. Lenny, this is Lizzy Turow and her husband, Jonathan."

She was a tall heavily made-up woman in her thirties. She reminded me of a woman who served on the cosmetic counter at Boots. UV rays had soaked her skin; in ten years or fewer, she would have the texture of dried toast. She lifted a delicate glass to her lips while she examined me. Her lipstick smudged the rim. She had the faraway look of short-sightedness. There was a tell-tale mark on the bridge of her nose.

He was middle-aged and slightly overweight. He hung on to a plate heaped with food. His face was round and friendly, slightly perspiring.

Julie placed a glass in my hand and slipped her arm around my waist. Lizzy raised her eyebrows and exchanged a quick glance with her husband.

"Is this . . . ?" Lizzy asked. Her brow remained quizzical.

Julie nodded. "My jazz singer."

"I think my taste in music needs widening."

Jonathan spoke while he gnawed on a chicken leg: "Am I missing something?"

The women laughed.

He looked blankly at me and raised his eyebrows. "What's going on here?"

"Your wife wants a Louis Armstrong collection for Christmas."

"Is that instead of the diamonds?"

Lizzy shot him with a stray glance then carefully placed her glass on the bar counter and touched my arm. "Come and dance with me, Lenny. You can tell me all about jazz. I'm a very good student."

"I bet you are," I said.

Julie smiled naturally and said, "Don't abandon me for too long."

In the other room, in the dark, Lizzy's hands were all over me. She wasn't nearly as good a dancer as Julie. Her movements were heavy and predetermined. There was no natural rhythm. Even so, by the time Simply Red had made a quick tour of 'Lady Godiva's Room' I had no secrets left. She had felt just about everything I owned except my wallet and even then some. While Elkie Brooks turned 'Lilac Wine' into an aphrodisiac she said, "Don't hurt her Lenny. That's an order."

"What's that supposed to mean?"

"It means that she's very fragile. You mustn't be flippant with what you say to her. Don't tell her you care unless it's true."

"I haven't told her anything. My being here was not my idea. This is only the third time we've met. You can't even count the first time."

She stiffened. "Now I'm surprised."

"What has she told you?"

"Perhaps she didn't tell me, but I got the impression that you were an item, the two of you."

"She came to the club," I explained. "The first time I didn't speak to her, the second she came to apologize for Paddy's behaviour on the first visit. That's it. Until tonight when I was dragged here by Nick. You know Nick?"

She nodded and shuddered slightly. "So there's nothing–"

"I didn't say that. Tonight has been pretty enjoyable. But we barely know each other."

She squeezed me. "I'm sorry I spoke," she said.

"How long have you known them?"

"About four years. We actually met Paddy in South America. When Julie arrived here, when was it? About eighteen months ago, we came to see her. He lived in America for a long time. I believe it was business that dragged him back."

The darkness hid my smile. She had to be kidding.

At the end of the next track we called it a day and returned to the bar. The two of them were still there. Jonathan had reloaded his plate.

As she handed me back to Julie, Lizzy said, "Lucky thing!"

The party was beginning to break up. The hall was crowded with people donning coats and hats. Julie took me back into the snooker room. Delaney was in there on his own, shoulders bunched over a small bar. He turned quickly as we walked in. His hair was rucked on one side, his eyes euphoric. He smiled awkwardly like a child who had been caught out.

"You know where I went today?" he said abruptly and loudly, taking us both by surprise.

I looked at him blankly. I felt Julie's eyes on me, waiting for a reaction.

"I visited my old hunting grounds: Whitechapel, Tower Hamlets, Brick Lane. Everywhere is derelict, neo-Nazi posters all over the fucking place, gangs of goosesteppin' bastards, and Pakis, I've never seen so many turbans in my life. I had to pinch myself to make sure I was back in England. England! It's more like India, or Germany. I can tell you, I was very depressed with what I saw. Someone needs to take over again. It was never like this when I . . . " He glanced at his sister then continued, " . . . when the twins were in charge!"

"It was always a shithouse," I said.

"Not that bad, though." There was a sanguine flush to his cheeks but beneath it was something cold and ugly.

"You've come to play?" he said.

"I'm not very good at games," I said, looking for an honourable retreat from his rollercoaster.

He was hyped up to explode but the rage wasn't hot; there was something frighteningly controlled about it. I was amazed that Julie couldn't see it. He moved off the stool, grabbed a cue and tossed it toward me. I caught it.

"One game," he said thickly. "Winner takes all."

I rubbed my hand along the cue and asked, "What's the stake?"

He glanced up slyly. "We can decide that after we've played."

I shrugged. Julie pushed me toward the table. "Go on," she urged. "Give him a thrashing. I've had enough anyway. I'm going up to bed."

Delaney's eyes narrowed before he nodded. "OK, I'll see you in the morning – before I go."

"Yes." For an instant her gaze dropped to the floor. When she looked up her eyes were dark and sombre. "Goodnight, Lenny, thanks for a lovely evening."

I turned back toward her. "Thank you for inviting me," I said.

I watched her leave the room and felt suddenly isolated and threatened. Before she could close the door Nick had stepped in and he closed the door gently behind her. He saw me and nodded. He stood motionless, hands behind his back, legs slightly apart and braced, looking for all the world like he was guarding the door.

"You break!" Delaney grabbed my attention.

I moved to the top of the table. After the cue ball had returned to within two inches of the cushion I turned back to Delaney feeling mildly satisfied. He was using a straw at the bar. A line of coke disappeared as I watched. He snorted a second line and wiped his nose on the sleeve of his jacket. He broke out another line with a razor-blade and offered me the straw. I shook my head.

"I don't use it," I said.

His expression dropped. "Don't insult me, Kid. Things are going along fine, aren't they?"

I took the straw and snorted a line. It wasn't the first time. My nostril twitched. I threatened a sneeze. As I leaned across the bar I stole a quick look behind the counter. Sure enough his glass pipe and cooking equipment lay on the side. The bastard had shot his load just before our arrival. About a grand's worth of crack was heaped on the side, a pile of tiny gems. A tiny rocky mountain. Know what I mean? None of your Coke cans for Paddy Delaney.

They call it 'more'. Crack. That's what they call it. Around King's Cross it's 'I want more. I need more!' If you're green and on your own, and often from Glasgow or the other northern cities, they'll give it to you for free. The first time. The second time, and the third, a rock will cost you about eight quid. A little later, when you really need it, the price goes through the roof. And if you can't afford the price and you're coming down head first, that's when you're asked to turn a little trick yourself. And in that sort of state, little tricks get bigger every day.

Delaney nodded and bent over the table. "Reme Columbian," he muttered, referring to the dust, not the crack. "The best!"

He made his shot. A red rolled into the corner pocket. He

45

looked up and smiled dangerously. Nerves tightened my chest. "You've been dancing with Julie?"

I nodded.

He potted a blue but got himself out of position. He scowled at the table and played for safety. He left a difficult red on.

"She dances well," he said. "Especially the slow ones, the groping ones."

The red went down, more luck than judgment, and left me on the yellow. I snookered him just behind it. He studied the balls for a moment. His lips tightened.

"Clever fucker!" he said beneath his breath, but I heard it.

I was hot; sweat gathered on my forehead. I could almost feel my blood racing. Everything seemed clear. He was going to miss the next red, open up the pack, and I was going to score. Fuck him! I knew my sudden invincibility was down to the snow. Even with the knowledge I still felt good. I watched expectantly as he lined up the angles.

"She moves like a fuckin' ballerina, you know that, don't you? Can you imagine pressing up against her arse?" he said. His eyes rolled up toward me. "Or gettin' her goin' down on you? Can you imagine pushin' into her cunt, the red hot pressure on your dick? Heaven, eh?"

"You're a vulgar bastard. It's your sister you're talking about." I was amazed at how calm my voice sounded.

He made the shot. The reds split and the black rolled over a pocket.

"Fuck it!" he said in dismay.

I smiled and moved in. The first red was easy.

"What about her lips sucking at your dick? The feel of her throat against the end of your dick, eh? eh?"

"Are you trying to make me miss?" I asked. I heard him snorting again. "It won't work, pal. Red, black, red, black, then we'll see!"

I heard him growl, "Cocksucker!" then the end of his cue smacked me around the head. It was the thin end but it still sent me sprawling. I bounced off the side of the table and landed on the carpet. My own cue hit the overhead light and sent giddy shadows across the room. I was stunned. I tried to get up but rolled over like a drunk.

"Go and get her!" I heard.

"Why don't we call it a night, boss? It's pretty late." Nick's voice was calm and soothing. "You'll feel better in the morning."

"I want to know what the fuck they've been up to. Don't fuckin' tell me nothing. Just go and fucking get her!"

"OK boss, OK."

I heard the door close.

Delaney moved across to the bar again and cut another line. "You ain't gettin' away with this, Kid." His voice dropped by the moment. "Abusing my hospitality. What the fuck do you think this is? A fuckin' whorehouse? I'll teach you cunts to fuck around with my friendship."

He began to cough. I looked up. Through a haze I made out a red stain on his handkerchief.

"I invite you to a fuckin' party and what happens? You start by fuckin' my sister right in front of me. A fuckin' liberty. Who else saw you? Eh? Who else is laughin' at me?"

His kick gave me a dead leg. I began to get up just as the door crashed open and Julie was pushed inside. She had come down in a hurry. The black dress was gone. Her ivory coloured slip was flimsy. She froze as she saw me. Her gaze went slowly across to her brother, then to the powder on the bar. She turned on Nick who was closing the door.

"What's happened?" Her tone was accusing.

"Don't you talk to the hired help!" Delaney said. "Just get your fuckin' arse over here!"

She stood her ground. Her eyes flashed defiance. Suddenly Nick was behind her, propelling her toward us. I struggled to my feet as Nick pushed her into Delaney's hands. He caught her by the hair and forced her to her knees. She grimaced as her head bent upwards.

"Now what the fuck's been going on?"

"What do you mean?" She squirmed, trying to loosen the grip on her hair.

"You give him a blow job, did you? Like a common fuckin' whore!"

"Don't be silly, Paddy. Nothing happened. We were dancing–"

"Dancing fuck! Dancing on his prick with your mouth!" He kneed her in the back, flinging her forwards. He dragged her to her knees again, wrapping her hair around his hand. "Show me!" he said. His voice was filled with madness. "Show me how you did it!"

I'd had enough. I tried to get out but stumbled as Nick blocked my way.

"You're going fuckin' nowhere, Kid!" Delaney shouted.

A switchblade flashed in Nick's hand. It came towards me with surprising speed and stopped as it touched my neck. I felt its sharp edge against the prominent vein that runs from behind the ear down to the clavicle. I twisted away from it and turned to face Delaney.

"You're a fuckin' madman," I said. The words came out in a whisper. I could barely swallow without gulping. For a moment I thought I would choke. The room seemed to spin.

Delaney pushed her forward. Her hands came up and clawed at my waist.

"Show me!" Delaney repeated. "I wanna know what you dirty fuckers got up to!"

I stood there half leaning against Nick. Without him behind me I would have fallen. The blade felt cold against my neck. The room continued to spin. I felt her hands shaking, heard the zip. Her hand felt incredibly cool as she pulled me out. I closed my eyes. This wasn't happening, I kept telling myself. Any second I would wake up, probably sticky. No, this was a nightmare. I'd wake up sweating out of fear, nothing else.

I felt the blade bite a little deeper. My Adam's apple must have moved for the point took away some skin. I felt the texture of her tongue, wet and soft. I couldn't stop myself squirming in embarrassment. She had a hold of what there was of me and that wasn't much. Limp, slack, floppy – that's the word.

I opened my eyes slightly, hoping to slow down the spin. The smirk on Delaney's face turned his nose upward.

I felt the warmth of her mouth as she closed her lips over the top of me. Her hair brushed against me.

The blade at my throat seemed to move fractionally and I felt something wet dribble down my neck like a fast little insect. I didn't know whether it was sweat or blood but I wasn't going to lower my head to check.

Her lips tightened and for an absurd instant I thought she

actually sucked. I tried to look down but the best I could do was see the top of her head. The pressure of the blade increased again. I felt my own pulse against it.

But it wasn't going to work and before long Delaney accepted it.

He stepped forward, bunched her hair in his fist and drew her away from me. Slowly, by the hair, he raised her to her feet.

"The dirty cow! Look, look at her fuckin' face. She enjoyed it!"

He hauled Julie aside. She seemed to bounce off the wall. For a moment he stood shaking then he turned to me and kicked out. His foot landed on my leg again. Bruise on bruise, pain on pain. The carpet burned my cheek as I went down. I stayed there, on my back. My dick was still hanging like a dead slug from my flies.

Delaney stood in front of her, shaking his fists.

"It was supposed to be fucking degrading, not something to fuckin' enjoy. You're no more than a whore." He turned to me. His face was flushed. The rash on his cheeks boiled. "You, get up!"

I staggered to my feet. Even dazed, I managed to zip up without cutting myself in half. He pointed toward his sister. "Now, you give her a smack. You gotta teach her a lesson, understand?"

I shook my head. "I don't hit women."

"You mean you haven't until now!"

"I mean I don't."

"And I mean you've got a fucking choice. You'll either give her a smack, or Nick here, he'll give you one . . ."

I turned to face her. Until then she had remained motionless, clutching the sides of her slip.

"Go on, in the mouth, or even in the tits. She'll enjoy it!"

Her eyes widened fearfully. Her lips quivered.

"Do it, Lenny," she whispered, almost pleading. "He'll hurt me a lot more than you will."

I turned back to Delaney. "This is ridiculous. I won't play your games anymore. You're sick, do you know that? Go get yourself a doctor!"

Nick's fist caught me on the side of the head. For a moment the heavens opened up, filled with starbursts. The pain lanced across my forehead. A deep headache began instantly. I gripped the side of the table to stop myself from falling. I tried to shake away the giddiness along with the sickness that crawled up from my gut.

Delaney said, "Nick isn't going to hit you again, Lenny. He's going to hit her, the whore!"

I watched Nick as he slid a silver knuckle-duster on to his fist. His other hand held on to the switchblade.

"He's goin' to hit her right in the face. He's goin' to mash her fuckin' face in so that no one will ever look at it again without throwin' up. Right!" He wagged a finger at me. "And it's down to you. You don't wanna play my game. Right?"

Nick approached her. She backed off until her back was against the wall and there was nowhere else to go. His massive fist drew back. She cowered.

"Stop!" I shouted.

All three of them turned towards me.

"All right, all right."

Delaney's smile was ugly. He nodded toward Nick. A gleam of satisfaction strayed into his eyes. Nick lowered his steel capped fist and moved aside.

I slapped her with my open hand. She was flat against the wall. For an instant she was surprised. Her cheek flared even as she lifted her hand to cover it.

"You think I'm fucking stupid?" Delaney said. "What was that? Eh? You call that a smack? No more chances, Lenny. You hit the bitch or Nicky will. What's it to be?"

Our gazes met again and she gave me the faintest of nods.

"Do it," she whispered.

I slapped her again. The side of her face smacked against the wall. Her eyes welled up.

Delaney screamed, "That wasn't hard enough. You're not even trying, are you?"

He stepped forward and punched her in the stomach. She gasped and sat down heavily on the carpet. Her slip caught the air and settled a moment later. There was no underwear beneath. She wrapped her arms around her stomach and began to rock. Her face screwed up and she let out a long cry.

"That's how you do it!" he said. He stood over her, shaking, his hands clenched so tightly they had turned white. He aimed a kick and caught her in the side. The force of it lifted her over against the wall. The slip bunched at her waist. Her pale buttocks shone in the table light.

Slowly Delaney turned toward me. "Get the fuck out of here," he said.

I didn't have a choice. The gorilla grabbed my collar and shoved me toward the door.

Once outside he dropped me and attempted to dust down my jacket.

"You all right?"

"Are you fucking joking?"

"It's just a job, pal. Pays better than the dole."

"Tell me about it!" I said angrily and walked past him to the front door.

He caught up. "I'll run you home."

"The fuck you will."

He shrugged and said, "It's a long walk."

I turned back to him. "You're Nick, right?"

He nodded.

"Jesus! Don't you have any feelings for her at all? How can you let that happen?"

"You did."

"Only because you were there. Think about it. If he kills her you'll be the one to cop it. That bastard will get by with mental illness. He's a fucking lunatic."

"Tell me something I don't know." Nick's smile was genuine. He shook his head. "He ain't goin' to kill her, Lenny." He hesitated then went on: "Just fuckin' leave it alone, stay out of it. You haven't got a clue what's goin' down in there, so just stay out of it. Understand?"

"I want to stay out of it. They won't let me stay out of it. I didn't come here by choice."

"Yes you did," he said seriously. "You might not think so, pal, but you fuckin' did!"

Once out of the drive I lit a JPS. There was blood in my mouth. The smoke flavoured it. In the freezing air the smoke followed me. I was in the middle of nowhere: ungodly shapes of winter trees and dark endless fields. The stars glinted like bits of ice. I began to walk in the direction of traffic noise. My footfalls slapped the hard, frosty surface of the road. Before I hit civilization again the first ghost of dawn crept out of the night.

I couldn't get Nick's final sentiment out of my head. As I walked toward a main road where the occasional headlamps flared past, Nick's words spun around in dizzy circles. Being there had been my choice, he had said. I had wanted to see the place where they lived. I had wanted to find out more about them, see her again, get an insight into their relationship. My choice, he had said. Even knowing the risk I had wanted it. Curiosity. Something more than that. The girl had got to me. Perhaps I had some crazy notion that I could protect her. If that were the case, I'd come down with a bang. I couldn't compete with these people. They came from a different, dangerous world. My pace increased; I needed to get back to the safety of my own.

SIX

"Don't say fuck all!" Roger said just after lunch. He still stood in the doorway of my flat. "Just grab a jacket and get in the car. I'm taking you for a ride."

I was still bleary-eyed, still trying to work out whether I'd dreamed it all and certainly in no mood to argue. It was the feeling you get when you stagger off a big dipper: you weren't sure whether you were going to throw up or fall over. Your feet seem to want to go in two directions, and they slap at the pavement. He led me down to his unmarked Rover. Every villain in the Smoke could tell it for a police-car at fifty yards.

We had gone a hundred yards when he said sternly, "A little bird tells me you went to Delaney's party last night; that you're sweet on his sister."

"Bollocks!"

"Well?"

"I was dragged to Delaney's party by his gorilla! It was the sort of invitation you couldn't turn down. Know what I mean?"

"What about his sister?"

"What about her? What is this, the third degree?"

He shot me a dark glance. "Tell me," he insisted. "Is there anything going on?"

I shrugged. "We danced. He didn't like it. On the contrary, he went fucking apeshit!"

"Did he use an iron bar."

He referred to the straight red mark that began just above my right eyebrow and disappeared beneath the hair above my ear.

"A snooker cue," I said.

"You must be fuckin' mad," he said. "That's twice they've taken you apart. Are you trying for three times lucky?"

"Where are you taking me?"

"You'll see."

He pulled up in front of the North Middlesex General.

"I don't need a doctor," I said.

"Yes you do, Lenny. A psychiatrist. But this ain't about your injuries."

We left the car in an ambulance-only area and he marched me through the main doors. Roger knew his way around. Two bare corridors, a lift, another corridor, and an arrowed sign marked 'ITU'. A Uniform sitting outside a single door and beneath another sign marked 'Intensive Therapy Unit' got to his feet as he recognized Roger.

"Anything?" Roger asked the PC.

The tall young man shook his ginger head. His thick polished toecaps caught the stark light. "They don't think he'll regain consciousness." He glanced at me. "Who's this?" His expression tightened.

"My brother-in-law," Roger said. When the policeman frowned, he added, "Fuck it, that's close enough." He indicated toward the door. "Anyone in there?"

The PC shook his head. His hair was plastered with gel and didn't even quiver. "His parents visited this morning. They spoke to the consultant."

Roger pointed to the window in the door. "Take a look," he said to me.

It was a small, bright room. A bank of monitors stood next to a single bed. Some of them bleeped quietly, others ran green lines across the screens. A drip fed into the arm of a man lying on the bed. Another tube ran to his nose. He seemed calm, his breathing steady. But what I could see of his body was covered in some kind of plastic sheeting, head to toe. Through it his skin seemed mottled and blistered. Other tubes ran into his other arm, round discs were stuck to his chest. Wires ran from these to the monitors.

"Take a fucking good look, man. That's a life-support machine. Switch it off and he stops breathing. They're not even bothering to move him to a specialist burns unit."

"You're going to tell me the point of all this?" I said.

"Third-degree burns, right through the derma into the tissue underneath. I'd say he's been cooked to medium rare. Sound good to you? Sound like fun?"

I gulped at the hot corridor air.

"Guess who his last girlfriend was? Can you do that, Lenny? No conferring? Starter for fuckin' ten?"

He watched my mouth drop open.

"I think you got it in one, my son!"

He led me slowly back to the car. We had to pause a couple of times because the hospital corridor had begun to tilt on me.

In the car he waited until some colour came back to my face before starting the motor. The engine spluttered before settling down.

"You think Delaney did it?"

He shook his head. "Nope. Not his style. He doesn't do his own dirty work?"

"His gorillas?"

"That's my guess."

"Tell me?"

"A whisper. Mind you, it's pretty reliable."

"When did she go out with him?"

"About a month ago, as far as I can tell. He took her to dinner at the Norfolk. Now that's a place an' a fuckin' half. The bollocks. Know what I mean? Don't know how serious it was. According to the mouth, it wasn't. They just went out the once. It isn't my case."

"Who told you all this?"

He gave me a screwed up look. "Are you kidding?"

I shrugged and asked: "Was she questioned?"

"Not yet."

"And Delaney?"

"I doubt it."

"What's the guy's name?"

"Nicholas, Nicholas James Linet."

"When did you find him?"

"A couple of skagheads found him under their bonfire. They were just about to light it. Two days ago. Over at the Cross. The immediate thought was that he was just another drunk and that some thugs had lit his cardboard box. But there were traces of paraffin all over him and no alcohol in his blood. There was also a wallet containing the best part of two hundred charred notes so he wasn't rolled."

"Did he say anything at all? I mean, was he conscious at all?"

55

"Not when we got to him. The skags said he was babbling on about some girl. It was hearing his voice that stopped them lighting the fire."

I felt a moment's panic clutch at my chest. I couldn't get the close stuffy air of the hospital out of my throat.

"Where did they meet – this guy and Julie?"

He smiled. "Fucking Julie, is it?"

"Yeah, yeah. Well?"

He shook his head. "I can have a look at the report if it's important, but I doubt there'll be anything. Their dinner date was over a month ago. Nothing to tie them together."

"Get me anything you can."

He turned to me and said seriously, "Once I heard the name, I figured you ought to know."

I nodded my thanks.

He flashed me a dark look and said: "If you want the information it means you're still interested. You intend seeing her again?"

"What do you think?"

"I think you're mad, Lenny."

"It's not a question of my seeing her again. They aren't going to leave me alone, are they?"

"Well, I'm fucked if I understand it," he sighed. "With their money and her looks, she can have just about anyone she wants. Why you? Have you told me everything?"

"Yeah, there's nothing else."

"I don't like the sound of it. You're gettin' shafted, man. For what, I don't know. It sounds like they're playing some kind of game with you. Why don't you get lost for six months? You've dropped out before."

"I was younger then."

"Yeah, and you had more sense."

He dropped me at the flat.

My answering-machine winked an orange message. I made some coffee and listened to it. After the bleep she came on. Her voice was smoky and hesitant.

"Lenny, it's me, Julie. Whenever I contact you I always seem to be saying sorry and making excuses for him."

I felt the weight of my frown. Even listening to her voice sent a mild chill across my back. I turned to check that the door was still closed and that Nick wasn't standing there with a broad grin across his wide, innocent face.

"No more excuses, Lenny," she went on. She paused and I heard a little catch of her breath, perhaps a sob. "Nothing could justify his performance last night, no amount of apologizing. I'm not going to say sorry. It wasn't my fault. He's gone now. He flew from Heathrow this morning. You can blame me, if you like. I'll understand and won't bother you again. And I won't let him bother you, either. That's a promise." She hesitated again before: "Please believe that I'm in a similar position to you. But I can't turn my back on it. I can't walk away. I wish I could. Will you please ring me, Lenny? Please?"

Apart from giving me the number, that was it. She broke off.

I rewound and listened to her again. I remembered the closeness of her, the fragrance, her hot breath against my neck. There was a narcotic quality about it all. Maybe four years, give or take the odd meaningless weekend, in the sexual wilderness had left me like a moth flying to the candle, unable or unwilling to stop myself.

I lit a JPS and thought about the man I'd seen in the hospital. Perhaps it had all been coincidence. Almost before the thought crossed my mind, I dismissed it. I'd seen Delaney in action. I'd seen how Nick and the other gorilla showed no hesitation in carrying out Delaney's instructions. I had seen Delaney's obsessive behaviour. For Christ sake, the man had just booked himself into the equivalent of Broadmoor. And now there was me. Hide! Run away! Roger had said, but his suggestion was not the answer. I wondered whether he had a more devious motive; he and Donna were having problems, that much was obvious. Maybe he put some of them down to me. Maybe he thought my absence would make things easier.

A doomed man making his last call. That was the thought that struck me as I dialled her number.

The telephone rang once before it was snatched.

"It's me," I said.

"Lenny?" She sounded excited.

"Yeah. I got your message."

"I'm sorry, I'm sorry, I'm sorry. Believe me?"

"Yeah."

"He's gone. He woke up in tears. He was still wiping them when he went."

"That doesn't help. How he feels the morning after is not good enough. He needs locking up, not just for a week. For the rest of his life, and then some."

"Meet me," she said. There was something in her voice. It grabbed me by the bollocks.

"No chance."

Silence.

I said, "You still there?"

Her voice was flat. "Yes."

"Did Nick and the other guy go with him?"

"Mario went with him. Nick's still here. Why?"

"He might have left some instructions. Like, for instance, go and break some arms and legs."

"He didn't."

"How do you know that?"

"I know," she insisted. "Please don't dismiss me without thinking about it."

"It might surprise you, sweetheart, but I've been thinking of nothing else from the moment I saw you dancing in the club."

Another pause, longer this time.

She said, "That's how long I've been thinking of you. Ever since you told Paddy off at the table."

"That was my first mistake," I said.

"What was your second?"

"I've got a feeling I'm about to make it."

"Meet me." She sounded like a little girl.

"I'm playing the club tonight. It's a free country."

It took a few moments to sink in.

"I'll be there," she said.

I hung up. Then I kicked myself.

Before arthritis crippled him, John Gresty played the alto sax. He still played it but not up front anymore. Now it was for his own pleasure, or annoyance, but he was still as good as anything I'd heard recently. He was Caribbean black and, apart from his wife and children, he had two loves in his life: the sax and Viv Richards, in that order.

I loved the guy. He was big and gruff, his face was always matted in a layer of white whiskers.

He had fought tooth and nail to stop me marrying his daughter. Six years later he fought tooth and nail to stop her divorcing me. We stayed friends. He often said, "You shoulda put up more of a fight!" He didn't realize how difficult it was to fight when you knew your wife was in love with someone else. At the end of the day it comes down to pride. Donna had been seeing her policeman friend for some time before I found out. But it wasn't only the affair. Things are never that simple. John Gresty never got on with his daughter's new husband. He sensed that the man was not straight. With Donna's father, honesty had always been important.

For over a year we had been meeting regularly on a Saturday afternoon while his wife, Mary, went out to collect the weekly shopping. During the week she had a part-time job cleaning some offices. It crossed my mind that she must have been close to retiring herself.

He asked about the skid marks on my face and I explained that I'd been introduced to a nasty bastard at the club who hadn't liked the way his sister said 'hello'.

"There's two kinds of people in this world, Lenny. There's people who blow and there's people who suck."

"You're going to tell me what the difference is, aren't you?"

"Yes, I am, and you'll be surprised to know that it's got little to do with air going in and out of your mouth."

He sighed and emptied a can of Sainsbury's bitter.

"It's passionate people I'm talkin' about, people who blow hot and cold. They've got hot breath. They're the people who produce the arias in the operas, the colour in life, the breath of fresh air that lifts you like an old Benny Green. The suckers, they're the cynics of the world. You can see 'em. The cold air findin' their fillin's. That sharp intake of breath every time they have to make a decision. The people who never take a chance in life. The people who'll die and look back and realize they never lived. They're the suckers." He paused and nodded. "You get one or two chances in life, Lenny. I mean real chances. And they don't happen so often. When they come up you gotta grab them with both hands and to hell with the consequences. Man, you gotta hang on. You gotta give it everythin' you got. You had one chance and blew it but that don't mean you shouldn't take another. Sure, you might not make it, but if you don't try you might as well lie down and play dead, 'cos you sure ain't livin'. You have to make your own decision, Lenny. Are you a sucker or a blower?"

Even though he didn't know all the details it was still refreshing to hear a voice that didn't warn me off.

I swilled some beer.

"Are they likely to come back?"

"Hell, I don't know." I shrugged and nodded. "Yeah, maybe."

"Well then, if they do, you might as well grab the bull by the horns," he said and then grinned. "Or the cow by the udders!" He nodded thoughtfully and opened another can. After a while he said sombrely, "They's takin' the kids away for Christmas."

"I heard."

He waved the air with his free hand. "Ain't you upset?"

"Yeah, I'm upset, but there's fuck all to do about it. I'm not sure I want to anyway. It's time you accepted that he's family, I'm the past."

He looked at me slyly. "It ain't over yet, Lenny. Not by a long shot."

"Meaning?"

"You never know what tomorrow brings. There's only two certainties in life, you know that? Death and prostitutes!"

I left him looking gloomily from his front window at the approaching grey dusk.

SEVEN

She turned up just before eleven. She wore a tight-fitting dark-green trouser suit with wide lapels over a white shirt. She probably chose it to hide her bruises. She had Nick in tow. His evening jacket bulged, two sizes too small across the chest. Peter led them to a choice table at the back and had a waitress serve them immediately before scurrying to his office and locking the door.

It was half an hour before the band broke and then I carried a drink across to them.

Nick stood as I approached. He seemed pleased to see me. "Hello, Kid. D'ya get home OK?"

I gave him my best shot at a contemptuous look. He raised his hands in mock surrender.

"I'm leavin'," he said. "I'll be over at the bar." He picked up his glass and walked stiffly away with a weightlifter's gait.

I turned back to Julie.

She said, "Please sit down. You're making me nervous."

I sat opposite and lit a cigarette.

"Don't we ever get to be alone?" I asked her and flicked a glance toward Nick.

"Is that what you want?" She arched her brows slightly and gave me an apprehensive look.

I examined her face for signs of bruising but couldn't find any. As far as I could tell she wasn't hiding anything with make-up either. Eventually I said, "I don't know what I want. Are you all right?"

Her eyes widened and fastened on to me. For a moment they remained child-like and dewy. She nodded and sipped at her drink.

"I've never known him to be as bad as that."

"I don't believe you."

She seemed hurt. "It's true. He's never done anything like that before. He's hurt other people, but never me. I lived with the odd slap, but last night was different. Things are so mixed up," she said. "I don't know what to do anymore."

"Any fool can tell you what to do. You get away from him before he kills you." I finished my drink and said, "Tell me about Nicholas James Linet?"

If she were surprised she hid it well.

"What about him?"

"You went out with him?"

She frowned. "That's not your business, Lenny. Who I went out with in the past has got nothing to do with you at all."

"It has if the same thing's going to happen to me. I'd say it's got a lot to do with me."

"What on earth are you talking about?" Her features remained innocent, bewildered.

"Are you telling me you don't know what happened to him?"

"For God's sake tell me."

"He's in hospital. He was found yesterday looking like Guy Fawkes, after the fire. There's a machine. When they turn it off his next stop is the chapel of rest."

Her mouth opened in shock. She was stunned. It appeared absolutely genuine.

"What happened?" she asked. Her face had paled.

"Someone poured paraffin all over him and lit a match. I don't suppose it was to keep him warm. Not even his best friend would recognize him now."

Her eyes dropped and she stared at her drink. Her frown deepened. "You think . . . ?"

"Yes, I do."

She looked up and shook her head. "I didn't know anything about it, Lenny." The shake continued. "Believe me, please."

"I do believe you. But I believe also that your brother and Nick over there, and the other goon, Mario, were responsible in some way."

"Oh my God," she said. She lifted her hand to her forehead as though feeling for pain.

"So, tell me about him?"

"I went out once, to dinner. It wasn't even special. I mean, I barely knew him. He was a friend of a friend. He asked me out and I said yes. I wasn't his sort. He didn't even ask me for a second date." She looked up as though struck by a sudden thought. "I don't agree with you. Listen, you're suggesting he was attacked because he took me out. Right?"

I nodded.

"If that were the case, they would have done it a month ago. Not now. Not when it's all over. I mean, what's the point?" She had a point but it wasn't convincing.

"When Paddy loses control, do you think it makes a difference whether it was yesterday or last year?"

"But he doesn't mind. He's always telling me to go out and enjoy myself."

"Oh yeah, is that before or after he warns me that if I touch you I'm going to be singing through a tracheotomy? You saw him last night. In that mood he's capable of anything."

She looked grave. "I don't agree with you," she said. "But now I'm frightened."

"Of what?"

"Things are moving in," she said sadly. "It's all getting too much. Let me tell you how it was." She folded her arms defensively and went on, "I was eight when my parents died. Paddy was fifteen. It was an accident; no one was to blame. Uncle Bob and Aunty Joyce took Paddy in. They would have taken me too, but the social work people wouldn't let them. It was the shock, you see? The shock of my mum and dad being killed . . . I was difficult . . . " She struggled and said finally, "I needed treatment at hospital." She paused and took a deep breath.

"This isn't my business, Julie."

"I want you to know. I want you to understand what's going on."

I shrugged and nodded.

"It sounds silly now, but in a way Paddy blamed me for leaving him. We were always very close. Before the accident we spent every minute together. He didn't go out with the other boys or have girlfriends or anything like that. It was always me. Or rather, me and Anthony. The three of us were inseparable. As soon as school was finished and at weekends we'd be together. We'd go to Uncle Bob's over at Epping. He had an indoor pool and a huge, huge games room. We used to play table-tennis and snooker and darts. Everything. We used to play in the pool until our fingers turned white and crinkly. When I had my breakdown, after the accident, I was taken away. Paddy blamed me for having the breakdown. Can you understand that? I was put into care. Paddy went off to South America. Eventually he found me a place in Cambridge where I could have treatment. Then he bought me the house in Mill Hill. He wanted to visit but it was impossible because of the police. He says they fitted him up. I couldn't go over there because of my treatment. So we were kept apart. Can you understand now why he's so frightened of losing me again? He's terrified that I'll get hurt again and be taken away. Now he's ill it's made him even worse."

"How old is Paddy?" I asked

"He's seven years older than me. Thirty-three."

I hid my surprise. He looked a dozen years older than that. "He never got married?"

She shook her head. "He did actually, to a girl from Rio. But it didn't last. He always talked about returning home one day and she always maintained she'd never come, so in a way they never really stood a chance."

She took a tissue from her handbag, dabbed at her nose then said, "I need the Ladies."

I pointed the way.

"You'll wait for me?"

I smiled at her apprehension and said, "I'm here for another three hours."

She walked toward the foyer. Her steps were youthful and easy. Her movements gave no clue to the beating she had taken. Even before she reached the door Nick had moved across to take her place.

"What do you think?" he asked.

"About what?"

"About you getting her the hell away from it for a while? She needs a break."

He smiled at my astonishment. He raised a huge hand and stroked his cheek. "Hasn't she asked you yet?"

I shook my head.

He nodded. "She will. All the way over here she was askin' me whether I thought you would. I told her to go for it. She needs a different scene. A break. Long enough to think things out."

I found my voice. "About last night–"

He put up his hands, palms toward me. "I seen it comin' for weeks. It's been building up inside him like a fucking volcano. They'll sort him out at the clinic. They always do. He used to fly to Switzerland from Rio. Different name, of course. He should have been back last month but this business delayed it. I'm tellin' you, Kid, him comin' back here was a mistake. In more ways than one." He paused before adding, "I wouldn't have hit her, you know. That show was all for your benefit."

"You could have fooled me."

"I did. Paddy too." His eyes narrowed and he said very seriously, "You've gotta talk her into leaving him, setting up on her own. Understand? Who knows when it'll happen again?" He shook his head. "Christ! If Paddy could hear me speaking now."

"Well I can barely believe it."

"Listen, I think she'll take your advice. She's gotta get away from him. Make her believe it."

"Where do you fit in?"

"I work for Paddy. Anything he says goes, to a point. But this is a two-edged sword. His madness didn't start until we arrived back here. Nothing like this happened in South America. It's her. Although he doesn't see it, she's the cause of his breakdowns. It's a fucking obsession." He stood and picked up his glass. "Do us all a favour, Kid, yourself included. Get her away for a couple of days. Show her that life exists outside of Paddy Delaney!" He pushed a card on the table. "That's my phone number. You can get me on that."

"Why do I need that?"

"You never know."

"Tell me about her last boyfriend, Nicholas?"

He looked puzzled. "It didn't work out," he said.

"Is that all?"

"Is there anything else?"

"He's in hospital."

He shook his head. "News to me. What are you saying?" He was almost convincing.

I shrugged weakly.

He had taken up his position at the bar again by the time she came back.

I bought us a couple more drinks and checked my watch. There were still ten minutes of break left. Ten minutes. With some people ten minutes could be like an hour. With Julie Delaney, Einstein came into it.

She looked brighter.

"Nick's been over," I told her. "He thinks you need to get away for a couple of days."

She turned to glance at him. He was hunched over the bar stirring his green drink with a straw. She turned back to me and said, "Will you come with me?"

"How will your brother feel about that?"

"My brother's not in the country. It's none of his business."

"He might not see it that way."

"He will." She paused. A smile fluttered around her mouth. She laced her fingers together. It became a fidget. "I want to sleep with you, Lenny."

My eyes must have widened.

"Is that so unusual?" she asked.

"Yeah."

"Well I do, so now it's down to you. Do you want to sleep with me?"

I nodded slowly.

"Will you pick me up tomorrow?"

"Where?"

"Come to the house."

I raised my eyebrows, almost in resignation, but there was nothing apathetic about it; my gut was turning inside out.

"About lunchtime," I said quietly.

She gave a little shiver and caught her breath.

They stayed for half of the next session, then she gave me a little wave from the back of the room and I watched them leave.

During the next break I told Joe Gabriel that I was taking a a night off. He bristled at the idea. Losing me for a night wasn't the end of the world, far from it, but getting a replacement at short notice was a pain.

"It's not done, man," Clarinet said angrily. "You shouldn't let people down like this. If you was ill then that's different. But you ain't, except in the head!"

66

"I want to get her away. All I need is a couple of days."

"Man, it's not just you lettin' us down, it's the situation. Can't you see that? You're playin' with somethin' worse than a headache here. You've already seen what he's like. What about us? Peter, or the rest of the band? What if he comes around here lookin' for her?"

"He's out of the country for at least a week. It's OK. Nick's squared it all."

"Nick? Nick? You believe him? He's just a minder, Sonny."

"Believe it or not, he's lookin' after her."

"That's what you say. That's not what I'm hearin'. Man, this is dangerous. I don' wanna come visitin' you in some hospital. And that's what'll happen. You think you're a fuckin' prayin' mantis, is that it? Or a black widow? The male gets eaten after he's finished shaggin'. Man, pain is a bigger sensation than comin' ever was, and it lasts longer. Keep that in mind."

He saw that he wasn't getting through and shook his head. "Sonny, Sonny, you're goin' to tell me that you're in love?"

"Well, fuck it, I've started playin' all the old King Cole records, and I've been listening to the words."

"Jesus, it's serious, then." He threw up despairing hands. "Bollocks! It's bullshit, man. People don't fall in love that quickly. You're still in the wet-dream stage. The dangerous stage." He shook his head in resignation. "Go on then. One night, that's all. I'll tell 'em your beatin' was worse than we thought. They'll understand that."

"Thanks, Joe."

"Don' thank me, Sonny. I have a bad feeling about this. I think you're askin' for a whole lot of trouble and I don' understand why. She ain't that special."

I flashed him a throwaway smile.

"Oh, shit!" he said bleakly. "Maybe she is. I don' know nothin' no more."

EIGHT

Julie was waiting for me to pull up. Nick carried her case down the two wide, marble steps and placed it by the boot. As I climbed out of the car, he looked at me seriously.

"You take care of her," he said and looked over his shoulder to make certain he was out of earshot. "Get any problems and you contact me."

I asked, "What sort of problems?"

"Anything," he said.

"You going to explain?"

"Nope."

"Didn't think you would."

He gave the Escort the once over. I'd spent an hour cleaning it out. I was never one for being car proud. To me one looked very much like another. You shoved fuel in one place and produced fumes in another. The dust tended to build up around the empty cigarette cartons. Leave a car clean and parked outside and it was likely to go missing. Fuck that. That was my excuse.

"It's got an MOT," I said.

He grunted and strode off around the side of the house. She closed the heavy front door behind her, smiled, and gave me a little tentative wave before skipping down the steps to the car.

"Where are we going?" she asked breathlessly.

"That's a secret. Don't worry, no one will find us."

"I'm not worried about that," she said.

"It was a joke."

"Oh." She laughed. "I didn't get it."

She undid her raincoat and threw it on to the back seat. She wore a knee-length dark-green dress, slightly flared. She pulled the seat-belt and snapped it shut.

"OK then, I'm all yours," she said.

The Great Cambridge Road begins or ends on the footings of London Bridge. The London end of it is a shit, traffic lights every fifty yards and none of them in sequence. It cuts through Royston and Cambridge on its way to King's Lynn. It passes over the Ouse and the Wissey and the Nar towards the salty air that comes in from the North Sea over the Wash.

"Did your brother phone?"

"This morning," she said. "Early."

"Did he give you trouble."

"A little, but he came round in the end. It's not you he's against. It's the idea. He thinks that he'll lose me, his little sister."

"It's about time he did."

"Don't be hard on him. He lost me once before. It took him a long time to get me back."

I nodded, hoping that she would go on, but she left it there.

"Look," she said, pointing forward. "There's fog ahead."

In the winter months a sea-mist often spills in from the wedge of grey water and dilutes the surroundings; the air becomes slippery and slows down the traffic to a crawl. The mist creeps in with the night and turns the night into a ghostly place and often it doesn't clear until the afternoon. It was just beginning to lift as we took a right on to the A148.

"I'm wearing white undies," she said. "I bought them in Harrods this morning."

I glanced across, surprised, and yet slightly thrilled. I tried to hide a fluttering smile.

"I went to see Nicky Clarke and his lizard skins first – you never said you liked my hair! Do you think it's too short?"

"No, it's perfect."

"Then I went to Harrods. I wondered what you would like and decided it had to be white." She smiled quickly, nervously. "They're from the Cacharel collection, trimmed with lace. I put them on for you." She paused again, briefly. "I think it's important to get things right, don't you?"

"Show me."

She gave me a little cat's grin and then drew the hem of her dress to her waist to reveal her bare legs and a white vee of cotton.

"Seen enough?"

"Unless you want a head-on collision."

She lowered her dress again and smoothed the material against her legs.

"Was I right?" Her voice thickened.

Mine was already treacle. "About what?"

"About you liking white?"

Without glancing her way, I nodded. I had to concentrate. Her legs were still getting in the way of the road.

"I thought so," she said.

We drove on, into a storm.

Sheringham is a tiny coastal resort that has grown out of a small fishing community. No more than a single road, really, that runs up to the coast, with shops and a few arcades lining each side. Behind the shops pre-war houses nestle in cosy rows. It is a tiny place and, at the time of year we found it, almost deserted.

The old hotel faces north, its white blistered façade leans into a wind that buffets in off the winter sea. The waves thrash a thick stone wall that stands just thirty feet from the grudging front door. Between the wall and the worn concrete steps to the door, a road sweeps around from the side of the hotel, edged by the narrowest of pavements. We followed the road around three sides of the old four-storey building and found a small car-park.

I pulled our luggage from the boot and fighting a strong wind that drew tears from our eyes, we ran around to the entrance. The door didn't close properly, the draught curled around its edge and paper notices hanging on the hall wall fluttered. I dropped the cases on a threadbare carpet and turned to her.

She was windswept, brushing strands of loose hair from her face. Her fawn-coloured mac was dotted by the rain. She wiped the tears from her eyes and smiled.

"You bring me to the best places," she said and peered around.

She didn't know that some of my roots were bedded in the hotel's foundations. I'd escaped here once before, just after Donna had left, and some old friends had put me back together. It was the safest place I could think of, and the last place her brother would expect to find her.

Before us, a steep flight of carpeted steps led to the upper floors. Beside them, the corridor continued to the kitchen. On our left, a series of windows looked into a dining-room and, to the right, a door led to the bar.

We left the cases in the hall and took the door. The room was rustic: low ceiling joists, wooden alcoves, sea paraphernalia, a log fire, rudimentary tables and chairs with split vinyl and loose legs. A couple of gaming-machines stood side-by-side winking coloured lights through the thick cigarette smoke. In the corner a Karaoke machine was silent, its monitor dusty. It stood next to a battered upright piano. The bar itself was in an annex near to another entrance from the side road. A few people stood there, leaning on its polished surface over pints of beer. In an alcove beside it, an elderly man sat beside a small wiry dog. The lunchtime trade had just ended for the room was a mess, the ashtrays brimmed with dog-ends and discarded cigarette packs and the tables were cluttered with empties.

"It's a hovel," she whispered. "Like something out of *Treasure Island*. Peg-legs and smugglers. Any moment now, someone's going to come in with a parrot. I don't believe it."

"Wait until you see the room. He charges extra for the mildew."

"Lenny, boy, what brings you to town?"

Max was a heavy-set man, barrel shaped, in his mid-fifties. His face was always gloomy, his disposition tetchy; it was an act, part of his humour.

He went on, "You made it just in time. There's a gale on the way. We've had flood warnings, high wind warnings, the lot. Mind you, I can't think of a finer place I'd sooner be stranded in!"

"We're only staying if I can have the penthouse suite."

He pulled a face. "Well, it's still there. At least it was the last time I looked." His voice lowered apologetically. "I'll have to charge you extra for the air-conditioning."

"That's the crack in the window," I explained to Julie.

She smiled nervously.

"You were lucky to see me again," he muttered. "I was thinking of retiring, going to Mexico."

I grinned and said, "Ever since I've known this guy he's been retiring. About twenty years ago he met a girl from Mexico and since then he's been going to look her up."

"Once you've tasted real chilli," he grumbled. "Nothin' else will ever do."

"You are talking about food?"

71

"What else?" He handed over the key with a knowing glint in his pale blue eyes.

"If you're about later, pop in for a drink. We'll mull over old times."

I nodded, then guided Julie to the door.

Our room was on the top floor. It was just as I remembered, holed carpet, cracked window, a damp patch on the ceiling discoloured by green mould, and a lumpy double bed covered with a faded green candlewick.

"I haven't seen one of those in years," she said, astonished or maybe horrified at the state of the room.

The bathroom was on the next landing down. There was no shower but the bath was huge, cast-iron. While you lay in it you could look up at the ceiling where a missing ceiling board afforded a dim view of the joists holding up the next floor. If anything moved up there, if anyone moved, then you got a reduction on the bill.

The wind whistled through the crack in the bay window. Across the heavy sea a single light blinked out of the darkness. I drew the thin curtains that didn't quite meet and turned on the electric fan heater.

"There you are, central heating."

She smiled and took off her raincoat. I caught hold of her hand and drew her toward me. She turned away from the kiss and surprised me.

"I need to bathe," she said. "Do you mind? It might thaw me out a bit."

I realized I had rushed her. "Of course. Be careful of the hot tap. Unless it's changed over the years, the water comes out scalding."

She undid her bag and took out a small vanity case. She paused at the door. "I won't be long," she said and gave me a promising look.

She reappeared ten minutes later. In that time I had used the small basin in our room to clean my teeth and splash some water about. Her hair was wet, strands of it clung to her cheeks. She knelt before the heater. The rush of air lifted her hair into streamers. I sat on the bed, quite content to watch her.

"There's a quiet little restaurant down the road," I said. "Shall we go and have dinner?"

She turned her head to look at me. There was a mixture of surprise and relief on her face. She nodded. The hotel had been too much for her, unexpectedly rough. I guessed that she had never seen anything like it before. She was probably worried about things with six legs, things that jumped and crawled. Little wonder that she had cooled toward me. My reasons for choosing it didn't didn't seem good enough. For a moment I wondered whether to find a pukka hotel. One with some stars and AA letters.

"We don't have to stay here," I said apologetically. "I realize it was a mistake."

She glanced back again, frowning. "Mistake?"

"You're not happy here. We can find a four-star. Our own bathroom."

"Don't be silly. It's an amazing place. I wouldn't have it differently."

She surprised me again. I thought she would have jumped at the idea.

" . . . And dinner sounds great," she went on. "Do I need to dress up?" She smiled beautifully.

"Is that sarcasm?"

She narrowed her eyes. "Maybe."

I watched her dress in a Romeo Gigli pinstripe trouser-suit and, by the time we hit the door, I was bucking like Gregory Peck in *The Big Country*. I'd seen that movie a dozen times. Even now I could picture my brother getting the hump as I asked him to play it again. For a while back there I was in love with Jean Simmons.

I took her along to a place on the main road, an excellent little restaurant run by a couple of old friends. She sat us in a secluded corner and he came up from the kitchen wearing his chef's crown.

"Lenny, Lenny," he said and embraced me in his thick arms. He was Maltese and had not yet learned English reserve. His wife was English but she didn't want to teach him, thank God. "Stay behind afterwards," he said. "And have some brandy with us."

I glanced at my watch. It was only just seven.

"It's been a long day," I said.

He glanced at Julie then back to me. "Well," he shrugged. "I understand. I'll pop up just in case."

Julie seemed suitably impressed by the fuss. The lemon sole was recommended along with the house pâté. Julie chose the Médoc. Once we were left alone she looked out from under long dark lashes with wide-eyed innocence and whispered, "What lovely people". She leaned closer, resting her arms on the table. "We are going to make love tonight, aren't we?"

There was something in the intimacy of the proposal, the shared secret, that left me breathless. Of course we were. That had always been the intention, yet somehow it had remained illusive, still to be broached. It was still a fantasy. Now she had put it up front with nervy anticipation. Her eyes gleamed triumphantly.

Under the tablecloth she slipped off her shoe and raised her foot. She pressed me with her toes and smiled wickedly when I responded against them.

At that moment my desire for her was so intense it was almost painful.

"Shall we go now? I've suddenly lost my appetite."

"No," she said quickly and shook her head. "I want to make it last all night." She pressed harder. "I want to spend the rest of the evening just certain of what is to come. Every time you move now I shall be thinking I will be having you later, that you will be between my legs, and each thought will send a little spasm right to the top of me."

"Bloody hell," I said.

"Will you undress me?" She spoke like a little girl asking to go to the fair. "While I stand still?"

"If that's what you want." I was puzzled and yet filled with admiration. She seemed somehow naïve, wholly innocent.

"That's what I want," she said firmly.

We used the side door to get back into the hotel. The road at the front was awash as the waves crashed over the sea wall. In order to get to reception, the corridor with a single table holding the signing-in book, we had to go through the bar. It had filled up. We had to fight our way in. Halfway across the room, a hand tugged at my arm and I looked down into a familiar face.

Ghost was a slight, grey man around fifty years old. A shadowy figure, his face sallow and lined, his long hair falling limply over his ears and neck, his eyes introduced him. Bland, opaque, his steady gaze eased from behind a deathly grey shroud.

He lifted his roll-up with nicotine-stained fingers and deliberately exhaled a stream of smoke upwards towards us. His thin lips parted to reveal, surprisingly, a line of sparkling white teeth. His smile was engaging. It cracked his face into a thousand lines.

I said, "See you had your teeth done?"

"Yeah," he said in a soft, Anglian accent. "Scraped, descaled, capped, you name it. All I need now is to have my gums out."

Julie let out a girlish nervous laugh. I'd heard it before.

He reached up and shook my hand. "You want a drink?"

I glanced at her while she looked apprehensively around the tightly packed, smoky room.

"What do you say?" I asked.

She looked directly at Ghost. "Isn't it a bit crowded?"

He chuckled. "It's a popular pub, sweetheart. Don't worry. I'll tell you some sea stories."

"I'm sure you will," she said coolly.

He stood up from his table and went off to buy the drinks. She watched him for a moment then turned back to me. "Who is that?" she asked in amazement.

"That is the Ghost. Not that it's anything to be proud of but he used to be a burglar. He got caught."

"My God," she said, astonished.

"In the old days we did a few gigs together. Some years ago we did a season at Cromer. That's just up the coast. He fell in love with a local girl and ended up staying. About three years ago his wife died and he moved in here. The first floor. He's been here ever since. Every time I do this coast I seem to end up here."

She mouthed an 'Oh', and shook her head.

"Don't worry," I reassured her. "He's absolutely harmless. Really."

I could see she was unsettled by the crowd. She seemed intimidated by the crush, even frightened. For someone not used to the press of other bodies, it must have seemed almost claustrophobic. "We'll just stay for a quick one," I said. "Any time you like we'll get out of here. OK?"

She nodded, the panicky look faded. My suggestion had given her the control she needed.

Ghost returned with the drinks. Julie sipped hers immediately, without questioning his choice.

"This is Julie," I said to him.

He looked her up and down and nodded appreciatively. Eventually he turned back to me.

"You making a living?" he asked. His weak lips curled around his glass of Scotch.

"Just about. You?"

"Not much. Gettin' too old. Thought about goin' out to the tropics, helpin' the starvin', but you know how I hate the heat. I thought about joinin' Greenpeace and savin' the humpback whale on account of that's my favourite word."

Julie fell for it. "Hump!" she said and gave him a little nervous laugh.

"No." He shook his head. "Whale!"

He left the puzzle spreading across her face. His pale eyes glided around the room and settled on the battered piano.

"Want to give it a crack?" he said. "Max's suggestion. Said you ought to be good for something." He smiled and his dead eyes came to life.

I shook my head. "Not really."

"Come on, be like the old days."

Over the heads of the crowd, I could see Max at the bar. He was pointing to me and then to the piano. I raised my hands in resignation and he seemed satisfied.

Julie was puzzled. She asked, "What's happening?"

"Max has a request," I said.

"He's sick of the Karaoke, or rather, the people who use it." Ghost grinned and turned back to me. "Come on, you know he's your only fan."

Julie seemed taken with the idea and pushed me forward. "I'd like to hear this," she said.

Ghost carved a way through the crowd to the piano, moved some empty beer glasses and an overflowing ashtray and sat down. He tried the middle C, grimaced, and shot me a look. His leg began to jerk as he used the soft pedal. He ran down the scale. Some people close by turned our way, amusement flickered on their faces. The hush spread from them and the room quietened. Julie moved to the other side of Ghost and watched me.

Ghost flashed me a quick look as he ran into a familiar tune. "Remember this?"

"Remember it? I've still got an old Vic Damone track at home someplace."

His fingers fluttered. He ran through the opening again. Some of the older punters started to hum and sing. One guy in the alcove began whistling and his wiry black-and-white dog started to howl. The youngsters looked on bewildered, open-mouthed, until it caught up with them.

I let him play it through again. Julie watched me curiously. It was an old Styne-Cahn number. *The* old Styne-Cahn number.

"Come on!" Ghost muttered. "This is gettin' monotonous."

"Mmmnn, 'Time after Time'." I grinned at him and made an intro.

After it was finished and the applause died down, we were left with shouts of "More! More!" Even the youngsters seemed keen.

Ghost said, "Well, they wouldn't appreciate jazz in here, would they? Try this one."

He started on 'Mona Lisa'. Some of the older girls yelled and began to murder it.

"I always said I'd never do his sentimental crap," I murmured.

"Come on, slum it for once in your life."

Halfway through the song he muttered: "You're sounding just like Bob Hoskins," and I laughed and missed the next line. It didn't make a lot of difference. Every customer in the room had joined in.

We were forced into a last number. There was no way we could get out of there without it. Max brought us some fresh drinks.

"You should come here more often," he said. Then, as an afterthought, shook his head. "Come to think of it you better not. I'd have to pay for an entertainment licence."

Ghost started on a new song. "We've done this before," he said.

"Yeah," I said and began immediately.

Julie watched me closely. Appreciation narrowed her eyes. She was impressed.

It was about building a dream. It came out of the American depression but even today it had the power to hit you in the guts:

ploughing earth, bearing guns, building railroads – got a dime, buddy? Things don't change.

Her gaze had turned child-like, wondrous. I grinned at her. She bobbed her black head in enthusiasm.

Everyone joined in. The room shook.

We stayed with Ghost, Max and the other regulars until closing time and then some. Julie felt perfectly at ease and joined in on the reminiscing, laughing at the tall stories. By the time we climbed the stairs we were both tipsy.

The sea roared. The foaming waves crashed over the wall. The road at the front of the hotel had become a gully. Dark water rushed down the slope toward the slipway. In the wash of light from the street lamps, it was a frightening place. Above, the clouds tossed and heaved and snuffed out the stars. The fierce black rain pelted our loose window.

I let the curtain drop and turned to her.

She stood shivering by the bed, even though I had left the fan-heater on and the room was warm and stuffy. I became all thumbs as I undressed her. It wasn't just nervousness. Her instructions had taken away the spontaneity. She closed her eyes. It was a fantasy: the savouring of every single touch, the fluttering of naked skin as her clothes were peeled away. Shoes, jacket, trousers, – silk scarf, a crêpe-de-Chine blouse that whispered as it dropped to the carpet.

The fan-heater blew a hot draught around her legs. Even so, goose pimples prickled along her thighs.

Her bra unfastened at the front. She drew in a quick little breath. Her breasts were smallish and delicate, the lower curves marked by a faint bluishness and traced with the hint of veins. Her nipples were small and rigid, really dark against her pale skin. I wanted to pause and kiss them but she wriggled her hips impatiently and opened her eyes.

"Now it's your turn to stay still."

"Is this a game?"

"It could be."

"I'm not very good at games. In any case, I haven't finished." I pulled the elastic on her white knickers.

She twisted away from me and kneeled down. She unbuttoned

78

my Levis. Her slender hand slid inside, incredibly cool against my belly.

She pulled me out, or rather, freed me, for I sprang out without her help. I was already sticky; I had been since dinner. I watched her tongue flick out to touch me, teasing. She looked up and smiled playfully.

Her lips closed over me. It reminded me of another time. For an instant the thought made me shudder. I shook it away. I felt the sharp edge of her teeth and then her tongue. Her mouth had become a vacuum. I felt that slow surge begin and pulled away from her.

She threw me a little knowing smile and crawled on to the bed where she lay to watch me undress. She stretched out languidly and slid one leg against the other, a sexy little move that sent my belly into a thousand flutters. I sat on the bed to get rid of the rest of my gear. Eventually I turned to her and found her momentarily preoccupied, staring into space.

"What's the matter?" I asked. It was that obvious.

"I'm so nervous. All of a sudden I feel panicky, tight. I can hardly breath. Look!" She raised a trembling hand.

I sat beside her and softly held her hand. "You don't have to be nervous of me. I'm not going to hurt you."

"It's not that." Her smile was fragile and uncertain.

"What then?"

Her brow creased and she shook her head. There was a real, unexplained fear in her eyes. Her body was tense, totally stressed out.

I hadn't expected this at all. She had been savouring the idea throughout the evening and now it had come to it, she had frozen. I was wound up, still throbbing, yet more concerned than disappointed.

I leaned across and kissed her.

Once we broke she said: "Will you do something for me?"

"Of course."

"Would you . . . ?" She flicked an embarrassed little smile.

"Go on," I encouraged.

"Would you just stroke me for a while?"

I smiled back. "That's easy. I think it's called foreplay."

"I didn't mean that."

"I know."

Not moving, she lay under my hands. I began on her shoulders and breasts and ribcage and gently moved down. I felt the tension draw out of her as she relaxed. At one stage I thought she had fallen asleep. It was a novelty for me, exploring every inch of a new body so slowly. I found it exciting and before long I was surging again, barely in control.

I pushed under her pants and when she didn't object I peeled them away from her and uncovered a faint bruise on the left side of her belly. As I removed them her hand went down to cover herself. Dark hair spilled around her fingers. Slowly, not daring to startle her, I held her hand aside and buried my face between her legs. She spread them slightly and shivered as I kissed her groin and found that fluttering spot. The texture was slightly rough, her musky perfume so subtle that I couldn't figure out whether it was natural or applied. Suddenly she writhed and without shame lifted her knees. I expected to find her indecently runny, at melting point, like me, but she was dry. She flinched although I had barely touched her. She twisted away from me and drew her legs up in a foetal position.

"I'm sorry, I'm sorry," she said. "I'm no good at this!"

"What on earth's the matter?" I asked anxiously, not wanting it to end. I was willing to try for ever. I could still feel the muscular spasms working across my thighs. The sensation was painful.

She didn't answer. She had her back to me. Her buttocks were as pale as ivory, her muscles clenched. The promise of night had been turned on its head. I drew up the bedclothes to cover us. The gale was still howling against the windows. The curtain moved gently into our space.

She slept. She hadn't moved away from me, nor had she resisted when I slid my arm around her and pressed myself against her smooth back in a close embrace. She slept, but it wasn't peaceful. Occasionally she would tense and her breath would catch, until, after a while, she would relax again and sleep on. I wondered in what sort of mixed-up world she was dreaming.

The first time she woke, perhaps half an hour later, she was sweaty, bathed in the heat from the electric blower. She murmured. Her breaths shortened and she gripped the bedclothes. Suddenly she let out a long drawn out sigh. She arched upward and went rigid and her breathing stopped altogether. Perhaps three or four seconds passed before she breathed out again and then sank back on to the bed like a crumpled doll.

It was about four in the morning when I realized she had woken again. I had turned off the heater before sleeping myself, but I sensed that I could feel the blow of heat. The next second or two were a bit hazy and I was only vaguely aware of what was happening. There were shadows moving and lights flashing, and then a sudden searing pain in my arm. I thought, in that moment of waking, that I had been stung, that a bee had found its way into the bed.

The pain cleared my head. I was coughing without realizing it. The room was full of smoke. Flames rose from the bed and licked at my arm. Even as I snatched my arm out of the flames and rolled off the bed I caught sight of her. She stood by my side of the bed, naked. The flames flickered a dim light across her pale body. She was striking matches, one after the other, dropping them as they flared. Even though her eyes were wide open, staring at the flames, I knew that she was in a trance. Her body was stiff, her movements jerky and unco-ordinated.

I leaped around the bed and pushed her away from the danger. She fell to the carpet and lay motionless. I grabbed the sheet, put out the flames, and carried it across to the window. The window catch was stiff. Layers of paint stripped off as I threw open the window. The wind gusted in. Sparks flew off the smouldering bedclothes. I tossed them out into the night. Before they hit the ground below, they were drenched. I left the window slightly open and let the Force Ten clear the room of smoke.

She was awake now; her mouth was pulled back and a strangled cry came from deep within her. Her eyes were wide open, the horror of what she saw stopped her from blinking. I pulled one of the blankets from the bed, examined it for damage, then put it around her shoulders. As I kneeled beside her, she gripped my arm. Gently, I put my other arm around her shoulders and drew her towards me. She was cold; I felt the tiny hairs brush against me. She sobbed; her tears cooled the blisters that were

81

rising on my wrist. She wept silently. Occasionally she shuddered. I sat up in the bed while she lay with her head on my chest and watched a pale dawn ghost in through the windows.

As the light intensified she stirred. She had slept for an hour or so, my arm around her. Once or twice I considered moving her; the burn on my forearm was beginning to throb painfully. Not wanting to disturb her I put up with it. Now her eyes opened. She saw my arm wrapped around her, the blisters not more than six or seven inches from her face. I felt her body go rigid and heard her voice. She sounded strange, high-pitched.

"I did that! I did it! I didn't mean to! Don't hurt me, please!"

"It's all right," I said. "I won't hurt you."

She began to scream. She broke free from me and her hands struck out between us, as if defending her space. She backed away and on all fours made for the door. "Stay away! Stay away!" she screamed.

Her scream barely covered the harsh knocking on the bedroom door and, above it, I could make out Max's voice.

"Lenny! What the hell's happening in there?"

And then the door opened and two or three astonished faces, Max's included, peered into the room, quite horrified at the scene of chaos before them.

"What's this?" Max said as he looked from the naked girl, still on all fours, whimpering now like some kind of wounded animal, to the burns on his carpet and bed, to the smoke marks on his wall and ceiling, to me, open-mouthed on the bed, holding my wrist as though it was broken. "What's this?" he repeated. "Some kind of deviation I haven't come across?"

NINE

On the answering-machine Clarinet grumbled: "You better be here tonight, man. This is just a reminder. A threat of real pain. Know what I mean, Sonny?"

Donna came on, slightly breathless: "Lenny, it's me. Roger's really worried. He didn't give me all the details. You know Roger, but he says you're in well over your head. Can you come round?" She was chewing on something and spoke with her mouth full. "If it's too late, don't forget we've got to talk about pressies. OK? Love you. No I don't. What am I saying? I mean, see you!"

Two more pips, a little silence, then: "Mr Webb, my name is Ellen Zahavi."

The name rang a vague bell.

"I'm a doctor. Julie Delaney has been referred to me. It's important that we meet. I'd be grateful if you'd phone me. I'm based at Cambridge. You can get me daytime at the university." She reeled off the number.

Nick must have given the doctor my name. It couldn't have been Julie. When Nick had picked her up at the hotel she hadn't known what time of day it was. He had wrapped a blanket around her and carried her down the stairs to a private ambulance as though she weighed nothing. He wasn't angry or hostile. Instead his eyes held on to a distant, almost resigned sadness. The only thing he said to me was, "This isn't good, Lenny".

Cambridge. Now I knew where I'd heard Ellen Zahavi's name before. Donna is a social worker. At the moment she's working through a six-month maternity leave. When we first met, she was a student into her second year of the social work diploma at the Anglia Polytechnic University in Cambridge. She was exciting, full of life, impatient to try out the world. She was too young to marry. It seemed to snuff out a part of her. But one of her modules at the university, a difficult one I recall, had been psychology. I linked Zahavi's name with that. Donna's studies, which had continued a further year for the degree, and my evenings at the club, meant that we rarely saw each other. We would meet up occasionally to discuss the bank account and, when they arrived, the children, but it was hardly a conventional marriage. It was one of the things that had led us to part.

I wrote down the number, reset the machine then took a swift walk toward the park and my ex-house, ex-garden and ex-wife. A frost was only just beginning to lift in the weak sun. The heavy rain that fell overnight had turned to ice. Little rinks dotted the park.

"I should have kept the key," I said when she opened the front door. She wore her dark suit: shopping clothes. She was on her way in, or out.

"Roger would love that idea." She smiled. As we went down the hall, she indicated a vase of flowers on the windowsill. "Look what he came in with," she said. "He's obviously hiding something." She eased past a pram near the door and led me into the kitchen. Roger was sitting at the table, bleary eyes into the sports pages of an *Express*, one hand toying with a half-full cup of coffee. A late breakfast plate was half hidden by the paper. The new baby lay across him, her little black head lolled in the crook of his arm.

He glanced up. "Look at this," he said. "Domestic bliss." He nodded toward me. "Hello, man. Take a seat."

I asked, "Where are the twins?"

Donna paused while she filled the electric kettle. "They put on their roller-boots and went off to do some ice-skating on the park."

"Ice-skating?"

"That's what they said. It is cold enough. I'm surprised you didn't see them."

"This morning I'm walking around with my eyes closed."

She gave me a dim look and plugged in the kettle.

"You and me both, mate!" Roger said. "I've just done eighteen straight hours, and seventeen of them were spent filling in forms."

"Well, you chose the police-force," I said light-heartedly. He shared my grin and said, "At Hendon they never told us we'd be fillin' in forms for most of the shift!"

The baby stirred, snuggled closer into his arm and carried on sleeping. He lifted his cup and finished his coffee.

"Somebody must have heard me asking about Delaney," he said abruptly. "There's something nasty going down. Quite a few people have been moved in from divisional to set up a Special Op Task Force, working with CIB. I've been warned off from even mentioning his name."

I shook my head. "CIB?"

"Complaints. Now they want to see me. I could be in the shit over this. I should have reported it, taken an official line. They'll want to know why I didn't. I shouldn't be telling you all this, Lenny. Official secrets, you know."

"I know. I'll keep it in the family. What do you reckon, then? Corruption? Is he paying the wages?

"Roger considered me for a moment, then said carefully: "That would be my guess, but maybe not. Maybe he's coming clean. Christ, supergrass won't be good enough to describe him! They'll have to dream up a new word."

I raised my eyebrows. "Bloody hell. That would be a turn-up."

"But I can't see it," he went on. "More likely they want to nail him and don't trust the people on his manor. Know what I mean? They simply want to know why I was askin' about him. I'm going to have to tell them about you, Lenny."

From the side, Donna gave me a questioning look.

"That shouldn't be a problem. You can put it under the heading of domestic quarrels. He didn't like the idea of his sister talking to me."

Donna put some coffee in front of me. Heavily. A splash of it hit the table. She gave me a dark, secretive glance.

"Are you sure that's all?" she asked coldly. For a moment I thought she was actually jealous.

"Yeah, I'm sure. There's no problem. You can tell them I didn't complain but that you asked about my bruises. That OK?"

"Funny you should say that. That's what I was going to suggest. We keep the other problem to ourselves, eh?"

He meant the attack on Julie's last boyfriend. He didn't want his snout talking to anyone else, especially not CIB. He might just spill the beans about other things. And he didn't want Donna knowing about it either. Maybe he didn't want her seeing him as anything less than incorruptible. Apart from Mike, I knew of a few dealers from the club scene that had been paying him a regular income. It wouldn't surprise me to find out that Delaney did too. Donna would be heartbroken if she discovered how her husband paid the rent and managed to take them to Florida in successive years.

"OK, man," he said and stood up. He gave the baby to Donna and said, "I'm going to leave you and get to bed. If I hear anything, I'll talk to you."

I nodded. He closed the kitchen door behind him. A few moments later we heard his footsteps as the ceiling creaked.

Donna settled the baby in the pram. I watched her from the kitchen table. She came in again with a curious expression.

"What's the other problem?" she asked seriously. She stood beside me, waiting for an answer. It had to be good. She reached out and touched my shoulder. I put my hand on top of hers. "What's the other problem, Lenny?" she repeated.

"It's not a problem. Mike was busted, possession. I wanted the details, that's all. Whether we had to find another drummer."

She nodded. After a few moments she seemed satisfied. I dropped my hand and placed it on her behind. She looked down at me and pursed her lips but didn't move. I stroked down to the top of her legs. She wriggled and broke free but from the kitchen sink she glanced back with a look that said maybe. She turned back to the sink and began to cut some sweet potatoes and yams into squares.

"It's about time you got yourself another girl, man."

"You'd just be jealous."

"Maybe I would. But I'd get over it."

"Remember a woman named Ellen Zahavi from Cambridge?"

She half turned towards me and frowned. "She was head of our tutor group. Yeah, I remember."

"She wants to see me."

The curiosity spread. "Oh?"

"Delaney's sister, the girl we were talking about, is a patient of hers."

She nodded. "She took our psychology class. Apparently she was a doctor of psychiatry, too. A live-wire. She frightens the government agencies more than the entire opposition."

"Why's that?"

"Her ideas. Her opposition to their ideas. I believe she's very controversial, anti-establishment. She was always causing ructions at Cambridge. She's written a couple of books. I think I've still got one or two. *The Psychology in Social Work*, that kind of thing. She specialized in learning difficulties, that's right." She smiled. "She'll certainly put you in your place."

"What's she like as a person?"

"She's really nice. Sensitive, earthy, pretty laid-back, but touch the wrong nerve and you better take cover. Why does she want to see you?"

I didn't want to go into details. "Delaney's sister had some kind of fit at the club. I presume it's about that."

She smiled. She didn't believe a word.

Kate stirred and began to cough and splutter. Donna wiped her hands, lifted her from the pram and carried her through the kitchen.

She picked up a disposable on the way to the living-room. She called through, "What about presents?"

"Yeah, I was thinking of getting Jack one of these Mega things. A computer."

"That'll be good. It will help with his school work."

"I don't think so, sweetheart. This is just a games machine."

Silence. Not such a good idea after all.

I asked, "You think a computer would be better?"

"They say they're never too young."

"Would they share one?"

"I think so."

"Right then, that's it."

She appeared at the door. Kate was wide awake, held at arm's length. Her tiny feet kicked the stinky air.

"I'll have to bath her," she said.

"I'll go."

"I thought you would." She smiled.

"I'll call you."

"No," she said. "I'll call you."

She saw my frown. "I don't want you waking her," she explained.

I gave her a silent 'Oh'. I didn't believe a word of it.

Just before I left for the club, Roger phoned me from the Yard.

"I couldn't ask before. What happened?"

"I booked in a hotel with Paddy's sister."

A long silence before, "Delaney know about it?"

"Yeah."

"What happened?"

"She had some kind of fit."

"Like brother, like sister!"

"I had to phone Nick to come and get her. Ambulance job, the works."

"You like to live dangerously."

"Did you find anything else about Linet?"

"He died, last night." Roger paused then said quietly, "The whole thing is being kept under wraps. No one's to be interviewed, nothing."

"Not even Julie?"

"Not even Julie," he said. "It's not that extraordinary. A single date, a month ago. No contact since."

"That's crap," I said.

"Yeah," he admitted. "You're right."

"Keep in touch, eh?"

"One other thing," he said.

"Go on?"

"This is important. Delaney, you said he's in Switzerland?"

"Yeah, he went the day before yesterday."

"You got that wrong."

"What?"

"He never even made the airport. He's holed up with the DPP somewhere. Very hush-hush. The word is in one of the London hotels. Surprise you?"

"Gobsmacked," I said.

"My information is that Mario went to Switzerland using Delaney's papers, and booked into the clinic using Delaney's name. They're obviously in on it over there."

"Where did you get all this?"

"It doesn't matter where, man. But you can take it as gen. The word is that he came home because he's dying! The man's got cancer. If he co-operates he gets to spend the last few weeks back here, with his sister. He can sort out her future. It's that simple. The man's dying. He's hasn't got much time, so what's he got to lose? A few weeks? Months? So, our people and the Yanks have come up with a deal: blow the lid, contacts, suppliers, organizers, which men in which places are having their pockets lined, you know the score. Come clean and you can come back and put your house in order. Apart from the fact that his sister came back on the scene and needed taking care of, I don't suppose he would have bothered. I mean, Delaney didn't care a damn about anyone else, did he?"

"Jesus," I said.

"Yeah. It throws it into a different league. If this gets out, there's going to be a lot of people looking for Delaney. They might even try and get to him through his sister. Know what I mean? You best stay away."

"Well, Roger, if you got to hear of it so quickly, it's a bit leaky, isn't it?"

"No sweat, there. Between you and me one of the plainclothes lookin' after him had a few too many and started to mouth off. Before he realized what he was doing it was too late. The buzz went through the Met inside an hour. Some people Delaney used to sweeten are getting very worried."

"Like you, Roger?" I said.

"Bollocks!"

"You better hope he doesn't spill the beans down to ground-floor level."

"Don't worry. We're fireproof."

"Are you sure?"

"Yeah. Delaney knows it would be too easy for us to leave a door open. Know what I mean?"

"Ah!"

"Yeah, but that don't mean it's safe all over. I'm just warning you that she ain't the safest date you've ever had."

"You can say that again."

"Just so you know. There's all hell breaking loose at Paddington Green as well as the Yard. Two detectives have been suspended already and apparently there's more on the way. There's talk of bribery in S-Eleven, the lot. I'm tellin' you, man, there's a lot of faces out there that want him shut up!"

"I get your drift, Roger. Have you seen the complaints people yet?"

"No sweat. It was as we thought. They just wanted to know why I was asking the question. Your bruises were good enough. I won't be asking anything else; Delaney's name is red hot."

"I can understand why."

"See you."

The phone went dead against my ear. I stood there for some minutes while the implications sunk in. None of them made sense but they left me with an increasing sense of dread that twisted my gut into little knots. The bastard was playing games but I hadn't got a clue what the rules were. I wondered whether Julie or even Nick knew what was going on.

TEN

By the time I got to the club none of it was any clearer.

Herman blew some smoke at me from his secret cigarette. "You could have this job for nothing," he grumbled and stamped his feet.

"Wouldn't know what to do with all the money," I said as I pushed through the glass doors.

"Nice of you to show," Clarinet said. "Are you shagged out, or will you manage a whole session and surprise us all?"

"Yeah, yeah."

"How did it go?"

"I should take up cards, Joe, 'cos my love life is a shit at the moment."

He showed me his teeth; his eyes sparkled. "Well, Sonny, I don't like to say I told you so."

"Then don't."

"Let's not have any more trouble. Let's go through a whole evening without interruptions. That's what we're here for. Peter's complaining."

"You tell Peter it was his fault in the first place. He was the one that got us doin' 'Happy Birthday'. Remember?"

I didn't see her arrive. She was one of those people that blended with the crowd.

"Mr Webb? My name's Ellen Zahavi. Julie Delaney is my patient."

She was about five-four with short brown hair, around fifty. Her tanned face was fresh, brown eyes lined, her wide mouth touched with a hint of lipstick. She was dressed in a dark-blue businesslike suit and flat heels. She carried a slim briefcase and a black raincoat. Given the present surroundings they looked faintly ridiculous and I should have noticed her. Everything about her was formal.

"You've made quite an impression on her," she said.

I pulled up my sleeve and flashed her my bandaged wrist. "She made a little one on me."

"Can we talk?"

"Sure. Would you like a drink?"

"An orange would be nice. Or anything soft. I'm driving."

So were most people in here, I thought. But it made no difference to them.

I said, "I thought all you uni girls drank bitter from pint pots?"

She raised an eyebrow, off guard for a moment, perhaps wondering how I knew about the connection.

She said coolly, "This university girl doesn't."

I bought the drinks at the bar and led her through to the quieter annex. A small table in the corner was free. Carefully she folded her raincoat and placed it on the back of her chair, then leaned forward to position her briefcase by her feet. Eventually she sat down. She brushed her skirt straight, shuffled her weight on the chair and then looked up.

Her gaze was vaguely searching. Meeting it was like looking over a GP's desk.

I asked, "Is she all right?"

"No, she's not. What on earth happened?"

"Didn't she tell you?"

"Not really."

"What about her brother?"

She shook her head. "Nick contacted me. I imagine he was in touch with Paddy first."

She saw my concern.

"Don't worry. Nick put in a good word. He's got Paddy believing that you can help. I didn't object even though I do have my reservations. Since you didn't return my call, Nick told me where to find you."

I was puzzled. It must have shown.

She said: "You do know that Paddy's ill?"

"Psychopathic, I'd call it. Julie told me it was the drugs."

"Well, yes, but there's more to it than that." She paused, reluctant to add anything further. "Let's just say that for the next day or so he's not going to be much help to us."

"One of his seizures?"

She seemed surprised. "Yes," she said softly.

I wondered whether she was in on it or whether she had been duped as well.

"How can I help you?"

"Do you know anything of Julie's background?"

I shook my head. "Surprisingly little since we spent a night together. She lives with her brother. He's been overseas for many years. When he came home he moved in with her, presumably to look after her. Or perhaps it was the other way round. After her parents died she ended up in hospital. He has a major problem with the white lady, and anything else he can snort. Apparently he's in and out of clinics to dry out or whatever they call it for junkies. They're loaded. She has her hair done by Nicky Clarke and wears designer labels. She has a hang-up about sex and likes to strike matches in the middle of the night. I think that just about covers it. For the record, let's just say that the hotel was her idea. She made all the running. Delaney warned me off, first verbally, and then violently, not that I can prove it unless you're into bruises. But I went along with her anyway. Maybe I need an analyst."

"You regret it now?"

"It was different."

A group of people paused by our table and she lowered her voice. "Are you willing to help her?"

"Of course. If I can."

She watched the group move away and sipped her drink. She had short fingers, no ring.

"You've told me what you know of her present circumstances. What about her history?" Her dark eyes fastened on to me. She wasn't going to miss a thing.

I shrugged. "Her parents died when she was a kid. An accident."

"What else?" she urged.

"Nothing much." I realized how little I knew. "Before the accident it seemed to be a happy family. She told me about the weekends she spent with her brother. An uncle or something, he had an indoor pool where they used to splash about. Then they'd play table-tennis and snooker. Apparently he had a massive games room." I shook my head.

Dr Zahavi considered me for a moment. Her hazel eyes

narrowed before she nodded and said, "She didn't tell you much, and what she did was largely fiction."

"When you said she was a patient of yours, what sort of patient?"

"I'm a psychiatrist. I deal in the treatment of mental and emotional disorders. Is that a problem?"

"Not with me."

She said, "I'm going to be totally honest with you. This isn't a betrayal of confidence because Julie is insisting that I give you an explanation. She asked me to talk to you."

"And Paddy Delaney?"

She took a deep breath and said, "At the moment he'd do anything to help his sister. As I said, whatever Nick said to him obviously struck home because he wants you to remain involved." She paused for a moment, flexed her fingers, then said, "Julie's parents died in a fire at their home."

The relevance didn't escape me. She saw my curiosity and said, "It gets worse. Our guess, and it is only a guess, is that Julie started the fire in which her parents were killed. It wasn't an accident. Her parents were. . . They'd had too much to drink and were sleeping it off. Paraffin was poured over them, the bed, the bedroom, across the landing and down the stairs, and...a match was struck. She was eight years old."

She studied me for a response. I tried to remain calm but I could feel my heart thumping against my bruises.

"Julie was committed into the care of the local authority. A child under the age of ten cannot, in law, commit a crime, and therefore she couldn't be subjected to criminal proceedings. Such cases are normally dealt with by care proceedings. She was put into secure accommodation while she was assessed, reassessed and eventually sectioned on the grounds of severe personality disorder. After the incident she was in an emotional tail-spin. Never mind what had driven her to it, the results of the fire left her a mental wreck, cracking up by the day. The therapy and counselling didn't really help. Not at that time. She just wasn't willing to discuss it. She was confined in various secure units until she was moved to an open hospital. She was eventually released in 1990 when she was twenty-two. She had spent fourteen years in custody. She went to join her brother in

South America but unfortunately the progress made here did not continue. Perhaps it was the new surroundings, perhaps the chemistry with the new doctors, I don't know. But it became obvious to all concerned that if she were to stand a chance of making a complete recovery, then it had to be here. Eventually Paddy sent her back, to Cambridge. To me. She stayed at a home near Cambridge for the best part of two years."

I offered her a JPS. She shook the idea away with something like disgust and waited while I lit one.

"She wasn't the girl that you spent the night with. Far from it. Oh, she had the same name, but that was about it. That length of time in an institution produces something akin to a zombie. When enough people tell you that you're mad, you begin to believe it."

"From what you've said she was mad."

She gave me a rather chilling look and said: "We'll come to that later. She had no choices, no concept of the word; in dress, in food, in anything at all. She couldn't take a shower when she wanted one, she couldn't brush her teeth when she wanted to, she couldn't choose what to eat or what to wear, when to get up or when to go to bed. Choice was taken out of life. She was dehumanized, institutionalized. You cannot begin to understand what this means. Her dignity, the whole concept of self-determination, had been stripped away. The first thing we had to do was to give her the confidence to . . . live. To make simple, everyday choices. Things like if you're thirsty you can have a drink and if you're not, then you don't have to have one. If you're tired you can have a sleep, and so on. It was nearly a year before she would venture beyond the grounds of the home, two years before she went out on her own. When she was ready, Paddy arranged the house in Mill Hill and she moved in there. She enrolled in a finishing school for the late developer, to prepare her for the outside world. A phased re-entry into society. She would come back to see me regularly. There were many moments of depression and panic. Having said that, her progress was constant. Just a few weeks ago Paddy came home for good and moved in with her. On the phone she told me about you, a jazz singer, she said. Made you sound like Al Jolson without the greasepaint. I told her to go slowly, that she didn't have to rush into anything. I must admit to being just a touch concerned about her getting emotionally involved so soon. So was her brother. To my knowledge you're her first real date. There were, of course, various liaisons and friendships in the hospitals, with other patients, but they weren't encouraged. I discussed it with Paddy and agreed that it was something that we would have to face sooner or later."

I was dumbstruck. My mouth dropped open and I waved the air. Eventually I found the words, "You must be joking? He tried everything short of murder to stop me seeing her!"

She nodded. "I did hear about that. But his actions that night had little to do with his rational thinking. In the calm aftermath he agreed with me."

"And now?"

"In hindsight it was a mistake."

"Anyway, you've got it wrong. There was a boyfriend before me. Delaney tried the same threats on him. They worked."

"She did tell me about another man, but I gather that it wasn't serious."

"It was pretty serious for him," I said. "He died from multiple burns a couple of days ago."

She frowned. Now it was her turn to be amazed.

"There's no evidence to suggest that Delaney or his thugs were involved, but I know that paraffin was used. Do you realize I could have ended up like her parents. What if I'd had one too many?"

"There's no good worrying over spilt milk, is there?"

"That's an old cliché dragged out when there's no excuse. The papers are full of nutters being let out too early!"

She said acidly, "Julie isn't a nutter. If you hadn't taken advantage—"

"Hold it there, doctor. Right there!" I wagged the stub of my cigarette. She sat back, momentarily surprised. "I didn't take advantage of anyone. As far as I'm concerned, we're talking about two consenting adults who decide to spend an evening together. That's it. She wasn't naïve, talked into it, or otherwise cajoled." I wagged some more, letting her see my anger. "Only now, now that you've told me, are one or two things fitting together."

Clarinet was wagging another finger but his was beckoning me toward the stage.

I turned back to her. "You'll have to excuse me, Dr Zahavi." I said. "Twenty minutes, OK? I'll get another drink sent across."

She smiled, probably glad of the respite. "Call me Ellen," she said and her features relaxed. Without the intensity she was really quite attractive. She indicated her still half-full glass. "I'll sit on this."

"I know," I said as I stood up, still bristling. "You're driving." Quite frankly, I doubted that Ellen Zahavi had sat on anything in her life.

I did a couple of Billie Holiday numbers and had to promise Clarinet that I'd look after the whole of the last stint before he'd let me go again. I left him changing clarinet for sax in order to give us his Sonny Rollins favourites from Colossus.

I collected another drink from the bar and, even as I approached the table, I could see that she was mildly impressed. She gently clapped her hands as I sat down.

"You're very good," she said but she didn't hide the fact that it would take more than a few songs to interest her in anything other than Julie Delaney.

Ellen Zahavi came from the breed of women who struck an irrational fear into the minds of many men: a totally self-sufficient woman, the sort that men liked to admire from a distance; the sort that in truth, and perhaps out of self-defence, we wish to emasculate and turn back into the acceptable weaker sex.

I lit a cigarette and coughed and watched the disapproval spread into her eyes again.

"You were explaining how a few things have come together," she said in a chilly voice.

I nodded. "Yes, there were times when she didn't act her age, or anything like it. She was building some kind of fantasy. Describing things that she would do, that we would do."

She interrupted. "Will you describe them?"

"Personal things."

She widened her eyes, waiting. Her coolness was quite intimidating. A slight tension filled the air over the table.

"She wanted me to undress her while she closed her eyes, while she didn't move. She wanted it confirmed that we would

97

make love later, not just once, but throughout the evening. She told me what colour . . . "

"Go on?"

" . . . underwear she was wearing. It was all a tease, I know. But it was like, like she was thirteen and flirting with the guys at school."

She smiled quickly. "Not when I was thirteen. Not at my school." She shook her head in dismay. "Did you follow the plan?"

"Come again?"

"What Julie wanted you to do?"

I studied her for a few moments. "This is strictly for medical purposes, isn't it, Doc?"

She coloured slightly. "Of course."

"Well, we didn't actually make love. There was no intercourse. At the moment of . . . truth, she became frightened. She froze."

"You didn't press her?"

"No, I didn't," I said sharply.

"Was it a sudden fear, or had it been building up? Were there any outward signs that she was beginning to panic?"

"She mentioned earlier, while we were fooling around–"

She interrupted: "In the bedroom?"

"Yes. She was short of breath, suddenly embarrassed."

"Like a little girl?"

"Maybe."

"Will you tell me what happened with the fire?"

"She told you about that?"

"I'd like to hear your version."

I shrugged. "I woke up, the bed was on fire; well, the top cover, really. She was standing there, flicking matches."

"At you or at the bed?"

"Not purposely at me, I think."

"What time was it?"

"Just after four."

"Had she been to sleep?"

"For a couple of hours, on and off. She didn't sleep well."

"Was she conscious of what she was doing, the matches?"

"No, not at all. She was in some kind of trance. She was still asleep."

"Her eyes, open or closed?"

"Open, wide. Frightening really. But funny, glazed, you know?"

She nodded thoughtfully. "The light was still on then, for you to see her eyes?"

"No, but there was a lot of light in the room. The curtains didn't fit and there was a streetlamp right outside. And there were a lot of flames."

She picked up her drink. I lit another cigarette.

I asked, "Why did she do it?"

"I beg your pardon?"

"Why did she kill her folks?"

"If I knew the answer to that one, I don't think I'd be sitting here talking to you right now. She would, or could, never tell us why."

"But she admitted it?"

"Oh yes, totally. I have all the records. There was never any doubt about her guilt. Only the reason for it. Did she hate her parents? No. Either one of them? No. Had she been punished for something? Was she upset? No, no. Was she under pressure at school?" She shook her head. "No, again. Her teachers thought she was a little withdrawn, but nothing to speak of. She didn't seem to have many friends, she didn't mix like most eight-year-olds do. So what was it? What suddenly snapped?" She shook her head despairingly and went on: "There was no hint at all of what was to come!"

She rubbed her eyes; the smoky atmosphere was getting to her. Ellen Zahavi was not used to night-clubs.

"During the investigation, she maintained that she didn't know why she lit the fire but that she was aware of doing it. That may well have been the case, but I doubt it. I think that suggestion, perhaps entirely unintentional, led her to believe that she had done it. Kids of that age are pretty vulnerable to suggestion. Don't get me wrong, she did light the fire, there was other evidence to substantiate her confession, but what is doubtful is that she has a real and not imaginary memory of it. Reports and assessments over the years have indicated that she wouldn't co-operate, that she refused to discuss that night. My contention is that she couldn't. The mind has a defence mechanism. It sometimes throws up what we call repression, the motivated forgetting that consigns a memory from the consciousness to the unconsciousness. Another of the mechanisms is denial. A refusal to accept certain aspects of reality. It's a Freudian idea. He maintained that the unconscious mind is largely composed of repressed memories, difficult to retrieve, but kept in storage. The main point is that although we are unaware of them they continue to have a huge influence over us. Other people have made detailed studies; Eysenck, Keane, Brewin, Baddeley and so on. The conclusions, generally accepted, are that powerful emotions, particularly negative emotions, do cause amnesia. You see where this is going?"

I nodded. "Was she examined when they found her?"

"Come again?"

"Medically?"

"Well, obviously."

"Sexual abuse, I mean?"

"Sexual abuse? At the time I thought so too. With children of that age there are usually obvious signs of abuse that would have led the examiners to take a closer look. Apparently the examinations disproved the theory. Why do you ask?" She was suddenly curious. She flashed me a sharp glance.

"She's frightened of sex, with me anyway. Mind you, if I was the first that might explain it. She takes part in the preliminaries without a problem."

Her eyes narrowed thoughtfully. "Like?"

"Well, I'm not going to spell it out."

"Please. Different people have different ideas."

"Foreplay, Ellen. Petting, heavy petting. That sort of thing."

"Did she participate?"

I nodded.

"Did she masturbate you?"

I carried on nodding.

"Did she have a problem touching you?"

"This is difficult."

"Why? You don't strike me as the shy type."

"I must be. This isn't easy."

"Please."

"I've forgotten your question?"

"Did she have a problem?"

I checked over my shoulder to make certain no one was listening. "No."

"Orally?"

"Yes, she talked me through it."

She gave me a doubtful, rather dismayed look and said, "Did you insert your fingers into her?"

I thought about that one before conceding, "I don't think so. My tongue, I think. Not my fingers."

For a moment she hesitated, a little surprised. Suddenly it was Dr Zahavi who was reticent. I held on to a smile.

"That's when we stopped. She was very dry, down there. Anything else would have been difficult."

"Did she stop it, exactly?"

I nodded. "I suppose she did, exactly. She turned over."

"Was she upset?"

"I think so."

"Were you?"

"I wasn't over the moon."

"Did you say anything? I mean, did you let her know that you were upset?"

"Well, I imagine she knew, but I didn't actually tell her. I didn't swear or anything like that. I actually put my arm around her. You know, 'Don't worry, everything's all right'."

"Did you tell her not to worry, that these things happen?"

"No. At her age I guess she knows that."

She smiled. "I guess."

"So, what now?"

"As I mentioned earlier, I have my reservations about your continued involvement."

I waited for more.

She went on, "On the positive side we have the fact that for the first time outside the family Julie has related to someone. She actually cares about you. Even though a lot of what she told you was make-believe, nonsense, she was frightened to tell you the truth. That means she cares about your relationship sufficiently to make up stories. She didn't want to lose you."

"What about the negative?"

"We saw what happened at the hotel." She looked up, and said curiously, "Would you like to see her again?"

101

I smiled. "Is that a medical question?"

She smiled. "Maybe it isn't."

"If I meet her, will you be there?"

"No, no that wouldn't work. It's got to be of your own volition. If it's going to work then she's got to confide in you. You've got to help her gain some confidence."

"You think I can do that?"

"Maybe. She needs to break away from her brother. Dependency in this situation is holding her back."

"You know he knocks her about, don't you?"

She hesitated. Her pause destroyed the possibility of a lie. She asked, "You've actually witnessed it?"

"Yes," I answered solemnly. "And sexual abuse." I thought about describing the events that took place after the party. I was still thinking when she spoke.

"Sexual abuse involving Paddy?"

"He forced her to commit an obscene act. I think that's the term. A blow job."

She was astounded. "On him?"

"No, on someone he'd seen her dancing with. It was some kind of punishment."

Her frown deepened. Her eyes flashed angrily. "Well, I can't explain that. Nothing can excuse violence, especially against someone who is helpless. Paddy blames her for the loss of his parents. He blames her for leaving him alone. She did leave him, or rather, she was taken from him. For ninety-nine per cent of the time he has it under control, is unaware that the problem exists–"

"And then?"

"And then, during one of his rare attacks, he loses it. Then he hits her, and anyone else in his way. And she puts up with it. To her it is a sort of punishment. It fits the crime. She won't entertain the idea of making a complaint. Not to me or to the authorities."

"So it's down to his habits, drugs and booze. He can't handle them?"

"In the beginning that might have been the case and they certainly don't help now. But the damage has been done and, contrary to what Julie believes, and what he tells her, it is getting worse." She looked at me seriously. "That is one of the reasons that she needs to become independent. She is running out of time."

"You mean that Delaney–?"

She nodded. "It's a progressive disease. He hasn't got long."

"Does he know?"

"Yes," she nodded.

"So what do I do next?"

"Come to see Julie and me at the clinic tomorrow, if that's OK. Tomorrow morning. I'll fit you in between tutorials. Some of our students are in trouble so we're having extra sessions tomorrow, morning and afternoon. Shall we say ten?"

"You do realize I'm here 'till four."

"Then you'll have to set the alarm," she said, smiling. She slid a small blue card across the table. "Bluebell Wood, the address is on there. Ask for me at the reception."

I watched her weave her way through the crush of people in the main bar. Her movements were slightly stiff: there was very little hip swing. The dark skirt of her suit barely moved from side-to-side.

ELEVEN

Bluebell Wood was a private clinic on the outskirts of Cambridge. It consisted of three large Victorian houses linked by covered walkways. Doors had been widened and steps replaced with ramps to accommodate wheelchairs. The place was surrounded by trees and gardens.

I followed a sign to the reception area and waited while a man remonstrated with a young woman behind the desk. A couple of patients – residents, Ellen called them – watched from their easy chairs. They were giving me dark, fearful looks. The one nearest me rocked in her chair.

The man's voice raised angrily as he leaned over the reception desk.

"You tell that One-Woman-Crusade that I need to see her now!"

He was about sixty, Asian, dressed in a dark suit and flowery tie. He was tall. His heavy spectacles gave him a pop-eyed expression. His face was slightly flushed.

Full marks to the woman. She remained deferential yet quite unmoved.

"I'm sorry, Professor Zahavi. At the moment she's in a lecture and then she has a meeting at ten."

"What lecture?" he snapped. "Why wasn't I told?"

The woman shook her head. The man banged the desk in exasperation then turned sharply and walked to the exit. He left the door swinging slowly shut. A blast of cold air swept into the reception. The residents shied away.

The receptionist shrugged her slim shoulders and turned to me.

"I think I'm the ten o'clock meeting," I said.

She smiled. There was a touch of gratitude in her expression as she said, "Mr Webb?"

"That's me."

"You're early."

I pointed at the door that had finally closed.

"Was that Ellen Zahavi's husband?"

She nodded. There was a conspiratorial glint in her eye as she leaned forward and whispered, "Only just."

"That explains the One-Woman-Crusade."

"Oh that. Not really. Once you get to know her you'll find that's quite a good description." She gave me a friendly smile. "You sound just like Michael Caine. Has anyone ever told you that?"

"Michael who?"

"You know, *Educating Rita*!"

"Oh, him. You're joking?"

"No, really. I suppose it's the London accent." Her smile became sympathetic. "Ellen Zahavi?" She wrinkled her nose.

"Yeah."

"I'll just find out how long she'll be."

"Thanks," I said and watched her walk off along the corridor. Her flat sneakers slapped the linoleum floor. Her behind moved beautifully. She skirted an approaching wheelchair and knocked at a door toward the end of the corridor. A moment later, she opened it and disappeared.

The wheelchair came on and stopped halfway across the lobby. An old woman sitting in it gave me the once over. Her head was lowered, bent forward, so that she stared at me through her untidy ginger fringe.

"Now, now, Mrs Collier, stop giving him the evil eye. You'll frighten him off," the receptionist said when she came back in. She moved behind her counter and said, "She'll be about twenty minutes. I'll just need . . . " She pushed a book towards me. " . . . you to fill in the visitor's book."

The page was ruled into columns: name, address, relative, friend, other, purpose of visit. I filled it in and pushed it back. She examined my answers and then pointed to another door at the far end of the reception. "You can wait in there," she said. "It's a sort of staff-room. The coffee's always hot. Like I said, Ellen should be about twenty minutes. She knows you're here."

I thanked her and went across to the door. The residents, especially the old girl with the ginger hair, watched me suspiciously.

It was a small, comfortable room containing easy chairs, a table and a work surface with steaming percolator, mugs, milk, sugar and biscuits. Another door was slightly open. Ellen Zahavi's voice travelled through it. I opened it a fraction more and glanced into the next room.

It was a similar room to the one I stood in, a little larger. Ellen was in the middle of some kind of tutorial. She was perched on the edge of a desk surrounded by a dozen or so students aged from teens to fifty.

"Don't tell me about back to basics, Margaret," she said to someone in the front. She lifted two fingers toward her mouth and made a vomit-inducing gesture. "The Tory concept of family life is what they expect from the rest of us, not from themselves. As soon as their kids are old enough to walk they farm them off to nannies and then boarding-schools and see them once in a blue moon! So much for the family being mother, or, according to them, father first, mother, and children. And yet behind that concept, the back to basics idea, lies their strategy on benefits – slandering the single parents, suggesting that the single parent is the cause of all ills, in education, in crime, in housing, in the balance of payments deficit. Politics is about hypocrisy, about being able to lie and thieve and get away with it. If you believe in their emollient reassurances that the welfare state is safe in their hands, then you must have been sleeping for the last fifteen years! I've said it before and I shall say it again: you cannot separate politics from welfare, just as you can't separate politics from medicine or justice. Social justice doesn't come into it. What is right is governed by the money the politicians are willing to spend, not on justice or morality or any fine ideal like that."

I began to understand why she was considered a thorn in the butt of the establishment. She was in her element, loving it. She shuffled on the table and glanced quickly at her watch. A ray of sunlight beamed in over the trees and caught her, deepening the colours of her clothes. She wore a loose flowery skirt and a thick mustard sweater.

"Let's get back to institutions," she said. "That's where we started. The Victorian age. The age of the institution. I began by telling you that they should be pulled down, stone by wretched stone, theory by wretched theory. They have been, and more importantly, still are, filled with people who were unfortunate enough to be in the wrong place at the wrong time: vagrants, the destitute, hard of hearing, people with learning difficulties, unmarried mothers. They were, and still are, the red-brick embodiment of the out-of-sight, out-of-mind philosophy. The slogan 'Care in the Community' is a nonsense, the much-hyped ideal of doing away with the institution is just a figment of the imagination. It's all very well to come up with an idea but unless it's backed up with the intention to finance it, then forget it. And what are we doing for these unfortunate people? Well, we're not listening to them, that's for sure. We're not asking them, individually, what they want. We're not giving them a choice, because a choice for them means spending money. For the present government, compassion is a weakness. Institution to institution. So, raise your voices and get angry. Make yourselves heard. If you don't do it while you're students then you never will."

There were some mutters of approval. She slipped off the table and stood up. "Right, tomorrow I've got personal tutorials and . . . " She waved the air. " . . . We've got to arrange dates for me to visit you at placement during the new term." The wave turned to a wag of the finger. "Don't let me forget that. I'm in enough trouble as it is!"

Some of the students laughed.

An older woman spoke: "I'm having nightmares with my child protection. Leslie lent me a copy of the orange book but he didn't explain how to use it."

Ellen told me later that Leslie was the group's tutor on the intervention module.

Ellen snatched the book that was held up. "I'm fucking sick to death of this," she said. Coming from an academic, the word came unnaturally and yet, as with many of them, at least one a session was obligatory. Humour, not shock, buzzed from the students.

She threw the book to the floor and said, "Well, it does make me angry! That . . . thing, should be burned. Protecting children should be seen from the child's point of view." She calmed down. "I'll speak to Leslie," she said. "I'll get him to phone you." She glanced at her watch again. "OK, I hope it helped. Just remember, no extensions, not even for injury or mental breakdown. All assignments in by two p.m., Friday. So you'll all be burning the midnight oil. And that includes you, Martin!"

Her last sentence was directed at a young man who seemed to be nodding off. He shook his eyes wide and gave her an apologetic smile.

She was heading my way. I moved away from the door and sat down. The door opened and she stood there, framed by the bright light that piled in the room behind her. For an instant her dress became slightly transparent and the shape of her legs pulled my gaze. She realized and narrowed her eyes in a half-accusatory, half-humorous fashion and moved out of the light.

"Have you been waiting long?" she asked breezily.

"Just a few minutes," I said.

"Have you had some coffee?"

I shook my head. She put down her briefcase and made two mugs.

"Sugar?" she asked while the spoon hovered.

"Please."

She stirred briskly and pushed a mug into my hands.

"So," she said as she sat opposite. "What do you think of the Wood?" She crossed her legs and held her drink with both hands.

"It's not what I'd call an institution," I said.

She raised an eyebrow.

A smile tugged at my mouth.

"What's the matter?"

I shook my head.

Her eyebrow remained high as she said, "Silly of me. For a moment I thought you were smiling at something I said. Why would you? You were obviously listening in?"

I nodded. "It sounded very controversial."

"Dear boy, without controversy, life is very dull."

"How is Julie?"

"A little subdued. She had a mild sedative last night and she's a bit groggy."

"How long will you keep her here?"

"There's no question of keeping her. She can leave any time she likes, today if she feels up to it. Realistically I imagine she'll leave when her brother gets back."

"Between you and me, her brother hasn't actually gone anywhere."

She frowned. "Explain," she said.

"He didn't go to Switzerland. He's in London, somewhere, in hiding, helping the police with their enquiries."

"It gets more complicated by the day. Why should he do that? Hide, I mean?"

"I imagine it's got something to do with some of his contemporaries who might think rather badly of him helping the police."

"From what I've heard of Paddy Delaney, he won't be volunteering his help."

"I agree with you. We'll have to watch this space."

She nodded thoughtfully and finished her drink. "Ready?"

She led me through the lobby. The woman behind the desk beamed as she saw me. Ellen noticed and glanced at me in an odd way. I said to the woman, *"Jaws Twenty-Six?"*

She frowned, momentarily flustered. "Pardon?"

"Michael Caine. He was in *Jaws Twenty-Six!*"

She giggled girlishly. Beneath their starch, they were all little girls.

"Not a lot of people know that," I said.

She broke up.

Ellen shook her head in mild exasperation and stifled a smile, still heaping up the formal bit. She pushed the door and led me out toward the next building.

"Gosh, it's snappy," she said glancing at the clear skies. "We might be in for a white Christmas."

I remembered someone else saying that recently. It seemed ages since the school nativity.

The next house along was more homely. There was no reception. The room had been turned into a communal TV room. A few residents, some of them in wheelchairs, had drawn up to watch the morning service. Some of them gave us curious looks, one waved and spoke to Ellen. His words came out as gutteral, strangled noises, but she seemed to understand and nodded.

"Later, Gordon," she answered briskly.

She led me down a bright corridor and stopped at the third door along.

"I'll pop back in half an hour," she said and tapped on the door before opening it.

The door opened on to a small single room: bed, dresser, tallboy, wardrobe and an easy chair. There were a few feminine touches, flowery curtains and lace on the dresser. There were a few clothes strewn around and a teddy-bear on the bed next to a photograph album. One or two of the snaps had fallen out beside it.

Julie Delaney stood at the window, hands fidgeting in front of her, long fingers laced together, opening and closing. A fragile smile fluttered across her lips.

She wore pale-green jogging pants and a sweatshirt. Her hair was combed straight. Without make-up, she looked pale. Her eyes were wide and apprehensive. She raised a hand to her lower lip.

"You've got a visitor," Ellen said gently and closed the door behind me.

For a moment I stood there awkwardly.

Julie dropped her hand and indicated the view. "It is beautiful here, isn't it?"

I nodded and approached to look over her shoulder. Outside the winter trees pressed in on a square of grass.

She turned back to face me. "I've been longing to see you again," she said. "But I was so embarrassed."

"There's no need to be."

With great daring she took two tentative steps toward me and stood nervously under my gaze. Her sweatshirt was bunched at her elbows. Her forearms were ivory pale beneath a hint of tiny dark hairs. The material was silky soft and wrapped the curve of her breasts. I felt her breath on my face as she reached up to kiss me. It wasn't lingering and, perhaps sensing my apprehension, she broke off almost immediately. She pulled me away from the window and sat by me on the bed. She held on to my hand. Her palm was cold and slightly moist.

There was an uneasy feeling in my chest. She had ceased to be an object of sex. The idea now was somehow faintly disgusting. It wasn't pity, or the fact that she was ill, but something more than that. Something deeper. The idea of consenting adults had been given a new twist. It was nonsense because, as far as I knew,

110

Julie was not mentally ill, although she obviously had an emotional problem. But it crossed my mind that those people whose mental age had not reached the age of consent were in a paradoxical situation.

"I didn't think you'd want to see me again," she said quietly. "What on earth must you think of me?"

"I don't think anything less of you. Can you remember what happened?"

"Bits of it," she said. "It's like a nightmare."

"Can you remember striking the matches?"

"I remember the fire. I can't remember lighting it. I remember the burn on your arm and panicking."

"What about before that, Julie? When we were making love. Why did you suddenly stop?"

She looked up gravely and shook her head.

"You can't remember?" I said.

She nodded. "I remember that." She struggled for words. "I didn't want you . . . "

"What?"

"It's so silly."

"Try me."

"I was suddenly terrified that you'd find out I wasn't a virgin. Isn't that nonsense?"

"Yes, it is."

"I'm twenty-six and yet suddenly I panicked. I could think of nothing else. Everything else just went out of my head. The one single thought that you mustn't find out was so fierce that it made me dizzy with fear. It was probably the drink. I don't know." She held my gaze, dropped her hand from mine and placed it on my thigh. "Promise me that it makes no difference, that you'll give me another chance?"

"You try and keep me away," I said.

She chuckled and pressed against me. She caught hold of my hand again and pulled it on to her stomach and downward. I felt the soft sponginess of her pubic hair through the material.

Trying to keep gentleness in my voice I said, "Why didn't you tell me about your problems? The clinic?"

She stiffened and let me go. "You'd be surprised how many people that would put off. In America, everyone has a shrink.

111

Over here it's still a mark of disgrace. It's like being a criminal. If it gets around you might as well use a branding-iron on your forehead saying leper or something. Because that's the end of your credibility."

"How long do you expect to be here?"

"Paddy's not due back until next weekend."

"There's Nick," I said. "He's at home."

"I'll speak to Ellen and see what she thinks."

I nodded. "When you're fit enough you could come to the club again. We can take it from there."

"That sounds good. You can show me your place."

"Why not?"

She nodded, satisfied, and leaned against me. The perfume of her shampoo, roses I think, lifted from her hair.

For an instant I wondered whether my feelings toward her would change once she was out of the clinic. I doubted it. She had become a little girl. The idea of touching her was mildly chilling.

She flicked open the photograph album. "I've been looking at these," she said.

She showed me a few snaps, children playing in a pool, splashing, diving, a very young Julie on the shoulders of an older, skinny boy – with his hair plastered to his head it took me some moments to recognize him as her cousin, Anthony – other people in their thirties, perhaps other relatives, relaxing around the pool edge, drinks on a nearby table, Paddy Delaney aged about fourteen doing a Tarzan act on the high board. It looked like fun. Childhood memories. Before it all went so horribly wrong. She pointed out the individuals, Paddy, Uncle Bob, her mother and father, Aunty Joyce, cousin Anthony, and other, remote relatives and friends from the past.

The half an hour seemed to go on interminably before Ellen Zahavi came to the rescue. She realised at once that our meeting had been difficult.

"That's it for today, Julie," she said. "You need to rest."

Julie accepted it without question and gave me a brief parting smile. From the door I glanced back at the sparse room, at Julie on the single bed. A sad little scene and, although Ellen would disagree, you just couldn't get away from it being a hospital.

"Come on, I'll buy you lunch and you can tell me all about it," Ellen said as she strode in front of me down a slight incline that led from the buildings to the car park.

Music drifted from an open window of a resident's bedroom.

As we crossed to the car she said, "You saw the lad in the wheelchair, Gordon?"

I kept pace with her surprisingly fast walk and nodded. "Go on?" I said, sensing that she was going to shock me.

"He's been here nine months. Crippled, communication shot to hell. For the first three years of his life his parents kept him in a cot. He never moved out of it. They barely spoke to him. His legs wasted and warped because he continually sat on them. His brain wasted through the lack of stimulation."

"Will you treat him?"

"Not his legs. They'll never work. But he's sharp enough."

"It didn't sound like it."

She flicked me a look. "It sounds like a noise, doesn't it? But that's how he speaks. If you don't take the trouble to understand him, then that says something more about you than him."

It struck me then that Ellen Zahavi spent most of her time picking up the pieces of failure. Children who had been left to cope because of the failure of their parents, or society, or both. Parents who had failed because of financial or educational restraints. It struck me, just for a moment, that an IQ test ought to be law for potential parents, and those failing it should be denied the possibility of parenthood. Then I realised just what I was getting in to and felt quite ashamed of myself.

She opened a Volvo Estate and drove quickly out of the grounds. She drove like a man, with relaxed hands. Women I'd seen tended to hold everything too firmly. Perhaps there was an unconscious sense that muscle power gave them control.

The pub was just half a mile down the road. The landlord knew her and exchanged pleasantries before she chose a table by a log fire that threw out a very welcome glow.

I gave her a detailed, almost word for word, account of the meeting. Her only query regarded Julie's fear of love-making.

"She was worried that she wasn't a virgin?"

Ellen was as astonished as I had been but for different reasons. "She told me that she was," she explained. "During our sessions

113

she has discussed all her sexual longings, even down to that one dinner date. Her untouched state, so to speak, has been something that worried her. We talked about it just a fortnight ago."

"Maybe she confides in me in a more intimate way," I offered.

Ellen shrugged, not accepting the possibility.

I asked, "Where do we go from here?"

"Well you've certainly given me something to work on."

I lit a cigarette. For the first time she accepted it without giving me a disapproving look. Maybe she'd already given up on me.

"Have you arranged to see her again?" she asked.

"Once she's fit, she's going to come to the club."

"How do you feel about that?"

"Uneasy," I admitted.

"I understand that. Why bother with complications when you have a choice?"

"Go on?"

"I can't imagine you being hard up for a date," she said.

"Huh!"

"Surely you have groupies lined up in your dressing-rooms? Or is this a new line you're trying out on me?"

"Huh! I share the dressing-room with four other guys, five on a guest night. And groupies? They're something out of the sixties, and they were never that hot on jazz anyway." I smiled recklessly. "For your information, it's been a barren time of late."

She raised an eyebrow. "You? Chaste? Who are you trying to kid?"

"What is this? You think there's a line of beautiful girls waiting at the stage door? I wish!"

She looked at me reflectively.

"Stop it, Doctor," I said. "I'm not one of your patients. For your information, after my ex-wife Donna and I split, I wasn't very good company for a long time."

"You were angry?"

"No, just on the defensive. I didn't need complications."

"Perhaps I know the feeling better than you think," she said. I remembered what the receptionist had told me and waited. She glanced up and said, "Who's jumping to conclusions now?"

"Well, you started it?"

114

"We officially separated five weeks ago."

"Unofficially?"

"Much longer."

"How long were you married?"

"Eighteen years. You?"

"Six. Compared to you, we were still on our honeymoon. Is he in the same line of business?"

"We're both on the board of Bluebell Wood. He's a consultant there." She noticed my curiosity. "Oh, all right! There was no third party involvement, nothing at all out of the ordinary. Simply two people who decided they were happier when they weren't together. All right?"

I smiled.

"Now you?" she said.

"She fell in love with someone else while I was doing a stint in Europe."

"How did your children take it? They couldn't have been very old."

"It happened four years ago. They were only two at the time so they didn't appreciate what was happening."

"Four years ago?" She sounded surprised. "You should have pulled yourself together by now."

"What makes you think I haven't?"

"You do. You're walking around with the world on your shoulders. Even you said you weren't interested in dating."

"I said that? For the first couple of years maybe, but lately there hasn't been much opportunity. Club hours are kind of restrictive."

"Poppycock! Lenny. Absolute poppycock!"

I smiled and said, "I think I saw your husband in reception. An Indian. My wife – ex-wife – came from the West Indies."

She sipped her drink and looked at me reflectively. The flames cast a glow on her face and made it softer, her eyes less intense.

"Himanshu is a Ugandan Asian, one of the many that Idi Amin Dada expelled in seventy-two. Doesn't seem like twenty-two years ago, does it? He was given ninety days to pack his bags and arrived over here almost penniless. But he had his qualifications. He got a job as Consultant in Psychological Medicine at Broadwater. That's where we met, eighteen years ago. Within months we were married. He's thinking of returning now. The new government, the NRM, is encouraging people to go and repossess all their confiscated property. Should he go, he'll be a rich man."

"Would you mind him going?"

"I'd miss him. Of course I would, even if it's just to know that he's all right. But it wouldn't be more than that. Too many bridges have been burned."

Our food arrived. I tossed the cigarette butt into the fire.

"So you met Julie when she was first hospitalized?"

"Institutionalized," Ellen reminded me. "Yes, Broadwater. There were two doctors to care for 800 patients. One of them had a breakdown and the Medical Superintendent advertised for a *locum tenens* to share the load until a consultant could be appointed. I applied, fresh and bright and thirty years old. They didn't want me. I was too young – in those days thirty was considered inexperienced, too radical, perhaps even too bold. I'll say bold, not rash." She smiled and paused while her lips closed over her fork. While she chewed she said, "I suspect that I was the only applicant because, much to my surprise, I got the job." She cut some more fish. "The hospital was a Victorian slum, a dark prison filled with the ghosts of generations of London lunatics. An asylum, miles of corridors that rang with the lament of madness and despair, a frightening labyrinth of unending screaming brick. I spent most of my time on the refractory wards, there were three of them. The majority of the women were simply old and rotting. They had been there for lifetimes. They were chased by phantoms, by their dead mothers and fathers, even by their dead children; they held animated conversations with ghosts, they stood in darkened corners chatting for hours on end. They screamed and shouted and sobbed. They stood in front of mirrors and slobbered and giggled. A few of the women, a minority, were violent and abusive. They were the cause of most of the problems. They attacked the others, led them into frenzied states. When it got too bad, of course, we always had the confinement ward, the leather straps, the padded cells, and we could lose people in there for days on end."

I could see she was joking, or rather, mocking.

"When Julie first arrived she was shy and innocent. The most surprising thing about her was her language. She tried to shock. But because she was so innocent her shock tactics were ludicrous. She was a skinny, attractive girl with long spindly legs. She shouldn't have been there. I fought tooth and nail to have her removed immediately. I had to act quickly because my temporary tenure was coming to an end. It wasn't that disastrous for her because Himanshu took over from me and arranged a speedy transfer to a more suitable placement. She shouldn't have been in hospital at all. There was no detectable psychiatric disorder, no unbalance, no illogical thought patterns. Sure, she was depressed and frustrated, there was temper and rage. But for heaven's sake, the girl was traumatized, not only from the deaths of her parents and the terrifying acceptance that she had been responsible, but from the hours of police questioning, and the various assessments which were little more than a series of accusatory questions. Little wonder that her emotions were uncontrollable. I did my level best to get her transferred to an Adolescent Unit or a private clinic and, after I left, Himanshu continued the struggle. Eventually he managed it, first to Cell Barnes on a temporary basis for more assessment and then to a secure home. It was another institution but you couldn't compare it with Broadwater. I don't know how much damage was done to her in that place, I don't know how much it set her recovery back. No one will ever know the answer to that one. But I would guess that it was many years."

She finished eating before me and dabbed her lips with a napkin. She caught the eye of a waitress and ordered some more drinks.

"Paddy went to live with an aunt and uncle. Had they been willing to take Julie, things might have been simpler. Because of the rumour and the generally held acceptance that Julie had started the fire their attitude, understandably, was pretty hostile. They wouldn't have anything to do with her and made it their business to poison Paddy's mind against her. Paddy grew up, inherited his father's share of the business and sold out to his uncle, the other partner. With the money . . . well, you probably know more about his business than me. He ended up in South America fighting numerous extradition battles. I don't know what changed his feelings toward his sister but, over the last few years, he moved her to our private clinic and picked up the bills. When she was ready he brought her the house in Mill Hill. He obviously made a deal with the authorities because two months ago he arrived back in this country."

"What makes you think he made a deal?"

"Well they didn't cart him off to prison without passing go, did they? There's been nothing mentioned about court appearances or charges. Until you mentioned he was helping the police, it's as though they weren't interested."

"So what took you to the Wood?"

"Once my tenure at Broadwater ended I moved to Cambridge to do battle. Himanshu had a house here anyway, and I took a lecturing position. The enemy was the state, the battleground was the columns of the influential press, the halls of science, any place that I could bend an ear. The battle won't be over until the last brick of those institutions is flattened. It will take years, longer than my lifetime. But in their places, in their grounds, I want to see individual homes built for the patients and inmates who are left. That is their world after all. They know of nothing else but those grounds. Those who want to stay together can do so. Of course, it will cost a fortune and the government will fight it all the way, just as they have been since Seebohm, perhaps until the majority of the patients have died, but we owe them that much. Before Seebohm, and even after that, people were thrown into these places on the whim of any authority; an expedience, a place where they could be conveniently forgotten. Seebohm did change things, a little, but far too slowly and not half enough. The metropolitan towns became a little more advanced and aware, but in the sticks things remained pretty much the same. These people, ordinary people, some with learning difficulties, some simply unfortunate, that we have incarcerated and bullied and tortured and dehumanized. All those lives stolen by the so-called authority; we owe them that much."

I felt ear-bashed. I lit a cigarette and swallowed half of my fresh drink. For a moment Ellen seemed self-conscious. Perhaps she was suddenly jaded by the sound of her own voice. I gave her a break and asked a question to show her that I hadn't noticed, "How serious is this set-back?"

"That remains to be seen," she said. "Something triggered it;

something that happened during the day or evening. If we can work that out we'd have a much better idea." She glanced at her watch and drew a quick breath. "I'm late," she said. "I'm sorry, but I've got to rush. What are your plans now? Back to London?"

"Yes, we've got a full house tonight and no special guest. That means extra work for us."

"Don't you get any time off?"

"We've had a full week at the club. We've got tonight and tomorrow and then that's it for a couple of days. Another band takes over. We'll get together for some new numbers but that's all. Apart from that I can get on with some housework."

She smiled. "I'll call you sometime."

"Yeah, do that."

She put the bill on her card. I held open the door for her. She walked before me toward the car, streamlined and determined, her cotton dress flapping in the cold wind. As she crossed the concrete standing, she struggled into her raincoat. The wind lifted her loose dress and showed me a few inches of thigh. Her hand moved deftly to cover herself and she caught my gaze. She shook her head in tight-lipped amusement and pressed her electronic locks.

"Get in!" she said.

I grinned. I love dominant women.

TWELVE

Wednesday night turned out to be a late one and I slept most of Thursday. I say slept but really a lot of it was spent with restless thoughts. Ellen, the One-Woman-Crusade, had got to me in a big way. Her anger was infectious. It got me thinking that I could give her even more ammunition to fire down those narrow corridors of political incompetence. I see some of it every night; every time I go to work in the early evening or motor home in those dark dangerous hours.

We've always had our share of winos and skagheads, sniffers, schizos and epileptics. Nowadays you can add crackheads to the list. We've always had them. It's just that we've got more of them now. Community Care had thrown them on to the streets. They had exchanged their hospital beds for park benches and shop doorways. Apart from the statement of the occasional headline, they are more dangerous to themselves than to the rest of us. At least that's what the experts tell us. Since they were kicked out of their various units they have killed over thirty people in the last three years. They wave at the polluted air, shout back at the voices in their heads, run from the ghosts that chase after them. Their drugs, procyclidine and dothiepean, still wait to be collected in some forgotten reception. This is the twilight zone. The city. Virginia Bottomley's community. There's a war going on and the one thing that's certain is that the Health Secretary and her friends are not in the front line. They're not even aware that it exists.

After they'd been here a while they started to look like the others: matted hair, vacant eyes, open sores; Waterloo's cardboard city, until it was kicked away by the kindly kozzers, was full of them, the no-hopers, cradling their Special Brews or Tennant's, or cider or meths; anything they could lay their hands on. Anything that would help them to forget.

In the late-eighties it was another group. The government

stripped the kids, the under-eighteens, of their benefits. Some of them left home because of the Poll Tax, some because they wanted excitement, others because home was unbearable and any alternative had to be better. They made for the bright lights of the capital to beg and hustle. Before they were closed down the hostels used to be a safety net and the kids had been directed to them by your kindly neighbourhood Sally-Anns: Arlington, Camberwell Spike, Mother Goose, even the Charing Cross on the Strand. But they were gone now. The kids had to get streetwise quickly and soon their younger brothers and sisters followed. The ponces waited for them outside the main line terminus stations, dealers and pimps and paedophiles.

The Sally-Anns still tried but they were fighting a losing battle.

No benefits, no hope. You gotta stay alive. You beg, you steal, and before long you turn to prostitution and dope. That's how it is on the way down. And when you've reached rock bottom, then you've hit the Cross.

On my way to work I see them parading in their skimpy outfits, shivering toms and rent-boys, some as young as ten, some as old as sixty, making deals with the pinstriped suits in their company cars, the businessmen who are working late at the office.

Thirty nicker! You can have it in the rain for thirty nicker leaning against a wall in the alleys behind the Cross. A tenner will get you a blow job from scabbed up lips. Forty quid will give you thirty minutes in your car, sixty in a local guest house. Argyll Street, Crestfield, Belgrave, Euston Road, any place in the Golden Triangle. The meat rack. You can pick up your dope at the same time.

On my way home the place has emptied. The punters are home in their semis snuggling against their wives; now it's just the homeless and the street cleaners with their sweepers hoovering up the condoms and the needles and the puddles of vomit.

The kozzers have lost the battle; the Yardies and Italians have taken over. Even the Maltese are back in business after a twenty-year absence. Dealers operate in broad daylight while the police are back in Marylebone or Bow Street filling in their forms. Those that you see are generally plain-clothed, white trainers and bomber jackets. It makes you wonder what they teach them in Hendon. If it wasn't so serious you'd have to laugh. I mean, it is some kind of sick joke. The whole damn city is coming apart and the kozzers spend most of their shift with their pens stuck up their arses.

But Ellen had got it wrong: unmarried mothers were no longer being blamed for causing the balance of payments deficit, and the Tory split on Europe, and for the power stations poisoning us all with radioactive gases. No, not any more. Now, according to Mr Major, it was the beggars in the streets of London. Next week, no doubt, it would all be down to the nurses.

Tell me about it.

I faced the day at about three in the afternoon, took a leisurely bath, shaved and, by the time I had eaten and watched the six o'clock, it was time to get ready for work. It was the last night of our week-long stint before Peter started throwing together his Christmas specials, mostly American imports, although George Melly was booked for Monday and Tuesday. I'd already decided to try to get down to see him myself. I'd also penned in an evening at Dr Bob Jones' Surgery in Rathbone Place. He was putting together some funk and jazz that sounded right up my street. But tonight Joe Gabriel was bound to turn it into some kind of party.

There were only ten days to Christmas. Retailers were getting jumpy, slashing prices; their shop windows were blistered with fairy lights and covered in feverish last-minute promises of special offers and free credit. January sales were pulled forward. The Tories had put a damper on yet another festive holiday, turning it into a nightmare for the average punter. People were nervous about using their plastic or their redundancy pay-offs.

The club belonged to another world far removed from the push on the frantic pavements or the worry of the January bills. It was a place that stood still. If time existed, then the music and atmosphere took you back a century or more and to a different part of the globe. Even the bar with its trellis-work and columns segregating it from the main nightclub resembled an old Mississippi river boat. Its paddle, about five feet long, and built into the end wall, turned slowly throughout the evening, and because of spotlights behind it, shadows were for ever sliding across the bar. A migraine sufferer's nightmare.

"All right, all right," Clarinet said happily as he saw me and slapped my palms. "My place Saturday night, seven, don't be late. Wanna run through some stuff for next week. Next week starts on Wednesday. We're supporting The Ronnie Scott Sextet on Wednesday. Thursday and Friday are party nights and they're all ours. You can have Saturday off. Got it?"

"Yeah, yeah."

He pushed a beer towards me. "You look like you need that," he said. "Problems? Don't tell me you're still hung up on the girl?"

"Right now, Joe, any girl would do."

"Man, you're better off without 'em. They's just bad news. To them you ain't nothing more than a vibrator with a cheque-book on the end."

I chuckled and gulped at my drink.

"But it ain't any girl, is it Sonny? That's the trouble. You're getting yourself obsessed with that family."

Mike cut in from the shadows. "Hey, boss, Saturday is Christmas Day!"

"Where did you get your A-levels?" Clarinet asked and checked that the others were ready before giving Peter the nod. Peter grabbed the mike and moved into the spot. The light bounced off his grease.

He cleared his throat into the mike and said, "Pleeease will you welcome some guys who have been entertaining us through-out the week, our resident band, Joe Clarinet Gabriel and–"

Mike hit his cymbals. Peter jumped. For a moment he juggled with the mike and caught it on the third attempt. He pretended to share the joke but, when he turned to us, his teeth were bared and clenched to hold in the obscenities. Mike sat looking at the ceiling as though nothing had happened. His eyes stuck out like a couple of split golf balls half buried in sand. Nick Faldo would have chipped them out with a wedge without touching the sockets. Peter turned back to face the murmur of chuckles and whispers.

"Ladies and Gentlemen, here's Wolves Aren't White."

Clarinet leaned into his mike and pointed my way. "That one is!"

The light slid across to me and before the applause had chance to register the band crashed into the fifties, blues and swing, a

Sonny Rollins burlesque as Clarinet hit his sax first with 'Toot Toot Tootsie' and then went straight into 'I'm An Old Cow Hand'. It left the room buzzing with energy. There was going to be a party.

I had three hours' sleep and a sticky dream and woke up with a stalk the size of the Post Office Tower. At least it felt that way and it was sending out all kinds of signals. Donna had finally gone down on me; I could feel the heat of her breath and her lips were just about to close when I woke up. I thought it was the throbbing that was banging in my ears but then I heard the door again and realized my mistake.

I struggled into a bathrobe and sat for a moment holding my thumping head. The door was banged again. I was still holding my head as I pulled it open and looked into the faces of two men. They were in their thirties, M&S suit-and-tie jobs, plain white shirts, polished slip-ons. CID. No doubt about it. The warrant card flashed in front of my spinning eyes confirmed it.

"Fuck off," I said.

The one with the card smiled and said in a mild west country accent, "That's not very nice is it? Will you ask us in?"

I shook my head slowly.

They walked in anyway and closed the door.

"Let's start again, shall we? Lenny Webb?"

"Yeah, yeah," I said as I moved into the kitchen. I checked the kettle for water and switched it on.

"That's nice," he said. "Coffee, with and with."

I yawned and lit a cigarette.

"I'm Superintendent Scott, this is DI Walker. You can call me Barry."

"I hate friendly coppers. I was working 'till four, hit the sack at five. That was just three hours ago. I'm not at my most sociable, know what I mean?"

Superintendent Barry Scott was dark-haired, square-featured, his blue eyes were humorous. In many ways he must have been his mother's delight: intelligent, good-looking, conservative, respectable, he had walked through the masculine rites of passage without a single hesitation. The other man, Walker, was quite the opposite: perhaps a little older and more intense, he was

124

greasy, open-pored, his eyes sunken and shifty. They flicked around the room, taking everything in. The sort of man it was easy to dislike.

Scott said, "This is not official. There's no trouble. We need your help but it's a bit tricky."

"I'm not into puzzles at the best of times. Speak in English will you?"

He smiled again and nodded. "Right. What I'm going to tell you is strictly confidential and it's got to remain that way."

The pain was spreading from my forehead into my eyes.

"I'm not happy involving you but I have no choice. You know Paddy Delaney?"

"So?"

"He wants to see you."

I met his gaze. "You can go and tell him that he can want 'till the fucking cows come home." I sniggered and added, "He wants to push me off a ski-slope, is that it? What the hell are you delivering his messages for?"

"Believe me it's not out of choice." Scott rubbed his ear and said soberly. "And he isn't on the ski-slopes. At the moment Delaney is dictating his memoirs from his sickbed. When he's finished he'll be guarded round the clock until certain people have been put away. You understand what I'm saying?"

I nodded and said, "You're saying he's not in Switzerland."

"Clever bastard, aren't you?" Walker said.

I gave him a fuck you look and said, "First-name terms already?" I turned back to Scott. "So his illness was just a cover-up?"

"No." The superintendent shook his head. "That's even worse than we thought. But meanwhile he gets whatever he wants. Even you can understand that. And right now he wants to see you. Do you know why?"

"Oh yeah, he probably wants to tear my bollocks off!"

"Because you took out his sister?"

"That's a good enough reason for Delaney."

Scott smiled. "I don't think so. In any case, I'll guarantee your safety."

That made me laugh but quietly.

I made some coffee to give myself time. I didn't bother asking what Walker wanted. He got with and with like the rest of us.

We sat down at the table. Scott spread his legs wide and looked at me in an amused sort of way. He seemed utterly convinced of his own magnetism. I accepted one of his Bensons. The kitchen was suddenly smoky.

"Will you come?" Scott asked.

"Do I have a choice?"

"Of course you do. This isn't even happening. I'll swear it never happened. So will my guv'nor." He smiled nicely and added, "On the other hand, if you were to turn down my invitation I'd be inclined to take a real close look at the car parked outside."

I shrugged weakly. "When?"

"Now, if it's convenient. Since you're up anyway." His smile flickered again. It was amused and honest. If he hadn't been filth, I might have liked him.

"I bet you're a fucking scream in the canteen, aren't you?"

Walker joined in on the laugh. He tasted his coffee and grimaced.

"Jesus! That's awful," he said and turned to the drainer to see what I'd used. When he turned back his tongue was flicking as though it had been mauled by a hot Madras. "Bitter," he muttered. "Piss." He stood up and tipped the rest of it into the sink.

Scott took another mouthful. He remained expressionless as he studied me over the mug. Finally he said, "Lenny, you realize how important it is that this remains between us? If it leaks before we're ready a lot of people would be in big trouble, including Julie."

"Did Delaney tell you about me and Julie?"

He nodded.

I said, "Don't worry, if it gets out it won't be from me."

I felt like telling him that at least two of his colleagues were already spreading the news, that it would only take a reasonable offer for either of them to spell out the details and leave a paper trail right the way to Delaney's bedroom door. But I didn't. Why the hell should I care?

Surprisingly they drove me away from the city centre. Roger had obviously not got all the details, or Delaney had been moved. The car was unmarked, another Rover. As soon as other motorists saw it, they slowed down to the speed limits.

We went north towards Hertford.

"So, why should a villain like Paddy Delaney want to see you Lenny?"

The question came out like small-talk but Walker wasn't fooling anybody. In the daylight his face had turned yellow. Nicotine yellow. Grease oozed out of his open pores.

Scott glanced at me through the rear-view mirror.

I said, "I guess he's playing the big brother act."

"His sister?"

"I can't think of anything else."

"How well do you know him?"

"He's a nutter. That's all I know. Anything else came from the papers: Rio, Biggsy, you know?"

Walker half turned in his seat. His narrowed eyes were almost threatening.

"Why is it I don't believe you?"

"That should worry me?"

He nodded. "Yes, I think it should."

I shook my head and looked out at the A10. "Fuck you," I said.

They fell strangely silent, perhaps aware of my mood. What they couldn't know about was the tension in my gut. In the back seat I crossed my arms to conceal the nervous shake of my hands.

We pulled up in front of huge, cast-iron gates set in an eight feet high brick wall. No Trespassing and Private notices were positioned either side. The gates were pulled open by a man in a duffle coat. He had recognized the men in front. Just inside the gate was another notice with a small map of the grounds. St Mary's Trust. Lately, life had been full of institutions, clinics and hospitals. I was getting faintly OD'd on the sight of red brick.

This was a large two-storey conversion that was once the centre-piece of a rather classy estate. The lords and ladies had retreated from the leaking roof, taking with them their grand collections, and the private trust had moved in, patching up, building extensions, replacing four-posters with single beds and the grand piano with an array of electronic boxes.

I was led to a side door opened by a uniformed policeman. He acknowledged the others and watched me closely. I followed them along a short corridor to another where another policeman sat outside one of the doors. The air held the smell of steamed meals and grease. The kitchens were not too far off. Steamed food; it evokes memories of empty ringing corridors and some flat-footed dickhead up front of a classroom spouting on about Harold the Twenty-Second and the second battle of Skegness in 520BC. Before Butlins moved in.

"He's in there," Scott said to me.

"Alone?"

The policeman in the chair nodded.

Scott said, "Don't worry, he can't move very far." He chuckled. "All you've got to do is shout."

I looked at him for a moment, not seeing the funny side.

"Go on in," he pressed. "The man's waiting." He opened the door for me and stood aside.

Paddy Delaney glanced up from his single bed. He was wearing spectacles. A copy of the *Sun* was opened in front of him. He was grey and weak, his eyes had a haunted look. Next to the bed was a control unit and next to that a cylindrical dialyser. Tubes ran from it into Delaney's left arm. Apart from the equipment the room came as a surprise; it resembled the chintzy suite of a hotel, Regency stripes and cut flowers. A side table contained bottles of Perrier and orange squash.

Carefully Delaney removed his spectacles and folded the newspaper. He wore pale blue pyjamas. Dark hair on his chest spilled over the top button. His brown eyes, paler than I remembered and sunken, slipped toward me.

"Surprised?" he asked.

I shook my head and said, "No. There's a grapevine out there and your name's hanging all over it."

He grunted. "I imagine it is," he said. He pointed at the machinery. "Apart from the fact there's a tumour on my liver the size of a football they'd treat me with drugs. Now they're something I'm an expert on. Apparently, because the liver's fucked, the drugs would send me into a coma. Can't break 'em down anymore. They accumulate. So, eight hours on this fucking thing!"

"Shame," I said.

"You could show a bit of fucking sympathy."

"Yeah, I suppose I could."

"All right, Kid. I deserve it." For a moment he grimaced. He sat up a little straighter and relaxed again. "I want you to do something for me."

"Fuck you!"

A flush of rage flickered on his face and his eyes hooded.

"Be careful, Kid. Just because I'm in here doesn't mean I'm helpless."

"I don't care whether you are or not. You're still getting fuck all from me."

"Why did you bother coming then?"

"Well it wasn't to bring you a bag of grapes, Paddy, that's for sure."

I sat down in a hard-backed chair.

"But I am getting the picture now," I said. "We thought you came home to look after Julie, but that's crap. You came home to die."

"If you like," he said. "But I'm not going to die strapped to some machine in some pathetic hospital bed. I can guarantee that much."

"You're boring me, Paddy. Why did you drag me out here?"

"I heard about Sheringham."

I nodded. A mild chill ran up my back.

"Now I ain't blamin' you for that. This Zahavi psycho tart reckons that you're Julie's best bet at finding out what's wrong. Julie trusts you. She trusts me but I can't get through to her on that level. Know what I mean? The shrink thinks her sexual hang-up is behind all her emotional problems. Since you're the closest she's got to a relationship, it's down to you."

"You're asking me to sleep with your sister?"

He snapped, "No I'm fuckin' not! What the fuck d'you think this is?"

I was perplexed. He realized it.

"I want you to get fucking close to her. Not that fucking close." He calmed down. "Get her to trust you so she can talk. Become her confidant. Work with this Zahavi shrink. Understand?"

"I'm already doing that for Julie's sake. You didn't need to ask me."

"Maybe. But I know what you show-business people are like. You're likely to lose interest overnight and where will that leave her?"

"Tell me something, Delaney. Why after all this time are you suddenly concerned for your sister? You spend eighteen years not giving a shit and now she's all important?"

"It wasn't eighteen years. And I've been paying through the nose for as long as I can remember. Zahavi knows it. Fuck me, she must have built the hospital on what I've paid her. But it's only these last few years, thanks mainly to that woman, that Julie has responded. Before that she hardly recognized anyone. It took me a long time to come to terms with it too. Remember that when you go around making half-cock statements. She killed our parents. My parents. How the fuck would you feel about that?"

"So what changed your mind?"

"I was told to think about putting my house in order. I was told that it was inoperable."

I nodded.

"The family, what was left of it, was suddenly important," he said quietly. He looked up and held my gaze. "Kid, to my knowledge you're the first man she's ever taken a shine to."

"If you want me to hang around, don't lie to me."

"Meaning?"

"Meaning Nicholas Linet."

"I heard about that too. You mentioned it to the hired help. Well, that was fuck all to do with me." He raised his hand. "Why? Tell me? Why would I bother with him?"

"When you were fucked out of your brain you didn't need a reason for anything you did."

He nodded. "I'll tell you something and you can believe it. Not one of my guys laid a finger on Linet. And neither did I. Why the fuck should I? There's no reason for it? Believe me, Kid. Do you think I'd be askin' you to see Julie if I had a hang-up like that? Think about it. Anyway, even when I do break up, I know what's happened. I can't control it, I know that, but I remember it." He shook his head. "What happened to Linet had nothing to do with us. And for your information the drugs are history. I was told yesterday that the next time will be curtains. A certainty."

"In that case I'll go cut you a line."

"You're funny. I'm startin' to like you, Kid."

"Don't. For Christ sake don't. Last time someone said you

liked me I got a Doc Marten's in the face."

"Mario?"

"Mario."

"Sorry about that."

"No, you're not."

"Uh?"

"You don't give a fuck about anyone."

"Wrong, Kid. I care about Julie."

"I wonder."

"What's that suppose to mean?"

"It means that I'm not convinced. But don't ask me to explain what other motive you might have. But even this scam isn't being fair on her. How's she going to react to the news that you're dying? And what about if this leaks? What sort of danger will she be in? You can guarantee that they'll try to get to you through her." I paused before adding, "You do know you're never going to get out of here, don't you? No one's going to let you get to court."

"They don't think I'll live long enough for that, anyway. They want names, Kid. Names and places. I'll spin it out long enough to take care of things."

"There's people queueing up out there to pay their last respects."

He smiled, a quick little smile that meant he had it all in hand. He knew what he was doing.

"I want to give you some money. I knew you wouldn't accept it off Nick without an explanation from me."

"For what?"

"Expenses," he said. "Looking after my sister."

"Would I get it in gold bars or drugs money?"

His eyes narrowed into sly slits.

"Fuck your money."

He raised his eyebrows, rounding his eyes again.

"Oh, you've got so much, have you?" He chuckled.

I leaned forward in the chair. "Listen, Delaney, I'm going to help Julie in any way I can. I'm doing it for her, because I want to. Not for you. Definitely not for you. Understand?"

His features firmed up. Back now was the contemptuous look that I recognized.

"If you need anything or if you need to get in touch again, just ask Nick."

I nodded and got to my feet. "When are you going to tell Julie you're dying?"

He shook his head. "No point in upsettin' her before it's necessary."

"She thinks you're in Switzerland."

He touched his nose. "So do a lot of people," he said. "Let's keep it that way."

I left him without glancing back.

THIRTEEN

On Saturday I went to Dixons and bought an Amstrad computer
that promised to do everything for you including the washing-
up. With it came a couple of free games, chess and something
to do with zapping aliens. I took it home, put a plug on it, and
killed off half-a-dozen nasties before I had to leave for Clarinet's
woodshedding; not that we had completely retired from the
musical scene but for Joe Gabriel two days was long enough.
We were not experimenting with anything new, either, for it was
simply a matter of running through a list of tunes that Clarinet
had put together, getting used to a riff so that individual solos
could compete for the applause. I spent most of the time watching
the others, joining in occasionally on the guitar. We broke up
at about nine. Anything later and the neighbours would have
started complaining.

When I arrived home Ellen was waiting outside in her Volvo
Estate. The streetlight caught her worried expression. She wound
down the window.

"What is it?" I asked.

"Damn you and your ideas," she said. "Have you got any
whisky up there or shall we go to a pub?"

"Come on in," I said. She secured the car and climbed out.
"How did you find me?"

"A slimy little man at the club gave me your address."

"Peter," I smiled.

"Is that his name? He made me crawl."

"Yeah, that's Peter. He makes everyone crawl."

As we walked to the door she said, "Julie went home this
morning." She seemed worried.

"There's been a development at my end too. You'll never guess
who I saw yesterday."

"I bet I will. Nick mentioned it when he picked up Julie."

"I might have known. Why have you damned me and my
ideas?"

She held her coat tightly at the collar. A northerly wind swept down the side of the flats.

"Wait 'till we get inside," she said.

We took the lift to the top floor. Her slim black briefcase made her shoulder sag and she bent down to place it on the floor. It was an easy movement but it made me incredibly aware of her body. Before I opened the door to my apartment she noticed the screws and gave me a funny look. I flipped on the light and stood aside for her. I tried to remember what sort of state I'd left the flat in.

It wasn't too bad. Lunch dishes weren't washed but there were only two of those, a few jazz magazines were spread on the table, and some CDs on the floor next to the stack. The computer was on the coffee table, of course, and bits of flex and a screwdriver that I'd used on the plug. The bedroom was in a mess but I couldn't really imagine Ellen Zahavi going in there.

The central heating had kept the chill off but even so I turned the fire full on before I took her coat to a rack near the door. She was wearing a long-sleeved navy-blue jersey jacket. It's gold buttons glinted in the light. Beneath it was a loose pleated skirt, two-tone green stripes edged with pink, which fell to mid-calf. On her feet were high-fronted suede slip-ons. She smiled at my look of approval.

"I can see you're a handyman," she said, indicating the spider table. As a temporary measure I'd stuck the leg with Scotch adhesive tape.

"Drink?" she said. There was something about her I found intriguing. With a simple aside or one of her looks she was able to reduce me to helplessness. And she knew it. Perhaps it was her age or more likely her understanding that I found unnerving. She had that 'not born yesterday' look in her eye which suggested, almost, that she couldn't be surprised.

She sat down on the sofa and crossed her legs. I poured some drinks and handed one across.

"Don't forget you're driving," I said.

She shot me a narrow-eyed look. I sat opposite in an armchair. The fire was already sending out its glow.

"Go on, then. Tell me?"

Carefully she reached forward and placed her glass on the

coffee table then opened up her briefcase.

"You put me on to it the other day," she said. "I don't know why I didn't spot it before. It's been staring me in the face for years. It's right here, on the front page!" She produced a thick buff-coloured folder and tapped it. "This is a part of Julie's file. Strictly confidential, of course. But I have her permission to involve you. This goes all the way back to 1975." She glanced up. "Before the fire."

I took the sheets as she passed them over.

"Have I got to read them?"

"Just one or two."

I shrugged and began. She kicked off her shoes and raised her feet beneath her. She picked up her glass again and settled back, waiting for me to finish.

It was a sheet of A4, typewritten.

Hilltop Hospital
22 September 1975

Dear Dr Eliot,

Re : Julie Delaney.

Admitted 23/8/75
Diagnosis: Renal Glycosuria
Discharged 7/9/75

This child was seen in the outpatients with a short history, approximately six weeks, of frequency of micturition. Dysuria was not evident. She also had polydypsia, taking 4 or 5 pints of fluid a day. She had recently lost approximately half a stone in weight. There is no history of diabetes in the family

She was found to be rather thin and underweight, slightly apyrexial, not dehydrated with no anaemia. Chest and cardiovascular systems were normal, the central nervous system was intact, the abdomen was soft, there were no palpable masses. On clinitest her urine showed 1.9% sugar and acetone was present. The blood sugar was 525 mgm/100ml, $3^1/2$ hours after a meal.

Her haemoglobin was 86% white blood count, 3350 per cmm, 58% neutrophils. A Heaf test proved negative. Urine

135

showed only a few leucocytes. Chest X-ray was clear.

She was treated with soluble insulin, 28 units a day for seven days, after which she became Ketone and sugar free. The hyperactivity and aggression may well settle down now that the infection is clear. If not then it might be neurologically determined and may require medication such as methylphenidate.

She was discharged on 7/9/75 and will now be monitored as an out-patient. There are no diet restrictions.

E F Conway
Paediatric Registrar.

I passed the sheet back to Ellen and shrugged.

"That was a letter sent from the hospital back to her GP. Eliot had obviously made the initial referral. We take it up again after the fire which killed her parents. First a note made at the children's home where she was first placed."

She handed over another sheet. Another A4, handwritten in ink.

Julie's behaviour is undisciplined. She was seen at Hilltop by Dr Sefton. He believes that she would be better placed away from the other children who know of her background. Their constant taunts are making it impossible for Julie to settle or progress. So far he has been unable to find a suitable placement at another children's home or adolescent unit and he wrote to Dr Freeman, consultant at Broadwater Hospital.

I turned over to a typewritten letter.

Hilltop Hospital
2 March 76

Dear Dr Freeman,

Re: Julie Delaney.

Julie's referral came from the Paediatric Dept of this hospital. Her behaviour has been severely disturbed since November of last year. She was expelled from her junior school in December

136

and she has just been excluded from a special class for maladjusted children in Hilltop. She is presently at Lady Christine's Children's Home.

The sequence of events is as follows: she was diagnosed in August '75 as suffering from polyuria and polydypsia etc. She was hyperactive and aggressive.

She was fully examined in hospital recently to see whether her behaviour disorder was the result of blood sugars or acetone but this was found not to be the case. Tests to exclude kidney infection are satisfactory.

The family situation is as follows: her parents died in a fire on 10 Oct '75. Investigations confirm that Julie deliberately started the fire in the house but the reasons remain unknown. The Coroner's verdict, apparently having taken her age into consideration, and worried about the flimsy evidence to substantiate her statement of guilt, was open. The police will take no further action or interest in the case. She has obviously had a psychological response and this seems to have affected Julie more than her brother. Her brother is 15 and is cared for by an aunt and uncle. They refuse to take Julie on the grounds that she is demanding, disobedient, abusive, and could be a danger.

I have seen her weekly since October and at interviews the most striking thing is her pressure to talk, which appears inconsequential but usually reflects her current preoccupations. She will not discuss the fire or anything relating to it. She cannot remember starting it, nor any reason that might have led her to start it. She is overtly sexual in her speech, wanting to shock at all times. This has sometimes come into the therapeutic situation but she had stopped trying to be provocative since it was pointed out as futile and childish. In the beginning she talked about missing her brother, Paddy, but not her parents.

At interview she has been able to reveal the depression behind her restless, talkative, exhibitionist behaviour. However, in recent weeks her conversation has been more inconsequential than usual. She has taken to using new strange words that she makes up and also shows a repetitive grimace of protruding her lower jaw, wrinkling her nose and opening her mouth. She has shown sniffing tics in the past but this is more severe than ever before. She also hums a tune, high-pitched, and this goes

137

on for up to half an hour at a time, the same tune, over and over. When asked about it she is not even aware of having hummed it.

A psychological test on 15 Feb gave the following results.

WISC	Full Scale	IQ	88	
	Verbal Scale	IQ	97	
	Performance Scale	IQ	79	
	Reading age	8		2/8 years
	Spelling age	8		3/8 years

My original diagnosis was of an affective disorder, with the depressive element more prominent although concealed by restless talkativeness. I feel this still is probably the case but I am beginning to wonder whether there is a more severe psychotic element entering into her behaviour recently.

I feel very strongly that it would be better for her to be treated away from the children's home, in her own interests and in the interests of the other children. Many avenues of placement have been explored through hospitals and local authority services, but these have proved unsuccessful. It seems imperative that she is admitted somewhere where she can be treated, as I feel the longer the situation is allowed to continue the more difficult it will be to help her.

I must again thank you for your help with this child and I look forward to hearing from you.

I B Sefton MD DPM
Honorary Consultant in Psychological Medicine.

The next sheet contained notes from the hospital. Julie had been admitted to Broadwater.

Has been severely disturbed since her parents' death in Oct 1975.
Displays various twitches.
Says she has been expelled from school for bad language.
Went to another school where they called her mental and killer.
Talks easily but not about fire.
Finds it difficult to get to sleep.
Brother is 15.

Misses him.

Has been seeing Dr Freeman at Hilltop since last Oct.

Hypomanic character disorder.

Haloperidol 1.5 mgm tds

Sod Amytal gms 3 nocte.

Interviewed 3 May 1976

Tense, emotional, tearful. Says she doesn't remember yesterday, how can she remember fire?

Julie has continued to be very difficult in the ward.

She is emotionally very unstable and usually fatuously euphoric.

She impulsively attacks other patients.

No longer fit for ward six.

Transfer to 16-up.

"And that," Ellen said, "is where I came in. Sixteen-up were the refractory wards. I had just taken over there and I met Julie for the first time. You know the rest. With the help of Himanshu we got her out of that place as soon as possible."

I shrugged. "I'm sure it's good stuff, Ellen, but none of it means much to me and it certainly doesn't explain why you should damn me."

"Oh yes it does. It's in the first letter I showed you. The letter back to Dr Eliot, her GP, from the Registrar. Firstly, it's what it doesn't say that's important. Secondly, Dr Eliot's referral is missing. It was never sent with the rest of her papers. Frequency of micturition, weight loss, infection and most importantly, hyperactive and aggressive behaviour. You mentioned abuse, Lenny. Remember? This is a classic case. And what's more, they didn't miss it. I did, because I took everything they wrote on face value. I didn't question it until you asked the question. There's been a cover up and it sent Julie to hell!" She sighed. "And suddenly everything falls into place, her sexual problems, the virginity business. Christ, it might even throw some light on the fire!" She rubbed her eyes and left them bleary. "Earlier I went across to Hilltop!"

"Go on."

"I wanted to have a look at Eliot's original letter."

"The missing referral?"

"Yes. It was on microfilm. I hate those viewer things." She

rubbed her eyes again.

"Well?"

She showed me another letter, a photocopy, similar to those I'd already seen. As far as I could see the only difference was that it mentioned discharge, inflammation of the eyes and a burning sensation when passing water. It was three pages long, mostly repeating what the others had said.

When she saw that I had finished Ellen said, "Before coming here I showed that, together with the discharge letter from Conway, to a friend of mine, a GP at Cambridge." She sniffed awkwardly and, almost reluctantly, handed across another sheet. It was handwritten, barely legible, definitely in the hand of a GP. "He was quite horrified," Ellen went on. "This is his summary." With difficulty I read:

Dear Ellen,

These are my first thoughts on the matter. You don't give a man very long!

The major difficulty with it all is the hospital discharge letter of 7.9.75. The clinical condition outlined in the letter does not really conform to a recognizable scenario, and the short-term treatment with insulin injections seems an extremely unlikely management of the situation.

I can confirm, from my researches into relevant medical articles, that it is possible to develop a temporary glycosuria (sugar in the urine) in association with an acute infection, in particular with a kidney infection, acute pyelonephritis. The glycosuria would not be as severe as in Julie's case, and there would not be a six weeks' history. The management for this temporary glycosuria would be the treatment of the kidney infection; as the infection cleared the glycosuria would settle. I have been unable to establish a connexion between glycosuria and acute gonorrhoea, and I suspect that any glycosuria occuring in association with that condition would be very transient. There is some evidence that a mild temporary glycosuria can occur after the ingestion of opiate narcotic drugs.

I didn't say this, but Dr Eliot is clearly complicit in the cover-up about Julie's sexually transmitted disease, and would have, presumably, overlooked the discrepancies in the discharge letter from Dr Conway.

Dr Eliot's receptionist, who would normally file the letter, would be unlikely to challenge its contents; other partners in the medical practice would 'smell a rat', but my impression from the reading is that Dr Eliot was (or still is – in any case easy to establish) a single-handed practitioner who may have conspired (by telephone) with Dr Conway to keep the more sinister elements of Julie's case out of the medical records.

I hope this is helpful to you. If I can be of further assistance please let me know.

Regards,
Bob.

I looked up. "Julie had gonorrhoea?"

"Yes," she said. "We're almost . . . No, we're certain."

"You can tell from these?" I waved towards the letters.

She nodded.

I shrugged, still astonished, and suggested weakly, "Let's ask her about it."

She shook her head. "No, not until we get all the facts, and even then it would have to be done very gently. My guess is that any abuse, like the fire, has been blocked out of her consciousness."

"It sounds bloody weird to me."

She smiled and stood up. "Where's your bathroom?"

I pointed the way. When she came back she said, "Where on earth did you get that bath? It's like a swimming-pool."

"It was here when I moved in. I can do twenty lengths now, morning and night."

She picked up her glass and moved to the window. The curtains were still open. She looked down across the rooftops opposite to the dark swaying trees in the park.

"I'm going to see Dr Eliot," she said thoughtfully. "He's still at the same surgery."

"You're going to show him these?" I nudged the copy letters. "That'll go down a treat."

She nodded.

"If you're right he's got a lot to lose. He could get nasty."

"I think I can handle people like Dr Eliot."

"Maybe. But to be on the safe side I think you should take me along."

She narrowed her eyes and struggled with the idea that she might need help. Finally she sighed and relented and said, "I'll give you a ring."

She left shortly afterwards. I walked her down to her car and waved her goodbye.

When I got back I poured myself another drink, a larger one, and sat in her place on the sofa, seeing the room from her perspective. In the dim light that hid the age of the wallpaper it looked quite good. A trace of her perfume was left in the flat but she had left a curious hole.

FOURTEEN

On Sunday, on the spur of the moment at Laura's suggestion, I took the kids to see *Aladdin*. We did the Cockney floor-show at the Wembley market first, the place where Londoners shop. We left Portobello and Petticoat Lane to the tourists. On the way home Jack and Laura were still full of the Gentle Genie.

"But how did the carpet fly, Dad?" Jack kept asking. Magic wasn't good enough. Nor was Laura's explanation of it being on strings. "If that was right, it would come up on each corner, wouldn't it, Dad?"

Donna saw us and smiled over the head of the new baby. The kids rushed up the path and started to question her about the carpet.

"Hold it a minute," she said calmly. She held the baby close. "Now just cool down and tell me what's going on."

Laura got in first. She always did. "If the carpet was flying it had to be on strings, didn't it?"

"What's all this then? What carpet are you talkin' about?" Donna glanced up at me. "What's goin' on, man? What have you done to my babies?"

I raised my hands and said, "Aladdin's carpet, of course. You better explain how it flies."

She grinned, "Thanks a lot, man. You comin' in for coffee?"

I shook my head and tapped my watch. Her face fell slightly. She turned back to the twins. They were arguing, still trying to work it out.

There was no message from Ellen on the answerphone. I was faintly disappointed and for a while considered ringing her. My head was still spinning with thoughts regarding Delaney and his sister. They seemed to have taken over my life. I thought of little else, unable to settle. It crossed my mind that I should pull back from the whole business and get some sort of normality back into life. But I couldn't do that. Julie Delaney was on the edge.

And I was too involved to leave her there.

I went to eat at Joe's café and arrived home to the telephone and all but ran to pick it up.

"It's me," she said. "I'll pick you up at four-thirty. He's not that far from you."

Dr Eliot was a little man in his early sixties. Ellen told me later that he seemed no less married to his job than was Conway, the Paediatric Registrar she had confronted at Hilltop Hospital. There was something in his bleak brown eyes to indicate that his soul had dried up; they weren't even cynical anymore. Years of dealing with patients whose only complaint was wanting a few days off work had eaten away at the Hippocratic oath. His face was rigid, blown, his hands quivered slightly, his dark-blue suit dusted with dandruff. He was surrounded by wooden trays of correspondence. On his desk an ashtray was half-full of half-burned tobacco from his dead pipe. His patients had ceased to be people. He was just working out his time.

"This is inconvenient," he said sternly. His eyes flicked across the two of us, slightly surprised at the mismatch.

"We'll do it another time if you like," Ellen said but she sat down anyway. We had been forced to wait an hour until the end of his surgery. His receptionist would have fitted in well with Nick and Mario. She didn't have their weight but her demeanour was just as threatening.

He finished scrawling a note and waved me into a seat next to her. Ellen crossed her legs. I remained stiff-backed.

Ellen took the copy of Eliot's letter to Conway from her slim black briefcase and pushed it on to the desk.

"I won't keep you long, Doctor. I really only have one question."

He glanced at the letter. His eyes blinked several times in quick succession and he shifted his weight in his chair before looking up.

"Go on?"

"Why is it that your letter to Hilltop never mentioned the abuse?"

He looked down to the letter again then slowly eased back into his leather chair. He studied Ellen carefully. The silence was almost palpable.

Eventually he said, "I take it that Conway gave this to you?" His back was to the wall. He hid his shock well.

"Among other things."

"It was a long time ago."

"But you do remember her?"

He nodded slowly. "I remember thinking it was diabetes. Micturition, pain, bladder infection, loss of weight, polydypsia. . . "

He paused, not finished, but she interrupted, "Don't forget the eye infection."

They toyed with each other. It was beyond me.

"That too," he acknowledged. "But that was before I sent her to Hilltop."

"The behaviour problems too?"

"Go on?"

"The overt sexuality?"

Now he knew where Ellen was leading him. Now there was no doubt. He shook his head.

"You prescribed an antibacterial not usually associated with eye infections . . . " Ellen went on, reeling him in. "What did you prescribe for the eyes?"

He interrupted, slightly flustered. "Protozoal infection, the bladder . . . Look, Metroni–"

"Don't try it on with me, Dr Eliot," she said sharply. "I don't have to spell out where my next stop is!"

He took a deep breath and looked into Ellen's eyes; for him they were twin barrels of a shotgun and he was looking right down them. Her gaze was cruelly unyielding. He swallowed loudly and played with a gold ring on his finger. He pulled it back and forth.

"I didn't know," he admitted. "Not until her brother came in a day or so later."

Ellen frowned. She would have been useless at poker. Her reaction could not have been more obvious had she been hit in the stomach. Dr Eliot was quick to seize on it.

"You don't know a damned thing, do you?"

"I know enough to have you in deep trouble." She was back on the offensive. You had to admire her. The thought of being a junior in her office made me shudder. And yet her students thought the world of her. For a while, back there, Donna had used her as a role model.

She barely paused for breath. "I know the police will be interested."

"I daresay," he said carefully and licked his thin lips. "But I think I might call your bluff all the same."

If Ellen's confidence had been shaken it didn't show. "You knew that Julie had gonorrhoea. She was eight years old. You knew that abuse was taking place. It was right under your nose. And yet you chose to take no action. You conspired with Conway to have it left out of the records. Even when the social services became involved, you maintained your silence. Why was that, Dr Eliot?"

He smiled slyly. "I think you'll have a job proving that. Falter just once and I shall sue you."

He had her. Her pause was too long. She had revealed her hand too soon. He was smiling even before she began.

"I think I have enough–"

I interrupted her. I wasn't brought up with the Queensberry rulebook. As far as I was concerned the Eighth Marquis never lived in the real world.

"Forget it, Ellen," I said. "Let's go. This medical line might not hold up, but he can talk to the police about corruption, about his name being mentioned in Delaney's pay-out book!"

Dr Eliot went white. It was amazing to see the colour run from his face so quickly.

"Fuck you, Dr Eliot!" I said.

Ellen turned to me, horrified at my outburst. Eliot's eyes focused on me at the same time as his mouth opened and closed.

It had been a stab in the dark really but I knew people like Paddy Delaney. I knew their philosophy and guessed it ran in the family. Threats first, and then the sweetener. After the threats, the sweetener always seemed like an excellent, face-saving, option. Ellen had got over her shock and looked at me quizzically.

I shrugged. "Well we might as well come clean. All this sparring . . . " I said to her for Eliot's benefit. "If we can get what we want from him we don't have to bother with all the form-filling. We haven't really got the time, anyway."

She raised her eyebrows, half understanding, nodded, and looked back at the wilting Dr Eliot.

His expression hadn't altered. He was still in need of Sal volatile. His rigid features had slackened considerably.

"What is it you want to know, exactly?" he croaked. "It was a long time ago. My memory isn't what it was." He picked up his worn pipe and sucked hard on the dead stem.

Ellen smiled sweetly and asked, "Who brought the children to see you?"

"The children's uncle, Bob Delaney, brought them in. He explained how he wanted to keep it in the family." Eliot glanced up, regretting his choice of words.

"I imagine he did," Ellen said icily.

Eliot went on: "He came on behalf of the children's father who couldn't face me. The mother was to be kept out of it altogether. She didn't know, didn't have any idea. It wasn't the money. He made threats. He promised to break my arms, and worse."

"I know the feeling," I muttered.

"The complaint was no problem. It's easily cleared. But she was showing all the other classic signs as well – signs of abuse." He sighed in dismay. "How do these things begin? I don't know. Bathtime, playtime? To the rest of us even the idea is repulsive. I suppose that's why we sweep it away, run away from it. There's no excuse, I know, but fear can influence many a judgment. I thought the best solution was to get her away for a while. That's why I approached Conway. He was the Paediatric Registrar at Hilltop. He agreed to take her for two weeks."

"Did Uncle Bob pay him?" I asked.

Eliot's eyes sparkled as they filled. "I looked after him," he said quietly.

"So the abuse was never recorded?"

He nodded.

"And when she came out, went home, it continued?"

"Perhaps. I don't know."

I glanced at Ellen. Her lower lip was trembling. She was fighting to hold in her emotion.

"Well, well," she said. "What a filthy little practice you run, Doctor. That little girl spent years in a mental institution because of you. It won't be a surprise to discover that your actions, or lack of them, in all likelihood led Julie into starting the fire. Where else could she turn?"

147

He looked down, refusing to meet her gaze. It struck me that he was not an evil man, simply a coward. That over the years the guilt had destroyed him. He had been threatened, perhaps assaulted. Fear wiped away the rights and wrongs. They didn't come into it. It took a brave man to stand up to the threat of acid in the face, or a switchblade waving in front of your eyes or, worse than that, the threat that it might happen to your wife or children. Given that scenario a lot of people would have followed Eliot's path.

I touched Ellen's sleeve. "Let's get out of here," I said. "There's nothing else for us here."

Without speaking she rose, snatched the sheet of A4 from Eliot's desk, and went in front of me to the surgery door.

"Is that it?" Eliot asked.

From the door I turned back. "That's it," I said and followed Ellen into the white corridor.

In the car she couldn't speak for some minutes. She wiped her eyes on a tissue then peered into the rear-view mirror to apply some lipstick. Her hand trembled.

"I thought the job made you immune to involvement, Doctor?" I said.

"So did I," she sniffed. "Something must be happening to me."

I glanced quickly sideways toward her then readjusted the mirror, fastened my seat-belt and ran through the gears.

"I'm going to see Delaney's uncle," I said coldly.

"What's it to you?"

"You can fight it for so long. Eventually you say bollocks. If you can't beat 'em you might as well join them. I want to find out what's going on, Ellen. Don't ask me why. As far as I'm concerned Paddy Delaney is capable of just about anything, but not this. Not standing by while his father fucked about with her or, come to think of it, with him either. There's something wrong. It doesn't add up. Not with the Paddy I know. Not now, and not when he was . . . "

"Fifteen," Ellen helped me out. "When Julie was eight he would have been fifteen."

I nodded. "Right."

She wasn't convinced. "You'd be surprised just how much of this goes on. And how much of it involves more than one person.

I've known cases where the grandfather, father and two brothers were all taking turns. Even the mother was frightened of getting pregnant again in case they attacked her."

She caught my frown. "In order to fuck the foetus," she said.

I grimaced. "That's a joke, right?"

She smiled quickly and nodded, "A social work joke. Off colour." Her expression fell again and she flicked me a look of concern. "You should stay out of it."

"Yeah? It was you that got me in to it in the first place."

"No it wasn't. You did that all by yourself by taking her away."

"Maybe. But I want to know why she set fire to me. Are you coming?"

She shook her head. "I've got a case conference this afternoon. I've got to get back. Drop me off at the car." She paused, then said, "Can I see you later?"

"I'll be at home."

She nodded. "Not at the club?"

"Not until Wednesday."

She smiled quickly. After a pause she asked, "How did you know he'd been paid? It never occurred to me."

"That's because we live in different worlds. My world is full of people on the make. It was a flyer. But on the assumption that Delaney needed him, there was no alternative."

She nodded. "I hate men," she said.

"I don't blame you."

The telephone directory gave me the address of Delaney's uncle. I dropped Ellen off and drove over to Forty's Hill in Epping. The road petered out to a deep-rutted dirt path between the bare trees and led to a concrete yard where red rusted machinery and dilapidated buildings pointed to a richer time when the business had thrived. But that was a long time ago. Before the economic boom had soured. A time when councils sub-let their beds and borders and bent councillors were putty in the hands of people like Robert Delaney. Uncle Bob. In those days the cutting-edges on the machines were sharp and glinting. Now the tractors and diggers were soft and flaking and the weeds that thrived in the sulphates had grown through the wheel arches to pin down the scrap. I rolled the car over the pockmarked grey surface of the yard and parked between a large two-storey house and a huge barn affair. A stack of rough tree trunks towered in front of me. The place seemed deserted but with all the scrap machinery about it was difficult to tell. The roof of the swimming-pool had long since fallen and tiles were chipped and covered in green algae. The pool itself was filled with leaves and rusted and rotting junk. Some of it jutted from a stagnant pool in the deep end. I walked across to the house. It had been patched up, weather-proofed, made ugly. Blue paint flaked on the door.

A plump, friendly looking woman in her early fifties opened the door. A long woollen jumper covered her from neck to knee.

"Is the guv'nor in?"

"You've missed him by a whisker," she said. There was a laugh bubbling away beneath her voice.

I wondered what was funny about it.

"I'm Joyce!" Her smile continued as though waiting for the punch-line of a joke.

I tried to picture her taking part in the cover up and couldn't.

"I'm sorry. Bob always calls me the guv'nor. Oh, don't mind me. Everyone tells me I've got a strange sense of humour. You want Bob? You'll find him down over there." She pointed beyond the barn.

"Can I leave my car there?"

"That's OK."

I left her on the doorstep and walked back through the yard.

By the shed I passed two grease-covered men working on a small pick-up. One of them, a dark-haired individual in his early thirties was vaguely familiar. It took me some moments to realize that beneath the black smudges and huge overalls that hung loosely from his slight frame, it was Julie's cousin, Anthony. He gave me the once over, scowling when our eyes met. His look of hostility was still puzzling me when I caught sight of Uncle Bob about a hundred yards on walking slowly along the side of a stream.

The resemblance between him and Paddy was quite remarkable. Give Paddy a miraculous thirty years longer to live and you'd be looking at his uncle. The hair was grey and short, but the features, especially the brown eyes, were just an older, looser version.

He waved at the black trickle of water.

"Used to be three, four feet deep," he said when I reached him. He rubbed his hand through his spiky grey hair. "When I first came to this place it was eight feet across, current, trout, the lot. Now look at it. I could produce more having a piss!"

He was shorter than his nephew, and stocky. He looked across the jungle of weed and bush.

"'76 it was when she dried up, that stinker. Never came back. Still shown on the maps, though. The River Welly."

I nodded. "My name's Lenny Webb," I said.

"What brings you out here?" Our eyes met for the first time. His were watery, shot through. Delaney hostility was evident. "You don't look like a kozzer."

"No. It's about Julie." I offered him a cigarette then lit them both.

"What about her?"

"She's had a relapse."

"Yeah, I heard." He grunted. "She always was a pain in the arse. Always. She's caused me more bother than the rest of the family put together!"

"That doesn't surprise me."

He looked up sharply. "What the fuck's that suppose to mean?"

"Abused children usually have emotional problems."

"She ain't a kid any more. What are you? Social worker?"

"Naw. I work at the hospital," I lied.

"Well?"

"Her old GP made a statement. Said you paid him hush money to keep it quiet, keep it in the family. He wasn't joking."

"I'm not laughing. Old Eliot said that?"

"Yeah. Do you deny it?"

"I ain't denying it. I ain't agreeing with it, either."

"Fair enough. Our only concern is Julie. We want to help her. Any information that we can get will help. It will remain confidential."

He nodded. "What does Paddy say?"

"He's got problems of his own. At the moment he's in hospital. He'll probably say something when he comes out."

Robert Delaney thought about that for a moment. He took a

deep drag on the cigarette and sent the smoke into a bunch of reeds.

"I don't suppose he'll be too happy," he muttered. "Yeah, well, my brother asked me to pay Eliot off. I didn't like it either. But there you are. Fuck all else to do, really. If that sort of shit hit the fan the business would have sunk without trace. You don't get councillors giving orders to people with that kind of form. Not up-front anyway. After the fire, well, you know about the fire. It ended there as far as I was concerned. No point in saying anything after that, was there?"

I nodded. If it hadn't been for Julie's incarceration, he was probably right.

"It was only about a fortnight later," he said. "And Julie was in hospital for most of that time. She'd only just come out. If he hadn't died I might have done something about it."

"You knew about your brother. Paddy was still at risk, wasn't he?"

He frowned. "Come again?"

"Paddy?"

He laughed. "No," he said. "Paddy wasn't involved."

Surprise worked its way on to my face. I felt the colour rise. Dr Eliot had been quite adamant that both Paddy and his sister had been taken to see him.

"You don't think . . . For fuck's sake, it wasn't her own brother! Paddy? Not a chance."

I shook my head, trying to get it straight. "I never thought it was Paddy," I said. "But Eliot said you took them both to see him."

Delaney shook his grey head. "The old man's obviously getting too old for it. I took Julie along to see him. I should know. Still, some things are best forgotten." He blew out some more smoke.

"I don't buy that. Eliot probably had nightmares about your visit ever since you made it. He isn't about to make a mistake like that."

Delaney squared up to me, suddenly threatening. "Well, Kid, if he wasn't mistaken, then he lied to you. You'll have to ask him why." Not concealing his irritation, he snapped, "Anything else?"

"Just for the record. After the fire you took Paddy in, why not Julie?"

He considered me for a while, drew on the cigarette and tossed the butt toward the stream.

"She was a damned troublemaker. Kicked out of school. Moody, violent, why should I?"

"Before the fire they used to spend weekends here, mess around in the pool, the games room."

He nodded.

"What changed?"

"I couldn't have favourites then, could I? Not when they were alive. Had to treat 'em as equals. When they died it was different. No need for pretence."

"I don't wear that at all."

He scowled. "You do know there was a question mark on their deaths, don't you?"

I shook my head.

"The thinking was that she started the fire."

"Yeah, I heard that. But it was never proved."

"Didn't have to be, did it? Even the police said there were traces of paraffin in the bedroom. The fire brigade. Even Paddy believes it and he's closer to his sister than anyone. That's a turn up for you, ain't it? Oh yeah, sweet little Julie, butter wouldn't melt and all that. They found her in the woods, hiding, paraffin all over her hands and clothes. She'd run away. She didn't sound the alarm or try to get help. She hid in the trees and watched the house burn, watched my brother and his wife burn . . . "

"Her mother and father . . . "

"Yeah. And she wouldn't say a bloody thing. She wouldn't say why she started it, or how. She never has." He shook his head in despair. "You tell me, Mr Fucking Wiseguy, if you know it all, before you come around here accusing me of not looking after the family."

I nodded. "Paddy was staying with you that night?"

"Yeah, and just as well, or they'd be fishing three people out of the cinders."

"Does your wife agree with you?"

"About what?"

"That Julie started it?"

"Maybe. Maybe not. You better ask her that."

"Didn't she want Julie either?"

153

"She does what I tell her. Listen, Julie needed help, whether we'd take her or not. I had a business to run. My partner had just been raked out of the ashes of his house. She killed him. My brother. My fuckin' brother! Would you have taken her in?"

"I guess not."

He shrugged and turned away. "I never had a head for business. My brother used to look after that side of things. I was the one that used my hands. He had the brains. Once he died that was the start of our troubles and they've been pilin' up ever since." He nodded reflectively then turned back to me. "Well then. Anything else?"

"No. Thanks for your time."

I left him by the dried-up stream.

"He confused the issue," I told Ellen later. She had knocked on my door at eight. She had come straight from work.

"This is getting to be a habit," she had said. "I hope you've got some food in the fridge."

"Are you all right now?" I had asked.

"I've calmed down if that's what you mean."

I explained what Uncle Bob had said and left her looking perplexed.

"I can't believe that Eliot would make a mistake like that," she said. "The thing's been eating him away for the last eighteen years. He wouldn't have forgotten."

I agreed with her. "That's what I told Uncle Bob. He said Eliot was mistaken or lying."

"Why on earth would Eliot lie? What could he possibly achieve by implicating Paddy?"

I shook my head. "Where does it leave us?"

"I don't know," she murmured. "I suppose we could ask Paddy about it."

I raised my eyebrows. "What if his uncle is right and he knows nothing about it?"

"Then the fat will hit the fire!" she said. "Perhaps it's not a good idea at the moment."

"Perhaps it's not even necessary. We're trying to help Julie, aren't we? Now that you know what's behind her problems you can try a new tack."

"I'd still like to clarify it with Eliot," she said. "I want to know just what Paddy's involvement is."

"I might pay Dr Eliot another visit," I said. "I think it would be better coming from me."

She drew a small diary from her bag and leafed through it. "Perhaps I could meet you at his surgery?"

I nodded. "Sounds good."

"Let's say six, tomorrow. That OK?"

"Fine. Does Julie know that you contacted Eliot?"

"We spoke about it before she left."

"How did she react?"

"There was no reaction, Lenny." She glanced up and explained. "You must remember that Julie has no recollection of what happened at that time. Not only has the fire been wiped out of her consciousness, but the abuse as well. If that weren't the case she would have mentioned it by now."

"Are you sure about that?"

"You mean could she be deceiving us? Why would she do that?"

"In order to cover up her guilt over starting the fire."

"But she's always maintained that she was guilty."

I nodded. "Right," I said.

"Come on, let's go and eat something."

"There's a little Indian down the road. Will that do?"

She smiled. "That'll do fine."

We were settled in a small booth by an Indian waiter. He served us with drinks before taking our order. The lighting was subdued; it gave Ellen a wonderful tan. She glanced around to get her bearings. A candle on the table flickered shadows over a mural beside us. Half-hidden by a complicated Oriental landscape in green and red, a great white slug of marble grinned contemptuously. She nodded toward the painting.

"Gautama," she said. "If his obesity is anything to go by then his desire for food was never abandoned, was it?"

I smiled but probably looked blank.

"Well, he said that sorrow was the universal experience of mankind caused by desire. He said that. With a gut like that I imagine he knew what he was talking about."

Behind our seats the booths were divided by carved wooden partitions. The carvings above her shoulders showed some gymnastic positions from the *Kama Sutra*. They kept drawing my eye. Eventually she turned to discover them for herself.

"My God," she said lightly. "You've brought me to a den of iniquity. How does anyone hold on to an appetite staring at that?"

It was a relief to get off the subject of Julie and her brother for a while.

I watched her crack a poppadom. It fell to bits and crumbled on the tablecloth. For a moment she seemed embarrassed. For Ellen Zahavi everything had to be just so, mastered; she couldn't handle anything less than success. It was a curious thought: that a woman whose life revolved around students and the care of her residents and the opening up of minds should have difficulty accepting her own shortcomings. She was used to people seeing her in a professional light, in charge, and when she hesitated, or broke a poppadom, then her defence was to draw the formal shutters. I wondered how much her recent separation had dented her confidence.

She asked in an affected voice, "What are you doing for Christmas?"

"I'm working 'till the small hours Christmas Eve. Nothing then 'till Boxing Day. Donna's taking the kids away to her in-laws. I'll spend Friday morning with them."

"That must be difficult?"

Perspiration touched her top lip as it quivered over a chicken Madras. She drank some lager.

I said, "It's a new experience for me. Up until now I've always managed to see them."

"I saw the computer. Is that for them?"

I nodded. "What about you?"

"I've no plans," she said. "It will make a change to put my feet up and hide inside a book. Not a text book. Something light and slushy. I shall gorge myself silly and drink myself to sleep and not think of anyone but myself. Does that sound good?" Her smile was enigmatic. It left me wondering.

"Maybe."

"I'm not like you, Lenny. The freedom of being on my own

again has not worn off. Right now I doubt if it ever will. I'm loving the space. The wonderful selfish space. I'm actually loving being a woman without a man. That's something you won't be able to understand."

"I'm not even going to try. Have you got children?"

Her expression fell. "No." She shook her head firmly. "That is one regret." She glanced up. "What about you? I can see that you're still full of regret."

"I went through a fair old time walking around with my guts trailing some yards behind me. Going through the motions of living, not accepting it. I'd find myself following her around, visiting places that I knew she frequented, that sort of thing. And hitting the bottle."

"What happened?"

"I pulled myself together. People do, or they don't."

"As Aristotle used to say."

"Eh?"

"When he was telling the future: it will rain tomorrow or it won't rain tomorrow. Oh, it doesn't matter."

"Well, anyway, I looked in the mirror one day and asked myself what the hell I was doing. Did I really want to maintain a relationship with someone who wanted to be with someone else?"

"Like most married couples?"

We laughed together.

Later, at her car, she said, "Thank you for a lovely meal. Maybe we can do it again sometime."

I watched her drive away. I was in a curious frame of mind as I caught the lift back to the top floor. Her company had been enjoyable but I wondered what she was doing. Her world was filled with scholars and dusty professors, her mind full of text books and ideas that I could barely comprehend. What then, I asked myself, was she doing with me? I was pretty certain that her scene was not centred around bebob, bob, and the crescent city.

FIFTEEN

I wanted to buy Donna something a bit tasty for Christmas. I don't know why. After we first split I could barely bring myself to think of her without a sense of outrage. But four years on, the memory of what she had meant to me overshadowed all else. She was the mother of my children. She always would be. That alone made her special. The blame had all gone, lost like everything else. It had been a two-way thing anyway. I had deserted her and that had been my choice. I was the one who had gone off for six months gigging around the European night spots, while she had been left at home with two babies.

None of the glittering shop windows sparked my imagination and I returned home empty-handed save for some wrapping-paper which I used on the computer.

I arrived at the surgery at about five to six. The place was deserted even though the lights blazed. Even the receptionist, the one with the swastikas tattooed on her breasts, was missing. The empty waiting-room hummed with the noise of a faulty striplight. For a few minutes I peered through the windows, watching for Ellen, but the small car park remained quiet. There were three stationary cars and one was mine. Headlamps flashed past on the main road.

Eventually I pushed open the waiting-room door. A short corridor led to Dr Eliot's office. I knew there was something wrong even before I got to his door. A layer of thick smoke, knee deep, was spreading out toward me, pouring from the crack along the bottom. Slowly I turned the handle and pushed the door open.

I suppose I stood there and took in the scene for just a fraction of a second, but from there on it seemed that I moved and thought in slow motion. Nothing would function. I told myself to slam the door shut but the message took an age to get to my hand.

I saw the receptionist first. She was on the floor right in front of me. Her body stopped the door from opening more than halfway. She was smoking. Her hair had disappeared, her clothes were welded into red flesh, her face was a black cinder. Her teeth jutted out; the skin around her jaw had disappeared. Her eyeballs were still in place but the lids and her cheeks beneath had pulled away. Little blue flames still flicked across her body, flaring occasionally as they hovered over bursting blisters of fat.

Dr Eliot was sitting in his chair engulfed in a fierce jet of fire. The ferocity of it pinned him down and forced his head back. As I watched his face blistered and peeled away and his scream died beneath the roar of flame. His hands, thrown up defensively, melted. A hole appeared, a deep black dripping hole, where his face had been.

The horror of it left me stunned, unable to move. The smoke and stench hit me like a brick wall. I saw the figure, no more than a dark shape in the smoke, turn slowly toward me. For a moment the roaring ceased and the fierce jet of flame died to a flicker. It moved my way, the gun, the flame-thrower, whatever. I watched it. Out of the swirling smoke a stream of paraffin headed directly for me, splashing into my face, soaking the front of my shirt. It felt incredibly cold. It was in my eyes and nostrils. I drew it in with my gasp. My eyes felt as though they were on fire. Almost blinded, I could still make out the flash as it lit up the smoke and then the ball of flame exploding toward me. Even as I pulled the door shut the heat propelled me backward into the corridor. The door rattled and flame licked around its edges. The door panel splintered immediately and smoke oozed through the crack. A blue flame travelled across the floor, leaping along the trail that I had left. It reached me just as I got to my feet. Suddenly my clothes were blazing and the flames rushed up toward my face. In that same instant I felt a blow to the face and I was soaked through. I heard a scream and saw Ellen, just a blur, as she came up the corridor. I could barely breathe as a mixture of water and foam hit me from all directions.

Ellen went past me, wielding the extinguisher like Steve McQueen in *The Towering Inferno*, chasing the flames back to the door and laying down a thick carpet of soap bubbles.

"Don't open the–" I screamed but too late. She had the door

open. The smoke came out in a dense cloud and she disappeared. Before I could reach the door the corridor had filled up. It was impossible to see more than a few inches. The heat was still unbearable but the smoke was too thick to see any flames. Something clattered in front of me. I stumbled over the receptionist and felt my hand burning as I clawed at the floor. Two more steps forward and I found her. She was bent double, gasping. I pulled her back through the door and slammed it shut. I didn't stop there. I pushed her through the corridor into the reception area and threw open the outside door.

We stayed there for a minute or more without moving, gulping the fresh air into blistered lungs, coughing and spluttering. For me everything was still a blur; my eyes stung and wept. I could just make out the smoke pouring from the back end of the building, a steady flow into the clear night.

I moved back into the reception area, reached over the counter for the phone and dialled three numbers. Moments later I said, "Fire, ambulance and police!" Within seconds I was back beside Ellen. She was crouching against the wall, still coughing, her arms wrapped around her chest. Her face was smudged by soot marks, her eyes reddened and wide. She looked up at me bewildered and frightened and she shuddered in a long sigh of relief.

The authorities arrived in a convoy of blue and orange flashing lights. The place was cordoned off. Firemen from two engines leapt into action, mostly at the back of the building but at least two hosepipes snaked up the steps to the reception entrance. The ambulance crew and a doctor who came with them weren't happy with Ellen's respiration and decided that she needed a few hours observation. With that they whisked her off to the North Middlesex. That left me shivering inside a blanket in a second ambulance. They bathed my eyes, put a temporary dressing on my blistered hand then sent me out to face a dozen uniforms.

The questions came thick and fast, some of them faintly hostile. For a while it seemed that I was under suspicion or that I was somehow hindering their inquiries. Out of desperation, almost, I asked them to contact Superintendent Barry Scott. If anyone could, then he was the man to cut through the police formalities. He arrived within twenty minutes and went directly to the man in charge. Five minutes later I was sitting in his car with the heater fully on. I told him exactly what had happened. At the end of it he said, "Whoever it was got out through the back window of a little treatment room. You can't add anything at all to the description?"

"Just a dark shape. I couldn't even tell you whether he was black or white, man or woman.

"He nodded thoughtfully and said, "You need a change of clothes. You'll have to make a statement. One of our guys will follow you home if that's all right. Try to remember everything you can. I'm going to get over and see Julie Delaney."

I nodded. "I guessed you might."

"Do you think it was her?" he asked seriously.

"It doesn't stretch the imagination too far, does it? On the other hand . . . No, I don't," I said honestly. "But I don't believe in coincidence."

"Nor do I," he said. "Still, we'll keep the Delaneys to ourselves for the moment. Get my drift?"

I nodded, then said, "Even so, I think you ought to wait for Dr Zahavi."

"Don't worry. I won't upset her. Let's just find out what Julie's been up to this last hour or so. If she's been at a church social since four o' clock we can rule her out altogether." He shook his head and muttered. "This is a mess. Divided loyalties, know what I mean? Fuck knows how Paddy will react."

He was talking to the OC again as I started my own car. Caught in the headlamps they both looked my way. The OC listened and nodded, his expression firm and unhappy.

The fire was out; the firemen began stashing their equipment. Above us the dark smoke had drawn a veil across the sky.

I led the police-car out on to the main road.

The Detective Inspector who came with me spent about half an hour making notes. He was interested in my description of the flame-thrower and, more particularly, the reason why Ellen and I had been there in the first place. I told him that we were following up a case of possible abuse and that Ellen could give him more details. He was obviously quite ignorant of Julie's affinity to fire, or anything to do with her past. He made it clear

161

that he thought that we were just in the wrong place at the wrong time. I knew that some of his colleagues would think quite differently.

Roger was on his way to work when he called. One of his mates had obviously filled him in. He waited outside for the other policeman to leave before knocking on my door.

"I just heard about it," Roger said. "I told you you was playing with fire messin' around with Delaney's crowd!"

"Ha! Ha!"

He looked into the red holes where my eyes used to be. "Fuck me!" he grunted. "Come on, man. Give me the SP. Was it her or not?"

I shrugged. "I don't know. Take her parents, her last boyfriend, the way she tried to turn my dick into a candle . . . Put all that together . . . " I shook my head.

"Why?" he asked. "Why? Without the fucking why it's nothin'."

"She could never tell you why about her parents but she told you she did it. She never told me why about my fucking dick, but I saw her doing that—"

He interrupted. "Yeah, but I can understand that. She was probably disappointed." He grinned.

I looked at him sharply. "Tell me something honestly, Roger."

His expression fell. I think he anticipated my question. "Go on?" he said.

"I've seen more of you this last week than I have for the last six months. You're fishing, I know that. I'm not stupid. If Delaney spills the beans, all of them, are you in shit street?"

"Lenny, Lenny, you're hurtin' my feelings."

"Screw your feelings! Tell me the truth for once."

He hesitated and stroked his firm chin before answering. Slowly he nodded. His face was as bleak as I had ever seen it. "Me and a lot of others," he said at last and gave me a critical, searching look. "Including a lot of the top brass. This special task force that's been set up won't even work from the Yard. You might not believe it, Lenny, but right now you know more than us about what's going down."

"So your interest in me lately has not been wholly about my welfare?"

"Man, you could say that."

"And before, when you said you didn't even know he was in the country?"

He shrugged and said, "Yeah, that was crap. Do you know where Delaney is?"

I nodded.

"Will you tell me?"

"Why?"

He tossed me a loose, embarrassed smile. "Let's just say I've been asked to find out."

"Not good enough," I said curtly.

"Come off it man. We's friends, ain't we? I mean, ain't I lookin' after your kids?"

That did it. He realized his mistake.

"I'm sorry, man. I didn't mean that," he said earnestly. "I'm just worried about the family, the future. I'd do anything for them, you know that."

The trouble was I did. I couldn't fault him in that department.

His eyes dropped lower. "I gotta go to work." He stood up and gave me a sad smile. "Lenny, will you do me a favour? Will you think about it?"

I lit a JPS and looked at him through the smoke. "Yeah," I granted vaguely.

Adrenalin used up, I felt totally knackered yet the questions still circled in dizzy spirals. I ran a bath and then showered and still the stink of burning flesh clung to me. It was in my throat and lungs. In my mind. I lay in bed, in the dark, and yet the woman's popping eyeballs and bursting skin lit up the room and the hole in Eliot's face glowed and sent sparks of burning fat towards me; the hum of the central heating became the sizzling and hissing of frying meat. I was still awake when the dawn began to creep through the curtains.

Ellen Zahavi got me out of bed in the morning. She hung on to the phone for some time while I stumbled about trying to find the arms of my towelling-robe.

"Lenny, they let me out at eleven last night. I nearly called round. It crossed my mind that I could sink into that swimming-pool you call a bath. But my clothes were absolutely filthy. I smelt like I'd been sitting on a bonfire!"

"You had as near as dammit."

"Funny!"

"And you using my bath is making my imagination run wild."

"Uh! Anyway, they fed me a pill but I still slept badly." She paused, either for breath, or for a response. When she didn't get one she said, "Did I wake you?"

"Yeah."

"Listen, that policeman came to the hospital after he left you. Did you tell him everything?"

"Just about."

"What about the abuse?"

"I just mentioned that we were checking a case with Dr Eliot. I didn't put Julie into the frame if that's what you mean. It was all pretty innocuous. He wasn't interested in that."

"Good," she said simply. "Julie was at home all evening. Nick vouched for her. So did a couple of other guys. Paddy's increased the hired help. I imagine he's worried that someone will try to get to him through his sister."

"That makes sense," I said and wondered whether my mentioning it to Delaney had got him thinking.

"She still believes that he's out of the country." There was a long pause before she said, "Listen, I've got an idea Lenny." She fumbled for words. "Nick's bringing Julie up to see me this morning and I want to try something a bit out of the ordinary. Can you get up here?"

"I suppose so. What have you got in mind?"

"I'll tell you when you get here," she said. "About eleven. That OK?"

"I've got to call in at the police station first and sign a statement, but that shouldn't be a problem."

"I'll see you later," she said in almost a whisper.

Given any other circumstance I might have read something into her soft, promising voice.

SIXTEEN

"How did it go at the police station?" she asked as we drove across Cambridge. Spits of rain from a washed-out sky dotted the windscreen.

"It was just a repeat of last night," I told her. "But in writing."

"Did you see the papers this morning?"

"Yeah, didn't they love it? Death in the surgery. Ugh! The police have picked up on the connection with Linet but they don't know what to make of it yet. Even so, it's only a matter of time before they knock on Julie's door, you know that don't you?"

She nodded and checked the mirror. In front of us the traffic had come to a stand still.

"This place is becoming impossible," she muttered irritably. "Traffic! Parking! Do you know there's not a parking space within walking distance of the centre?"

I had a feeling there was more to her mood than traffic. She was worried, perhaps even a little frightened.

"If we ever get there – eventually – what you're going to see is the proof of my failure. I'm clutching at straws, willing to try any damned thing. But it's failure."

"I'm sure I'll understand what you're on about sooner or later."

She threw me a sideways glance.

"Well, if any of my colleagues find out what I'm doing I'll be a laughing stock. Credibility zero."

"Yeah, yeah."

As she worked the clutch her dress rode above her knees. Her legs were slim and toned.

"The quick-fix appeal is booming," she said solemnly. "Stop smoking, lose weight, get rich and win the pools, that sort of thing. I've fought against this for years. For years Fraser-Andrews has been trying to talk me into letting him loose with one of my patients."

I wondered who the hell Fraser-Andrews was but shrugged

and said, "Maybe he has other reasons."

"Such as?"

"Well, maybe it's you he's interested in."

She gave me a funny questioning look. "You should seriously think of changing your job; taking on mine."

We parked on a concrete standing in front of a three-storey Victorian town house just off the city centre. Julie had already arrived. She sat in the passenger seat of a sparkling blue Jaguar. Nick sat beside her. We grouped between the two cars.

"I'm going to stay out here," Nick said anxiously. "How long will you be?" His glance took in both sides of the busy street.

"An hour. No more than that," Ellen told him.

He checked his watch and climbed back in the car.

Julie gave me a little, nervous, happy-to-see-you look. She still seemed fragile and lost. Standing beside her Ellen was physically dominant even though she was six inches shorter.

"Are you ready?" Ellen asked and led the way.

There were three bells beside the heavy door. Ellen pressed the top one beside the name Fraser-Andrews. Moments later a man's voice crackled from a speaker.

"Hello."

"It's Ellen Zahavi," she said simply. The door clicked. She opened it and ushered Julie in. I followed. We climbed five flights of carpeted stairs to another open door.

Fraser-Andrews met us just inside. A heavy man, about six-two or three, with a shock of long white hair and eyebrows that had flared out of control. His eyes were almost incongruous in his large fat face, small and round and pale blue. They glinted with a simple boyish humour. His nose was stubby and red, like something out of Red Nose Day, and dark hair curled down from his nostrils. He wore a long green check sports jacket, corduroy trousers and tartan bedroom slippers. No socks. If you met him just once, you'd never forget him.

Ellen introduced us and he shook my hand vigorously. "Come in, come in," he said and closed the door behind us.

The room was a gloomy clutter of antique furniture, sofas and chairs and tables. One wall was taken over by three Welsh dressers displaying at least a hundred pieces of porcelain. The other walls were covered in original watercolours, mostly nudes, reclining figures and bits of bodies. The place reminded me of an antique shop, it had that same musty feel and it was just as confused.

He moved across to a window and drew back a pair of heavy curtains. Light streamed in and picked out floating specks of dust.

He turned to us and smiled expansively. "That's better," he said happily. "Now sit yourselves down. Tea?"

We gave him our orders, with and with and without for Ellen.

While dishes rattled in his kitchen Ellen leaned across to me and said, "We're going to try hypnotism."

"Ah," I said, suddenly falling in.

"Eugine Bliss of Salt Lake City University said that it is based on the ability of the reticular activating systems to focus attention on the inner operations of the mind."

"Well, in that case, it must be all right," I said.

Ellen grinned. Fraser-Andrews had heard me. As he placed a tray of tea and fairy tea-cakes between us he raised a critical overgrown eyebrow.

"Did I hear a note of scepticism?" he said doubtfully. "Shall we start? You sit over there, Julie, and relax." He pointed to a battered leather armchair.

Ellen fished in her briefcase and pulled out some photographs. Fraser-Andrews took them and made a few pencil notes on a scrap of paper. We watched him closely as if waiting for a sleight of hand.

Ellen looked worried. She sat in a hard-backed chair, leaning forward, arms folded, her hands bunching the cotton of her jacket. Her face was drawn tightly in concentration. I sat behind her.

Julie watched me, smiling awkwardly. She seemed tiny as she rested her head back against the roughened leather.

Fraser-Andrews sat in an armchair facing her and crossed his legs. He bridged his stubby fingers under his chin and nodded reassuringly.

He said in a quiet low voice, "Now, Julie, I want you to close your eyes and concentrate on what I'm saying. I want you to listen to what I'm saying, concentrate on what I'm saying, listen carefully to every word, I want you to listen carefully to every word that I say to you and concentrate on every word. Your eyes are closed, you are relaxed, feeling very comfortable, listening to what I say, concentrating, thinking of nothing else but what I say, nothing but what I say, your eyes are closed, you are relaxed, comfortable, feeling very comfortable, you are thinking of nothing, nothing but what I say to you, you hear my voice, you're listening to what I say, thinking of nothing else but what I say, concentrating. Your arms are heavy, they feel heavy, your legs feel heavy, you are relaxed, your arms and legs are relaxed, relaxed, your head is heavy, relaxed, your entire body feels relaxed, the muscles in your arms and legs are relaxed."

His voice dropped a notch and became monotonous, there was a drone about it, and his words came slower. Incredibly, I shook away a moment's drowsiness.

"You are moving into darkness, the light is fading, and you're moving toward the darkness, and as it gets darker you are more and more relaxed. It's becoming darker and darker, you're moving into the darkness and as you move into the darkness you feel more and more relaxed, more and more relaxed, thinking of nothing but my voice, thinking of nothing but what I say to you, listening to what I say, thinking of nothing, nothing, listening only to what I say, listening only to my voice. You are relaxed, comfortable, very comfortable, as it gets darker, you are moving into the darkness, listening only to my voice, the sound of my voice, and you are relaxed, completely relaxed."

His voice dropped further and became softer.

"You are breathing easily, deeply, deeply, thinking of nothing but the sound of my voice, breathing deeply, deeply, in and out, in and out, moving into the darkness, hearing nothing but the sound of my voice, relaxed, comfortable, very, very comfortable, and you are thinking of nothing but the sound of my voice."

The sound of his voice had dropped very deep and was whispered.

"Nothing, nothing but the sound of my voice, relaxed, and as it gets darker you begin to feel sleepy, drowsy, very sleepy and heavy, relaxed, and you are thinking of nothing but the sound of my voice. You are breathing deeply, relaxed, in and out, in and out, and you are so sleepy, you are going to sleep, a deep sleep, a deep, deep sleep, a deep, relaxing sleep, breathing deeply, deeply, breathing deeply, and your sleep is getting deeper, deeper, deeper, and the darkness is complete and your sleep is getting deeper, deeper and deeper, you are going into a deep, deep sleep, deep, deep, deep, deep sleep, relaxed, deep, deep, deep, sleep, sleep, sleep . . . "

Fraser-Andrews leaned forward and gently lifted Julie's arm. It fell back limply. He turned to us and raised his bushy eyebrows and gave us a quick confident smile. He turned back to Julie.

"Can you hear me, Julie?" he asked in the same deep voice.

For a moment there was no response, then her lips moved and she said in a strangely unemotional voice, "Yes."

"Do you know who I am?"

Again a long pause before, "Yes."

"Julie, listen carefully to my voice. It's your birthday. You are eight years old today. It's a party, cakes and lemonade and fancy hats. It's your party." He studied the photographs on his knee. "Lots of people by the swimming-pool, you're wearing a pink dress, a beautiful dress. Are you having a good time?"

"Oh yes, oh yes." It was not Julie's voice, it was too high, breathless, that of a child.

Fraser-Andrews looked at the photographs again and glanced at his handwritten notes. Before he could say anything further Julie was rocking in the chair.

"Push harder, higher, higher," she said. "Dimwit! Higher! I don't care. I'm not coming!"

Fraser-Andrews frowned. "You're not coming?"

"No! I don't care either!"

"Where don't you want to come?" he asked softly.

"Don't be a dimwit. You just said, didn't you?"

"Yes."

"Well then."

Fraser-Andrews turned to us and shrugged his heavy shoulders. He turned back and said, "All right then, I'll go on my own."

Julie relaxed. For a moment we thought that was the end of it. The silence lasted ten, maybe fifteen seconds. Then she shouted out, "You'll be sorry! You'll be sorry! He'll be angry!" She split the last word, as youngsters often do. It came out as 'annnn-gry'.

"Who will be angry?"

"Dimwit! Dimwit! Who's a dimwit?"

She began to hum. At first it sounded like a series of disconnected notes, but then, as she hummed louder, I recognized them. Fraser-Andrews didn't and he shook his head.

"Julie, your birthday is over. It's summer again. You spent all day at Uncle Bob's, playing in the pool, splashing. Sliding down the slide. You're home now. It's dark. It's the night of the fire, the horrible night. You're in your bedroom. Have you been to sleep yet?"

Julie stopped humming and for a while remained silent. Her eyes fluttered against her lids. She began to cough. Little coughs, clearing her throat.

"Can you hear me, Julie? Answer me Julie. Have you been to sleep? Are you awake?"

"Yes! Yes!" Her voice was clear and sharp.

"You woke me up! What are you doing? What's that funny smell. What . . . ? Put it out! Put it out!" Her voice raised to a shout. "Mom! Dad!"

We were horrified, half-raised from our seats. I gripped the arms on my chair. My blood was surging; I felt the heat pouring out of my collar. Fraser-Andrews raised his hands to calm us.

Her breaths came quickly. She rocked in the chair. Her fingers gripped the arms so tightly that they turned white.

"Mom! Mom! Mom! Don't! Don't! I did it! I didn't mean to! I didn't mean to! Don't hurt me . . . " Suddenly she was screaming.

I was out of my chair, shocked. I had heard those exact words before. That exact voice. 'I did it! I didn't mean to!'

I exchanged glances with Ellen. She looked horrified, utterly horrified.

Fraser-Andrews clapped his hands loudly. Julie's scream continued. Ellen was at his side, willing him into some kind of action.

"Oh shit!" he said and leaned closer to shake Julie's shoulders. With his mouth only inches away from her ear he said, "When you hear my hands clap you will awaken." He repeated it.

Her screaming stopped. His voice seemed to calm her.

"That's it," he continued. "When you awaken you will feel refreshed and happy. You won't remember your dream at all. Your sleep is getting lighter now, the darkness is fading and the light is coming in. Lighter, lighter."

He clapped his hands.

Julie's eyes blinked open. She looked from Fraser-Andrews to

Ellen and then to me. She must have wondered at our expressions that mixed concern with a very real fear. She seemed a little disoriented, like someone who had just emerged from a drugged sleep.

"Just relax. Everything's all right," Fraser-Andrews said in a very apprehensive voice.

"I'm OK," she said shakily.

Slowly Fraser-Andrews turned and looked at us sheepishly. "I'm sorry about that," he said. "That was quite extraordinary."

"It was more than that, Fraser," Ellen said and sighed loudly. "It was so much more than that!" She shook her head in dismay. "You know who you are. But who are you? Can we assume that he – it – was male?" She turned to Julie. "Can you remember anything at all?"

Julie's forehead wrinkled. She shrugged, not understanding.

Fraser-Andrews jumped in. "No, she wouldn't Ellen. And as for it being a he, you mustn't assume that at all. Julie would put her own interpretation to my voice. To her, only the words were important."

"Who then?" Ellen asked, as though Julie was not present.

"Will you tell me what happened?" Julie asked.

Fraser-Andrews ignored her and said, "I'd like to try it again. But I want a lot more background first. Can you let me have that?"

"We could get together later," Ellen suggested.

"Good, good. Then perhaps we can arrange it for after Christmas. I think we're on to something here. Something rather thrilling."

"Actually Fraser," Ellen said coldly. "I could think of a better word."

Julie's frown deepened. Eventually I said to her, "Sweetheart, I'll tell you about it later. Ignore these people and they might go away."

She smiled quickly. Both Ellen and Fraser-Andrews shot me with curious looks.

"Could that have been play acting?" I asked Ellen as she drove me back to the Wood where my car was parked.

She answered curtly, "You saw it. What do you think?"

"In that case the police ought to be involved immediately.

Someone else started the fire and got away with murder. Someone she knew. One of the family. There were a dozen or more people in the photograph but I'll guarantee not many of them would have a motive."

"If Paddy's father was into as many rackets as Paddy, there'd be a whole heap of people willing to light the match."

"Maybe. But not that many that Julie would recognize. It's family. It's gotta be. And it's gotta be mixed up with this abuse business. Think of Eliot for Christsakes! It's gotta be Uncle Bob."

"Maybe. Unfortunately, I'm afraid the police won't take much notice of alternative medicine," she said. She turned and gave me a sharp smile. "You're seeing her tonight?"

"She said she'd come to the club. It depends on how she feels."

"She'll be there. She's infatuated. Be careful."

"Don't worry, Doctor. I won't take advantage."

"I wasn't thinking of you taking advantage," she muttered. For a few moments there was a difficult silence, then she said sombrely, "You recognized the tune, didn't you?"

I nodded and gave it to her.

Ellen raised her hand and smacked her own forehead. "Oh my God, of course!" she said and joined in on the last line. We were building railroads and begging dimes again.

I said, "That was one of the songs I did in the bar in Sheringham. Just before we went up to bed. And I'll lay you odds that it was the same tune she was humming in hospital. The tune that the geezer in Broadwater mentioned in his report."

"I hadn't forgotten," Ellen said quietly. "Remember I told you that we were looking for the something that triggered Julie's attack? I think we've found it."

In the club, Peter had moved the corner table and set up a massive Christmas tree decorated with winking lights, golden balls, tinsel and fake snow. The business. He stood admiring it as we walked in.

"What do you think, boys?" He held his hands together and shuddered in delight.

People getting the bar ready paused to catch Clarinet's reply.

"Not bad," he grunted. "I suppose you're going to be sitting on top of it?"

The rest of the band laughed. The people behind the bar

sniggered.

"On top?" Peter frowned before it sank in. "Oh, the fairy," he said. His hands spread out before coming together in a little clap. He chuckled and coloured up. "Don't be so hurtful," he said then did a little pirouette before tiptoeing toward his office.

Clarinet finished admiring the tree and said to me, "George put on a real good act. I thought you was coming."

"Yeah," I nodded. "I was a bit busy."

"The girl?" His voice was edged with disapproval.

"She was part of it."

"Listening to George Melly would have done you more good," he chided. "You could learn something about style an' timin' ... "

"Yeah, yeah. I'll catch him next time."

Later, Peter caught me alone. "When was it?" he said. "Saturday, maybe Sunday, there was a woman in here looking for you. I gave her your address. I had no choice." He lifted his hands defensively. "I thought she was going to hit me. She marched in here like the fucking female liberation front rolled into one. Talk about a chip on the shoulder. I told her, I did, I told her it wasn't my fault she wasn't born a man!"

I laughed out loud. One or two people turned our way. "I bet that went down a treat," I said.

"She demanded to know where you were, where you lived–"

I interrupted him. "She's a doctor."

"Oh, well, that explains it."

"She looks after Delaney's sister."

Peter flinched at the sound of Delaney's name and locked himself in his office.

Wolves Aren't White were supporting the big names tonight, The Ronnie Scott Sextet, so we didn't have a lot to do, except listen and enjoy the show.

Mike kept on saying, "Cool man, cool, man."

"You see how professional they are, man?" Clarinet told him. "Do you see any of them falling off chairs? That's why you never get invited to Ronnie's place!"

Julie came in earlier than I expected and I had to break away from the others. Clarinet rolled his eyes to the ceiling. Alan nudged Keith and smiled at him affectionately.

Mike said, "Cool, man." His popping eyes raked her, up and down.

I led her away from them just as Peter emerged from his office. He skated past and gave us a second, surprised look, realized who she was and did a quick U-turn. He would make do with the speakers in his office to listen to Ronnie.

I said to her, "Can we agree that we won't talk about what happened this morning?"

Curiosity flickered in and out of her expression.

"You're being mysterious," she said.

"No, I don't mean to be. It's Ellen's domain. She'll tell you all about it when she's ready. I don't want to put my foot in it."

She nodded her understanding and said, "You like her, don't you?" Her voice was marked by a faint touch of jealousy.

I reached forward to the ashtray and stubbed my cigarette. "Yes," I conceded.

"I know you do. She's so positive and confident, everything that I'm not."

"That's silly. I've seen you pretty confident. In the hotel, for instance, with Ghost and the others. You were the life and soul, remember?"

The memory brought a smile. She sipped at her drink.

"Do you remember much about Broadwater?" I asked.

"Of course." Her eyes lowered.

"Is it painful to talk about it?"

"Not to you," she said quietly. "I'll tell you if you want me to."

"I'd like to know what it was like."

Slowly she looked up to meet my gaze; her eyes had moistened. "I didn't know it was a mental hospital to start with. Not until the sister told me we were all mad. All of us in there. I was in a long dorm, beds on either side, thirty of us to the room. All the others were older than me; most of them real old. One was eighty-something. Most of them seemed pretty ordinary, just overweight and unable to get about properly, just old and maybe a bit stupid, but they weren't mad or nuts. One or two of them tried to get a bit too friendly and I kicked them. It was a stupid thing to do; they were so old they wouldn't have managed anything. But remember, I was only just turned nine. But having some old woman without any teeth and only strands of grey hair leaning over your bed – that was pretty frightening. But kicking them got me sent into the locked ward, the refractory ward."

"That's where you met Ellen?"

"Yes, funny how things work out. She was the one who got me out of there. In the locked ward it was different. There were the same number of beds but there was no privacy at all. The bath, the shower, even the toilet, were open. You couldn't be alone for one minute, not unless you got PR. Do you know what that is? Padded cell! Then you could be alone. In the locked ward everything smelled of toilets. We were allowed one bath a week, one towel between four of us. If you were last in line you put more water on to you than took off. Most people in there were really mental. They screamed and shouted, talked to the walls. You learned very quickly to keep out of the way, make, like, invisible. The worst thing . . . "

"Go on."

"The worse thing, Lenny, was that even in a little while you realized you were becoming like them, you couldn't stop yourself from acting like them. Maybe it was to survive, to be one of the crowd, but I think there was something more to it than that. Ellen used to tell me that if enough people tell you you're mad, you'll start believing it and acting like it." She shrugged. "I was only there a few weeks before they moved me. Eventually I ended up in a secure unit and that was run by social workers. Then the clinics, then the Wood. I lived at the Wood longer than anywhere else in my life."

"Do you know why you were sent to Broadwater?"

She looked directly at me, "Because I started the fire," she said matter-of-factly.

I shook my head and asked, "Can you remember starting that fire?"

Her quick rueful smile surprised me. "The number of times I've been asked that question. It must run into hundreds."

"What was your answer?"

"Ellen must have told you."

"Maybe, but I'd like to hear it from you."

"Remember the night at Sheringham?"

I nodded.

"I turned over. We talked about it the other day."

"And?"

"The next thing I remember is the ambulance. The flashing light. It was the same the night of the fire. I remember the flashing lights. I was in the woods, freezing, and the flashing

175

lights got closer. That's what I remember about the fire."

"In that case, Julie, tell me why you're so certain that you started it?"

"The words were in my head. I did it. I did it! I was covered in paraffin. I'd run away. Of course it was me. Everyone said so, the police, the social workers. Even Paddy thought so."

"Remember a few minutes ago you told me something that Ellen had said?"

"What?"

"That if enough people tell you you're mad you start believing it and acting like it."

"Oh Lenny, I wish you'd talk to me like this all night. I want to make love to you so badly."

"I don't want you to do it badly at all."

She grinned and said earnestly, "We will try again, won't we?"

"I think that's a pretty reasonable bet," I said. "But let's just take things as they come, slowly."

Before Nick took her home just after midnight I said to him quietly, "I've got to see Paddy again, like yesterday."

He looked at me sternly, mildly surprised.

He said: "The word is they're going to let him home Christmas Eve. Have him back Boxing Day. Put a dozen kozzers in his garden to keep him safe. Can you believe that? With me and Mario there, they're worried about his safety!"

"No, that's pretty unbelievable."

"Still, fuck 'em. Maybe I'll get to see Christmas myself."

"How about tomorrow?" I insisted.

"Can't it wait 'till Friday."

I shook my head.

"I'll get a message through," he said doubtfully. "I'm sure he'll be thrilled."

Clarinet had us run through our complete repertoire. The club remained full and boisterous until after four. Eventually Peter called a halt to the proceedings. We left the club with eyelids the weight of lead and throats the texture of sandpaper. Too much booze, too much smoke, too much blowing and puffing, and a hectic day that had lasted twenty hours; I was dropping before I reached the bedroom. Showering and cleaning my teeth were done by instinct and I was barely dry before I hit the pillow.

SEVENTEEN

My message got through to Nick's boss and Superintendent Scott telephoned me. He wanted the reason for my visit and I gave him 'personal business' which really thrilled him. Before I was allowed into Delaney's room I was frisked by Walker while two uniforms scowled. In their eyes anyone who had personal business with Paddy Delaney was a villain.

Delaney was fading quickly; the difference just a few days had made was astonishing. His skin was grey and loose, his brown eyes heavy and deep, unable to cling on without slipping. Even his movements seemed slower. He was off the machinery, resting against the headboard. The bedcover was pulled up to his waist.

"Hello, Kid," he said. For a second his eyes held a trace of affection. Taken aback I could barely remember what I'd come for. Eventually it came back to me and I decided to come straight to the point.

"A mate of mine is a copper."

"Bent as arseholes then, eh?" A smile tugged his slack mouth.

"Sort of."

"Do I know him?"

"Roger Aremetei."

"The coon," Delaney nodded. "I know him. Bent as arseholes as I said." He glanced up. "Mate of yours? That does surprise me. He's quite a vicious little toerag." He saw my frown and asked, "What is it?"

"How come you've got your finger on everything local? I mean, with you being overseas for so long?"

He tapped his nose. "Business, Kid, the world's a small place now. Now you got satellite links, cables under the sea, faxes. It's a fuckin' wonderful world, you know. You can even talk to someone from your car, or a boat, or even the fuckin' moon. As long as you got people you can trust you can control your business from anywhere in the world. That simple. Just because I left doesn't

177

mean I gave up being chairman of the board. And I've got a good personnel department as well. In here." He tapped his head. "I know the coon, and I know how much he's earned himself these last few years. He must have a nice little nest egg somewhere."

I asked, "Is he going to feature in your memoirs?"

"Well he don't actually rate a chapter, does he? I mean, he's hardly a star."

I shrugged.

Delaney narrowed his eyes and said simply, "If he gets off so does his boss and half his squad. Is that what you want?"

"How do you work that one out?"

"If they go down they'll implicate him as well. He'll probably end up copping it as ringleader. He is a coon, isn't he? Figure it out for yourself."

"Have you given their names in yet?" I asked bleakly.

He shook his head and winked. "Keep the most important stuff 'till last," he said. "That way they can't make you redundant."

"But it keeps you in the firing line."

"Fuck it, Kid. Look at me. I ain't foolin' anybody and that includes myself. I'll be lucky to see the New Year, won't I?"

"Have they told you that?"

"So who gives a fuck?" He sighed and nodded thoughtfully. "I ain't got much, but I'd like to take those bastards with me!" He looked up. "I'll tell you what I'll do, Lenny. You make the decision for me. He's your . . . What the fuck is he to you?"

"He married my ex-wife."

Delaney smiled. "So if he goes down you'll have to pick up maintenance payments again. Ha! You old bastard! And I thought you were straight."

"It isn't that, Paddy."

"You make the decision, Kid. I suppose I owe you that much."

"I'll think about it."

"Not for too long, eh?" His glance was doubtful. "Is that what you came about?"

"There's something else, but it's tricky."

"Try me." He lay back against his pillow.

"I don't want you to go loopy. Give me trouble and I'll call in the kozzers."

He frowned and sat up again, sensing that I was deadly

serious.

"Go on."

I took a deep breath, stood back a pace out of his reach, and said, "If you're not straight with me now then I'm going to walk out of here and I won't be back. To hell with you, your sister, and the rest of the Delaney crowd. Understand?"

His frown deepened. The colour in his face darkened a shade as his eyes narrowed to a cruel glint. "I'm listening, Lenny," he growled.

"You're not going to like it."

He waited, his body tense.

"Ellen Zahavi got hold of some old medical records. They dated back some time before the fire, before your sister was admitted to Broadwater."

He nodded firmly.

"They showed that she had been abused."

"What?" His mouth dropped open in astonishment.

"Sexually abused," I said. "She was taken to Dr Eliot with discharge, inflammation of the eyes, burning sensation when passing water, and so on. Gonorrhoea."

"What the fuck?" He raised himself up, threatening to leap off the bed toward me.

"Calm down or I'm off," I said. I meant it.

Slowly he eased himself back on to the pillow. "All right! All right! I'm calm, see? Sit down, will you? You're going fucking nowhere!"

I raised my hands to shut him up, dragged the single chair away from the bed and sat down.

"Now tell me," he said and wagged a finger. "Make some sense!"

"We saw Eliot. He said that both you and Julie were taken along to see him and that you both had gonorrhoea. He believed that your father had been abusing you both. Your Uncle Bob threatened him with death unless he kept it off the record. He saw him on your father's behalf. Your mother and your Aunty Joyce were to be kept out of it completely. Presumably some excuse was made to keep them happy. I don't know about that. Up until that time your sister had been in trouble at school and had been referred by Eliot for psychiatric tests. Until she turned

179

up with Uncle Bob he hadn't put the two and two together. Eliot decided that the best solution was to get Julie away from your father for a while until things settled down and he had her admitted to hospital for tests. Are you with me so far? Comments?"

Delaney concentrated hard. With each sentence his expression had fallen further, away from disbelief to one of shock and sadness.

"Give me the rest of it," he said in a shaky voice.

"I went to see your Uncle Bob, Robert Delaney, out at Epping. He confirmed the story with just one exception. He said that you had not been involved, that they hadn't taken you to the doctors with Julie. As far as he was concerned, you knew nothing about it."

Delaney nodded slowly, taking it in bit by bit.

"Now that leaves us with a problem. Either Dr Eliot had got it wrong, and that to us seemed pretty unlikely, or he was lying and wanted to implicate you, or Uncle Bob was lying. Trouble is, I can't check it with Eliot. Before I got back to him someone pumped up a flame-thrower and turned him into a fucking kebab. You still with me?"

Delaney seemed dazed. The colour that had so quickly darkened his face had now drained and he looked grey again.

"Is he dead?"

"Dead? Yeah, I'd say he is. What's left of him would go in a little silver box on your mantelpiece. Somebody's doing their best to put the local crematorium out of business!"

Delaney's hands began to shake.

"With all these fires going down you'd think it was bonfire night, wouldn't you? Your parents' house, the boyfriend's, Dr Eliot, Sheringham. You see where this is going don't you?"

He rubbed at his temple, trying hard to relax and make sense of it.

"Bob wasn't lying," he said eventually. "I never knew a fucking thing about all this."

"Why would Eliot want to put you in the frame?"

He shook his head.

"There's more," I quipped. "It gets worse."

He shot me a dangerous look and said, "How can it get fucking worse? You come in here and tell me my father was fucking around with my kid sister? How the fuck can it get worse than that?"

"I'll tell you then you can tell me. Once Ellen realized that the abuse may have triggered Julie's behaviour she tried another test. Yesterday. I won't go into the specifics, 'cos I didn't really understand them, but the outcome was that your sister didn't start the fire that killed your parents. She walked in on it. Somebody frightened her, there was some kind of scuffle and she ran away."

If he had been merely shocked before, now he was shocked rigid. There might have been a thousand questions in his head but not one managed to get out. As the implication sunk in he began to shake. I left it until I thought he was about to explode then got to my feet.

"I'm going to get someone," I said.

The words had an immediate effect. The shaking stopped and his eyes reddened with emotion. He reached for his watch.

"I'm getting out of here," he said. "Things need doing."

"I don't think they'll let you," I said.

He gave me a sharp, curious look. "Mister," he said. "They'll let me do anything I fuckin' well like! Haven't you heard? I'm royalty around here!" He swung his bare feet to the carpet. "Come on, you can help me get dressed. Is your car outside?"

"Paddy, we'll never make it."

He pointed to the window. "Yes we will," he said.

I shook my head vigorously. "Oh no, I'm not getting involved in this."

"You're already involved, Kid," he said sharply. "You can drop me off in town. You worry too much."

"Whatever it is that's so important, can't I do it for you?"

"No chance," he said as he struggled into his trousers. He buttoned up and reached for his jacket. "Help me on with this." He couldn't get his arm round far enough without being stabbed by a pain in the gut. I caught hold of his jacket and directed his hand into the sleeve.

"What about a shirt?"

"Come on, I've got plenty more at home."

I peered out of the window. The grounds were empty. A few trees stood in front of the wall just twenty yards away. The car was parked away to the left, perhaps fifty yards. I flipped the catch and pushed the window to its full height.

"You go first," Delaney said. "You're going to have to help me out."

I dropped down on to soft earth. Delaney followed, gasping out loud as he raised his leg above the sill. "Jesus!" he said and for a moment remained quite still. He took a few deep breaths and tried again. I took his weight and pulled him clear. For a few seconds he crouched by the wall, his face screwed in agony. When he gazed up his eyes were tearful. "That was a bastard," he said.

"This is going to kill you," I muttered.

"I'm all right now. Come on, where's the wheels?"

I pointed the way and keeping low, below the line of other windows, we made our way along the wall. Luckily the car was the last in the row, out of sight from the gate.

"Open the boot," Paddy whispered.

"You'll suffocate."

"Don't be bloody stupid," he insisted. Keeping an eye on the surroundings I turned the key and opened the boot. He rolled in next to the spare. In a foetal position he looked up and smiled, "That was easier than the window. Getting out again might be another story."

I closed the boot on him and climbed into the car. At the gate the man in the duffle coat gave me the once over before letting me through.

Once we reached the Smoke he insisted on calling Nick from a phone box, then sat in my car to wait for him. It was about ten minutes before I recognized the sleek blue Jaguar pulling towards us. Delaney had the door open before Nick had stopped.

"I'll see you around," Delaney said to me through the open door. "When the kozzers turn up just tell 'em . . . tell 'em to fuck off!"

I watched them roar off before motoring carefully across to Bruce Castle. I kept telling myself not to worry, but it didn't help. I'd dropped myself right in it. Shit was about to rain from the heavens.

Superintendent Scott and DI Walker were not very happy with

me. They walked into my flat an hour later just like Rory Calhoun and Dale Robertson would have done in one of those black and white B pictures. Expanded chests, jutting jaws, hands hovering over six-guns. Wonderful, really, men, know what I mean?

"I know, you've come for some more coffee," I said.

Walker remained tight-lipped and went to check out the other rooms.

Scott said, "You've been fucking stupid. Where did you take him?"

"I dropped him off in Mill Hill, the Broadway. Nick picked him up from there."

"Why did you help him?"

"He insisted. He gets whatever he asks for, remember?"

"From us, maybe. Not from you."

"Why not from me? My arms break just like yours." I hesitated before asking, "Was he actually in custody?"

Scott shook his head. "Helping with our enquiries. That's the term."

"And even they were unofficial, so I wasn't breaking any law, was I?"

Walker came back and butted in, "We're going to be watching you very carefully."

"Yeah, yeah. Tell me about it." I shrugged. "Listen, Delaney said he'd be in touch with you as soon as he's sorted out a little problem."

"Do you know how many people are out there looking for him? You know what they'll do if they find him?"

"He knows."

"Time is not on our side," Scott said.

"How long has he got?"

"A week, at most. That's if he lays off the booze and dope."

"Does he know that?"

Scott nodded.

"He'll contact you," I insisted. "Christ, he needs you to stay alive even that long. Think about it."

That seemed to satisfy them. They headed for the door.

"Don't you want to stay for coffee?"

Walker turned on me. "You're joking aren't you? You call that coffee? Piss!" He slammed the door behind him.

It was another party night. I imagine the economic gloom outside and the little faith most people had in the government's ability to pull it round, increased the need to forget it all for a while. In Peter's place that's what his customers did. They pulled crackers and put on party hats and drank as though prohibition was coming in with the morning. Perhaps nothing would surprise them with what John Major and co might do next.

A bunch of women from Debenham's took over one side of the club. Gusty and noisy and shouting out requests at every moment. They were into Neil Diamond and thought that the sound-track from *The Jazz Singer* was what jazz was all about. Beside them some of Peter's regulars insisted on a Dixieland revival. At one stage bread rolls were used as artillery shells.

Mike said, "Cool, man," as one missed his head by a foot and showered him with crumbs.

But it was Christmas and Clarinet tried to please everyone. What in the early evening promised to be a disaster turned into a swinging party and the two groups joined up and talked about the New Orleans white bands and the cost of lamb chops and cheese. They were still talking and shouting out requests when we packed up, said bollocks to Peter, and headed home at four thirty. The milkmen on double rounds had just started their shifts.

Donna woke me up. She called in from the living-room.

"Stay in bed, it's only me!"

Years earlier I had given her a key to take care of the mail while I was on tour. You'd be surprised to know how much joint mail, mostly junk, still turned up even after all this time.

"I came to collect the pressie," she shouted. "And to bring one for you."

I glanced at my watch. Nine o'clock. Things were hazy. I stumbled into the bathroom, splashed some water and used a mouth-wash. One of Mike's bass drums was knocking out a two-bar phrase in the back of my head. I took Donna's advice and crawled back under the duvet.

"The present's in the hall cupboard," I called to her. "Give me a call in four hours!"

"What shall I do with your present?" she asked.

She stood at the open bedroom door looking across at me. A ray of light shafted in over the top of the curtains and coloured her sympathetic smile in gold. Her straight teeth flashed. "You look terrible," she said. Her raincoat was buttoned to the throat. She seemed taller. I glanced down at her blue high-heels.

"You're dressed up for the town. Where are you off to?"

She glanced down at her shoes and grinned before taking a step forward. Her coat parted over her thigh.

"I've brought your present," she said. Her slim fingers fiddled with the buttons on her coat. Each one revealed a little more.

Slowly she drew open her coat and showed me my Christmas box. Just below her navel and above her bush of jet-black hair a single pink ribbon was tied in the prettiest bow I'd ever seen.

"Do you want to open it now?" she asked thickly.

I looked down at her stomach, firmed up by her work-outs, and at her beautifully tapered legs.

"For goodness sake, man, you're making me embarrassed!"

"My God," I said. "I'll get up for a present like that!"

She giggled. "I thought you might." She dropped the coat to the floor and climbed into my bed.

'On top of the world, mama!' Jimmy Cagney's voice shouted above the thump of Mike's bass. Brilliant!

I felt wonderful; sticky, covered in her, breathing in her familiar musky scent, running my fingers along the length of her spine to the perfect rise of her behind. She lay on top of me, her breasts flat against me, her finger tracing my lips. She had a question but found it difficult. She hummed and hawed before coming out with it.

"Tell me straight, will you? Is Roger bent?"

I was caught off guard and hesitated too long. In the end I had to make the best of it. "All coppers are bent, you know that." I put a joke into my voice.

"Seriously?"

"I'm not going to answer that, Donna. You'll have to ask him yourself."

"You've just answered it," she said solemnly. Her eyes flared. "Why didn't you tell me before?"

185

"I'm not even telling you now. I don't want to be accused of sour grapes!"

"I'm not accusing you of anything. I don't know what's going on anymore. Nothing makes sense. What's happening to me, Lenny?"

"Only you can answer that."

"Dad wants to know whether you'd like to go over and have Christmas lunch with him and Mom?"

"There's only one person I want to spend Christmas with. Or at least, one and two halves."

"I know," she said softly. "Christ, I know that. And do you know what the most stupid thing in the world is? That one and two halves wants to spend it with you." She sniffed, then went on, "What about Dad? Will you go?"

I shook my head. "No. We'd sit around and get pissed and reminisce about the old days. Fuck that. I've been trying, without much success, to forget about all that."

"This is crazy. It's just made things worse."

"No it hasn't. Not for me. I'm going to be flying for the rest of the day. I never stopped loving you, you must have known that."

She moved up. Her kisses peppered across my face and reached my ear and she whispered a single magical word.

"Good."

She glanced at her watch on the small MFI bedside unit and panicked. She struggled off me, all arms and legs. I peeled away from her stomach like a sticky plaster.

"Oh my God, I'm late! I've got to pick the kids up. I've still got some shopping and wrapping to do. I'm going to be late!"

She pulled underwear from her coat pockets. I watched her get dressed, bra first.

"I'll shave and shower and come and see them," I said.

Ready to go she paused at the door. "Don't be long," she said and gave me a sad, wide-eyed look that fluttered in my gut like a long smoky breve.

EIGHTEEN

As soon as Donna had closed the front door, I sprang out of bed ready to take on the day and anything the next thirty years might throw at me. Mike's drums had faded; I trod air to the bathroom. The power shower stabbed me but I never felt a thing. I watched her left-overs hit the waste with the bubbles, clockwise, like fake snow on Christmas tree baubles.

Donna had taken one look at the size of the computer and told me to drop it round. Coming for it had only been an excuse anyway. I put it in the boot then drove down to the high street and parked in a little side road next to a veg stall. I fought my way along the pavement to Boots and bought a bottle of Coco Chanel. What was good enough for the Delaneys was good enough for Donna. It cost over a ton and I had to use plastic. But it came gift-wrapped, like a pair of socks would on the Continent.

Roger met me in the drive. He had managed a few hours' sleep after his shift but still looked bleary; his eyes shot through. He was loading the car with a mountain of colourful presents.

He looked at me quizzically and said, "You thought about what we talked about?"

"Yeah, I had a quiet word in Delaney's ear. Between you and me, I think you'll be all right."

"That's not good enough, man. There's others involved."

"Well that's all you're getting."

He took a step towards me. It was almost a threat. For an instant his mask slipped and I saw the man Delaney had spoken of. He got it together quickly, raised his hands and smiled.

"Hey, man," he said. "I'm worried, that's all."

Donna opened the front door. She still had that secret glow. Her eyes were bright, hovering between reserve and anticipation. She gave me a tiny fleeting smile that dimpled her cheeks.

I glanced at Roger again and felt a sudden awful rush of

187

jealousy. I pictured him strapped across her and my throat went dry. I lit a JPS.

The twins rushed past her and tugged me down to kiss them. I undid the boot and they helped me carry the box to Roger's car.

Ten minutes later I watched them lock up and drive off. I was left with homemade cards from the children. Crayon drawings of a tree and a sock and red streamers. A matchstick man floated between the sketches. An arrow pointed at him from a single word written in Laura's hand. Dad. Inside was a ballpoint note from Donna. 'It won't be a happy Christmas. Ring you Boxing Day!'

I went home, had some lunch at Joe's café then crawled back into bed. Filtering through the window taped carols came from the local church loudspeakers. Bells rang a message of curious goodwill across the frantic city. People squatting under their cardboard shelters probably heard them. Skagheads in doorways, the homeless and the down-and-outs queuing at the Christmas missions heard them too. The sad clear notes of goodwill. And they were probably grateful that, in this festive season, on this special night, people thought about them and cared. Know what I mean?

Outside the club Herman said, "Evening Lenny. It's a lovely evening isn't it? Christmas Eve and all that."

I glanced up at the heavy sky and then back into his eyes. "You're taking the piss?"

"Yes," he said

"Well done."

Peter's was half full and buzzing with good spirit. There was a determination out there; eyes glittered, faces were already flushed and happy. I was early so I hovered by the bar to soak up some of the emotion. During the next ten minutes the others arrived. Alan and Keith came in together. We grouped at the bar for a pre-session drink.

"It's going to be a heavy night," Clarinet mused.

"It's been a heavy two weeks," Cell said.

We all looked at him. He rarely spoke.

"You on somethin'?" Clarinet asked him.

He looked blank.

We spoke about our plans for the morning; who was home, who was with in-laws, who had kids coming. When I told them I was spending the day in bed Clarinet wanted to know who with.

"Just me," I said. "Do you know I haven't sent a single card?"

"Tight bastard!" Cell said and surprised us again. Twice in one night. It was becoming a habit.

Alan said, "You mean you're spending Christmas Day on your own?"

I nodded meekly.

He glanced at Keith. "We've got a turkey, and a Christmas tree, and lots of cards. You can come and read ours and share our turkey."

Mike said, "You can come to me. I'll just give the old girl a bell to O.K. it."

Cell sniffed.

Clarinet said, "Bollocks!"

"Thanks all of you but I really am all right. Do you know I'm quite looking forward to taking it easy, watching the box and getting quietly pissed?"

A couple of girls had pushed to the bar beside us. All teased wool, dangling jewellery and long bare arms. The elder of the two turned to me and said through garish lipstick, "You sound just like that actor, what's his name?"

"Michael Caine?" I offered.

The others turned to listen.

"No, silly, the good-looking one, the younger one." She shook her hands in front of her then smiled brightly. "I've got it! Bob Hoskins, that's him!"

The band fell about laughing and left her with a deepening frown.

The alcohol had thawed some of the tension the day had twisted in my gut and suddenly I was laughing with them.

The girls retreated. They thought we were all mad. They were absolutely right, of course.

Mike glanced at the clock between the rows of down-turned bottles hovering on their one-sixth of a gill rotors and excused himself for his pre-session sniff. It was time to get underway. We hit the stage and went through the ritual: scalar warm-ups and tunings while Clarinet put his bass together. The room had filled

189

up. There wasn't an empty table.

Right in front, staring up at us with a grin that cut his black face in two, was a very familiar face. Clarinet saw him, raised his hands in delight and shouted, "Oh man, all right, all right, get your fat ass up here!"

Simon Glen, known as Simple, was in town for a couple of gigs over the holiday. He had a reputation as a solid bebopper, ballads and blues picked from Ellington. He lived in New York and Clarinet was an old friend. Now the fat guy helped the fat guy on to the stage. They slapped hands and hugged.

"Cool, man," Mike said as he crept on to his stool and silenced a couple of quivering cymbals.

Peter Selvey watched the two fat friends from his position at the mike, realized after a while that Simple was there for the night – he carried his trumpet with him – and spoke into the mike: "Ladies and Gentlemen, we have something a little bit tasty tonight, a bit of a surprise guest all the way from the Big Apple . . . " He pointed an unsteady finger. "Will you welcome Simple Glen?"

The crowd whistled and shook the room with their enthusiasm. When it died, Peter went on, "Now, pleeease welcome the band, Joe Clarinet Gabriel and Wolves Aren't White!"

Mike thumped out some noise, his hands guided by black mankies. Tonight he'd spent out, his hair was beginning to stand on end. The spot did a dizzy turn around the room and landed suddenly and forcefully on me.

"That one is!" Clarinet shouted from the darkness.

The applause started up again. We were into our first number before we could hear ourselves. The session went well; it was about reeds backed up by Mike in a positive mood. Whatever they were the amphetamines produced a control we hadn't heard in a long time. He surprised the lot of us and knew it. His smug look grew more apparent with every number. Even Clarinet nodded his approval and allowed him, at long last, to have a bash at his own composition. His red eyes buzzed. He nearly choked on the mike.

His voice was clotted cream, coming out in lumps, sending a hush across the room. He began in a whisper, like a cold wind, and it reached into every corner.

"There were a few skirmishes last night, but nothing much,
"Just a few friendly little fights, but nothing much,
"We gave the residents a fright, but nothing much . . . "
I saw Peter at the back of the room. His eyes were wide, his mouth open. He looked horrified. His trembling hand pinched at his bottom lip to check that what he was hearing wasn't in some horrible dream.

The rest of us came in, rocking, having a ball. Now, Peter knew that it was a conspiracy. I thought he was going to cry.

"We're the heavy metal followers of Pan,
"And we're looking for the evil in man,
"Collector of the soul, electrified warlock,
"Rock . . . "

Mike's eyes popped. He chewed on more of the mike. His hair began to fizz.

"We're the heavy metal warriors from hell,
"Come to electrify the filth can't you tell,
"Collector of the soul, electrified warlock,
"Rock, and rock,
"And Rock and rock..."

It wasn't jazz. But it was Chirstmas.

During the breaks Clarinet and Simple had a lot of years to catch up on and we left them alone. They worked something out for, when we resumed, Clarinet picked up his own trumpet and they chased each other through half-a-dozen numbers. Their improvisation produced whole clumps of repetitions and climaxes that suddenly snaked away to start again.

"Cool, man," Mike said a dozen times as they ran through the Duke's repertoire.

It was something special. You could tell by the hush in the club. People held their breath to pick up the sound of the night, the souls making pacts with the devil, the ghosts gliding through the graveyards, the painful sounds of lament from the grieving trumpets. This was more than music; it made you shiver, turned the hairs on your neck into nerve ends; it caressed your spine, took it out of your back and rubbed it up and down with a velvet glove; Anna Ford was blowin' news into your ear makin' you sit up straight, wanting the six o'clock to go on for ever; the old guys were in charge, sweatin', drippin', on fire.

When I left the club the night was glinting. It was cold. Herman, the doorman, was moving on a beggar, an old woman who had found the cold too much. Her clothes were in tatters, newspaper was stuffed in various holes. The blue neon turned her open sores into black holes. Her grey hair hung down like clumps of dusty cobweb.

"Fuck off!" he said. "Fuck off!" He raised his hand to point. His Senior Service burned orange and sparks jumped like glowing fleas.

She moved stiffly away, not protesting, not even looking back.

"That could have been my mother," I said to him.

"Your mother's dead," he grunted, refusing to see the point. He dragged on his cigarette and produced another cluster of sparks before cupping it behind him.

"Fuck you," I said and ran to catch her up. She cowered and threw up her hands to shield her face. I offered her a fiver. For a moment she looked at me then at the note. Her grimy gnarled hand reached out to take it.

"Bless you, mister," she said. Her eyes were wet, matted over.

"Good luck, girl."

She nodded and went on her way.

Herman stamped his feet.

"That's done it," he shouted. "She'll be hanging around here every night now! You're fuckin' mad, Lenny. Mad!"

"Happy Christmas, Herman," I said. "Happy fucking Christmas!"

NINETEEN

Christmas morning arrived sharp and clear. Early bells rang through the chill. In shop doorways people stirred; the occasional empty bottle nudged over by someone turning rolled and clinked toward the gutter. The streets were still silent, the street-lights still glowed, fusing with the creeping dawn to produce an eeriness that was quite unsettling. Take-away cartons littered the pavement. Outside the pubs puddles of vomit were stirred by the weak vitamins of the sun to burst with an occasional tiny bubble of gas. The occasional car swept by; night workers returning home, nurses going to work.

"What are you doing?" she said into my ear.

"I'm just going to bed. Eyes are held up with matchsticks."

"You can't do that. It's Christmas."

"I've just got in."

"A party?"

"The club," I said. "You could call it a party."

"Look, I've got this twenty-pound turkey, and chestnut stuffing and sausage meat, and a bottle that just better be good at the price I paid, and no one to share it with. Why don't you bring round your Bennie Greens and you can doze in front of a real coal fire while I get it ready?"

"Real coal? I thought all the pits had closed."

"Ha! Ha!"

"I snore."

"I won't mind."

"I'm on my way."

"I'll give you the address."

"That will help. If I'm stopped I'll blame you."

"How's that?"

"I'm already well over the limit."

"Can't you get a cab?"

"To Cambridge?"

"Take care."

I wrote the address down and hung up.

While I was shaving and examining the reflection of death warmed up in the mirror the phone rang again. I reached it just as the answerphone had taken over.

"Daddy? Daddy?" It was Jack.

"Hello, boy. Happy Christmas. Did he come?"

"Dad, Dad, you got us the computer. Whose games is whose? Is mine the Aliens, isn't it?"

"Hold on a minute, sweetheart. The games are for both of you as well. You'll have to share them."

There was a moment's silence while he took that in.

"What else did you get?"

"Skateboard, money, books, tapes, a stereo player from mum."

"Blimey!"

"Here's Laura."

"Daddy? I got a typewriter, one you plug in."

"Blimey!"

"And money and books and lots. Is the Aliens mine?"

Donna came on. "Happy Christmas, Lenny."

She sounded subdued, distant.

"Can anyone hear you?"

"Yeah, there's a house full. Thanks for the perfume. You shouldn't have . . . "

"Yes I should. A long time ago."

"I didn't sleep very well."

"You were probably excited."

"Is that what it was?"

The background noise grew more intense, laughter and festive voices.

"Ring me when you get back," I said.

"Yeah." She hesitated then added in a whisper, "I'm hating this."

I went back to the bathroom and shaved one side before the phone rang again.

"Lenny?" Julie's voice was breathless and smoky.

"Yeah," I said. "Happy Christmas. How are you?"

"I'm fine. Just fine." She sounded strange, stoned. Perhaps it was Buck's Fizz. "I just wanted to say Merry Christmas, and thank you."

"For what?"

"Everything, Lenny. Paddy's here."

"Is he all right?"

"He's fine. He's looking great. He got back last night."

"Can I have a quick word?"

I heard Julie call him. Moments later he came on. "All right, Kid?"

"Yeah. What about you?"

"I sorted it!"

"What do you mean?"

"You'll hear all about it sooner or later."

"Does Scott know you've surfaced?"

"Yeah, him and half his task force are camped outside. I'm enjoying this, fuckin' up their Christmas."

I chuckled. "Are you home permanently?"

"I suppose I am. There is something I want you to do for me though. You or that psycho tart."

"Go on?"

I heard a door shut, then, "You still there?"

"Yeah."

"Just making certain I'm out of earshot. I want you to break the news to Julie. It'll be better comin' from you."

I guessed what he meant but wanted it confirming.

"About me," he said soberly. "It's time that she was told."

"I'll speak to Ellen."

"Make it fast, eh? Tomorrow."

"Boxing Day?"

"Is that what it is?" He paused then said, "There's something else. I've got you a Christmas present."

"You shouldn't have bothered."

"That's funny. This one you'll like. You'll have to decide what to do with it. Get my drift?"

"Yeah. But I'm not certain I want it."

"Well you're getting it anyway, Kid. So you got no choice in the matter. I told you it would be your decision. Nick will deliver it."

I broke another moment's silence with, "How are you feeling?"

"Like I'm dying," he said. He paused and added, "Make it tomorrow. Understand?"

195

"Yeah, I think so." I hung up. There was shaving cream on the phone. I stared at it for some seconds before replacing it then I went slowly back to the bathroom.

While I was on my way to see Ellen, the local radio station came on with a news bulletin. In the early hours of the morning a man had been rushed to hospital with multiple stab wounds. His throat had been cut. His condition remained critical. He was the owner of a landscaping business based in Epping. He was named as Robert Delaney. As yet police were unable to establish a motive for the attack but have not ruled out London gangland connections.

I knew the man as Uncle Bob. And now I knew what Paddy had been up to.

A mist had cut visibility to a hundred yards by the time I hit Cambridge. Ellen lived in a detached two-storey with a garage built in to the ground floor. Her front door stood next to the steel up and over. A big bay window was frosted with magic snow. The net curtains glowed from blinking fairy lights on a Christmas tree that stood just inside the window.

I pulled on to the concrete in front of the garage door and climbed out carrying two bottles of Chianti and my collection of Bennie Greens. The front door opened and Ellen smiled a welcome. An apron covered the bottom half of a pale peach low-cut dress. Her face was made up, gold glinted subtly around her neck and on her ears.

"You found me all right?"

She closed the door behind me and took the bottles. "Let me get them up to room temperature," she said.

Her home came as a surprise. I'd expected a shrink to live in a Victorian cottage full of old furniture.The hall was bright and airy, tastefully decorated. The living room was on the left. On the right stood an elegant Queen Anne-style writing desk. A heavy old-fashioned black telephone stood next to an open diary. I followed her down the hall past a flight of stairs. Opposite the kitchen was a door to the garage and another to a small downstairs loo.

She had been busy. The work surfaces were covered in dishes, various vegetables had been cut precisely; the aroma of cooking turkey evoked childhood memories: my mother and father were laughing ghosts as they hunted out old woollen socks and placed sherry and mince pies on the table, just so. Ellen placed the bottles on the side so that they caught the heat from the hob, then led me back into the living-room.

A coalfire breathed an ancient life into the modern room. Before it a white sheepskin lay on pale grey carpet. Dark oak Elizabethan dining furniture stood at one end by a hatchway into the kitchen. The wall units were almost floor to ceiling, leaded glass, traditional, moulded handles. The table was already set with two places. Silver glinted. Candles were ready to light. Two M&S crackers lay next to the placements. A single step led down into the living-room area where the fire threw its glow on to a flowery cushion printed suite. Matching curtains and frilled pelmet framed the tree with its gold baubles and blinking lights.

Ellen had obviously not heard about Julie's uncle, so I decided to keep it to myself. There seemed little point in complicating the day with a heavy discussion.

She poured Glenfiddich and passed me a glass. "Happy Christmas, Lenny," she said happily and lifted her drink.

"Happy Christmas, Ellen."

"Call this a nightcap," she smiled. "Now I'm going to spend the next hour or so in the kitchen. You can spread out here. I'll wake you when lunch is ready."

"Isn't there anything I can do to help?"

"Yes. Lie down on the sofa and close your eyes. Better still, there's a spare room upstairs with a single bed. You might have to move some books but it will be more comfortable."

"This will do," I said. "The drive has woken me up."

I might have dozed once or twice but you couldn't call it sleep. I nosed into her Christmas cards which covered every available surface. There were hundreds of them, mostly from students past and present. She had stacked her presents on a small coffee table in the corner. Chocolates and perfume, bath salts, a fragile glass elephant, that kind of thing. A bag of torn wrapping-paper stood beside it. Under the tree there were half-a-dozen unopened presents.

Behind some of the leaded glass her bookshelves contained works ranging from *The Noel Coward Diaries* and Ackroyd's *Dickens* to the unexpurgated text of *Sons and Lovers*, some Oscar Wilde and a whole section of poems by Eliot, Milton and Hughes. Then came her textbooks, rows of them with titles like *Psychology*, *A Child's Mind*, Coulshed's *Social Work Practice* and Piaget's *Developmental Psychology*. Some of the titles were vaguely familiar. They had been lying around in Bruce Grove during Donna's studies.

Over lunch Ellen told me more about the Wood. She was on secure ground, completely at ease. The meeting with her students had only hinted at her self-assurance. Here was a confidence that was almost unnerving. She was at her best when directing proceedings, in charge, so to speak. Enthusiasm about her work lit up her eyes. It was almost toxic. It made her carefree and slightly daring.

"A lot of our residents are transferred to us from secure units," she said. "Our job is to get inside their heads by exploring what happened in the past. You talk to them but listen mostly. You wait for that one moment of acknowledgement, their acceptance of what has happened, whether it be guilt, or the memory of some incident. Without acceptance you can't move forward. So you listen and you keep listening. Sooner or later they will tell you what hurt them. They will tell you about their feelings. And they learn, slowly, how to express their distress and anger and hatred, in ways that are acceptable, within themselves rather than in outbursts of uncontrollable action. It takes a long time. Many years."

"Who pays for all this?"

"The Wood is mostly funded privately by the likes of Paddy Delaney." She chuckled. "But we do have a small grant. What that means, unfortunately, is that, unless you come from a rich family, you'd be very lucky to get in there."

"But you still lecture, you still take your social work students?"

"For me that will always come first. They will carry the fight into the next generation."

"The political fight?"

She said sharply, "The fight for justice and equality in mental health care, in care for the aged, in care generally. If I've got to take that to Westminster then so be it. If they don't like the truth, then tough. The Tories have wiped out the idea of a caring country so now it's left to the individual."

"You think the socialists will make a better job?"

"Not necessarily. They screw up far too often. But at least their heart's in the right place. At least they have a heart." She sighed and straightened her paper hat. It had slipped forward on to her eyebrows.

"I'll give you one example of Tory thinking," she said. "We already know the names of the people who will be convicted of about ninety percent of the criminal offences that will take place in ten years' time. We know them. We can actually name them. We can give you their addresses. Some of them come from the less well-off families, but by no means all. Some of them come from broken families. Some of them have been abused and battered. Even now some of them are truants. No one is chasing them. They are getting lost, falling through the system. They are grouping together, as youngsters do, and forming the first semblance of gangs. Some of them are being introduced to booze and drugs for the first time, some of them are starting to steal from shops, before long it will be houses. Some of their parents have less than ideal moral values. Ask them what their kids are up to and they won't be able to tell you. Tell them about their truancy and they will blame the schools. Talk to the teachers and they will blame the parents. Talk to socialist MPs and they will blame poverty and the government's record, talk to the government and they will first deny that there is a problem, and then, when they cannot get away with that any longer, blame unmarried mothers, or the police, or anyone or anything other than themselves. And while all the rhetoric goes on, while everyone is blaming everyone else, more and more kids are falling through the gaping holes in the net. So, what's the answer? The government has come up with it. They're about to spend a billion pounds on six new prisons so that in ten years time when these kids become criminals and are caught, we can lock 'em up. Wonderful. I mean, that is foresight. That's why we have a government. So they can plan for the future!"

Her passion had turned to anger. That spark of enthusiasm so evident in her eyes had caught fire and now it blazed. She gulped at her wine, trying to settle herself. Eventually she looked up and said shakily, "Sorry!"

I grinned and said, "You're a very angry person, do you know that?"

Her intensity broke and she laughed at herself. "My God, how can you turn everything into a joke? I wish I could bottle some of your character, Lenny, and spray it around some of the meetings I have to attend."

Throughout the afternoon and evening we talked and listened to records and polished off a number of bottles. At about eight she stirred herself and put out some salad, cheese and cold meats and a small, beautifully iced cake. It was about nine when she turned to me on the sofa and said suddenly, "Do you think sex can be fulfilling without an emotional attachment?"

"Between strangers, you mean?"

"Not necessarily. But without a commitment, without other feelings coming into it?"

"Yeah, married people do it all the time."

She frowned.

"Sex without feeling," I explained.

"But can it be meaningless, just an act that you can walk away from? Can that be fulfilling?"

"If it satisfies a desire I guess it can."

"OK then," she said. "I'll put the dishes in the washer. Then you have a choice. We can watch some television – there must be something on – play your Bennie Greens through again, sit in front of the fire talking some more, or you can screw me silly. Your choice."

For a moment I was speechless. I couldn't believe it. Save for the disaster in Sheringham there had been nothing to speak – or dream – of for the best part of a year. Now twice in two days.

I found my voice and said, "In that case there is no choice."

She remained thoughtful for a moment, then nodded, then stood up before me and fiddled with a zip. I sat back in the deep sofa and watched and wondered how far her nerve would take her. I was convinced that sex outside of her marriage and certainly this side of her separation was a totally new experience for her.

With her dress drawn open at the back she walked to the door and flipped off the main light, leaving us in the glow from the coloured fairy lights and the licking fire. Her perfume was all about me even though she had come no nearer than she had been before. She moved back to her previous position and pulled the dress from her arms. It fell in a heap on the carpet. She wore stockings and suspenders. I don't know why that surprised me but it did. Nylon whispered. She undid her belt with deft quick fingers and threw it aside. She stood in front of me. At a time when gravity and age were beginning to tug she remained as confident in her body as she was in everything else. She reached behind, one-handed, and unfastened her bra. Her gaze into my eyes was quite penetrating as she slipped out of it and let it fall. Her breasts were smallish and slightly flat. A tiny birthmark, a pin-point really, broke the circle of her left nipple. My look of admiration seemed to satisfy her for she slipped quickly out of her pants and stood upright again, legs slightly parted so that I could see the orange glow of cinders between them. She reached forward, took my hands and pulled me toward her off the sofa. She undressed me, slowly and clinically, then lay back on the deep sheep-skin. We kissed deeply for a while while we explored, then I went down on her with my tongue, splaying her legs and licking every part that I could reach. She moaned and writhed unashamedly. I looked up between her legs and saw that her eyes were shut tightly. I moved up bringing her legs up with me until I was pressing against her. Her eyes blinked open as she felt the pressure.

Her voice was deep and quivered. "There's a packet of rubbers on the shelf," she said. "I'm suppose to be sensible and responsible!"

I lay there for a moment while she relaxed. I still throbbed against her leg. The shelf seemed a long way off. I used her knees as levers and rose up above her. She left her legs open for me.

"Hurry," she said.

Three strides took me to the shelf. The pack of three was half-hidden by a Christmas card. I ripped open the tin foil and held the rubber up.

"They call them passion killers," I said.

I followed her gaze down from my face.

"It hasn't made any difference yet," she said. "Bring it over here. And the rubber."

I laughed, moved back across the pile and took up my original position. Her cool hands spread the rubber then she reached up and pulled me towards her. Her tongue buried itself in my mouth. Her legs rose again. Her slender hand fiddled between us to guide me. She was slippery but tight and I stretched her. She tensed up as if waiting for pain. She relaxed then tensed then relaxed again. She held me so that I moved at her pace. But there was nothing feverish, no frenzied pull of passion. She lay beneath me almost still, meeting me on every stroke but pulling back just before the full extent. She was distant, engaged in her own feelings, lost in her own sensations or reverie. I was just a tool. There was nothing personal in this at all. Even when her breaths quickened she wasn't conscious that I was there. Not entirely. Oh, she felt me, that was obvious enough, but Clarinet had got it in one, at least as far as Ellen was concerned. I was just a vibrator, a warm one. Forget the cheque-book on the end.

I imagine the isolation came from her marriage. Long ago she had learned to do her own thing. Presumably her husband had done the same. They were faithful, I bet, yet even in coition they remained apart, utterly selfish. They wouldn't even ask each other 'How was it for you?'. They wouldn't have been that interested. Satisfied with their own release they would turn over, perhaps touch behinds, and drift into the safety of sleep.

For some reason I wanted to hurt her, perhaps for some kind of involuntary reaction. I wanted her to lose control, realize that I was there. That her sensations had something to do with me. The feeling was odd. Perhaps it had to do with her being an older woman, but more likely it was to dent her self-assurance, bring her down to mortal levels.

I let go of her legs and took hold of her hands, pinning them to the floor either side of her head. A tiny frown appeared and her eyes flicked open. For a second she was puzzled but when she saw my determination her frown deepened. She realized that she could neither restrain nor control things and the thought produced a moment's panic. She was going to say something; I could see it coming.

There was a ludicrous fear in her eyes. I pushed my lips down on to hers and heard the muffled sound as it disappeared into my mouth. It might have been 'no' or 'stop' or even 'yes'. But I guessed it was no. She struggled beneath me. At one stage she bit my lip but I continued to kiss her. The rising pace of her movements, the sudden thumping of her heart and her hands pulling on my behind set me off. I peaked an instant after her and drew back from her mouth to take a great gulp of air. She let out her breath in a long, tremulous moan. Her features had relaxed. She smiled, a quick, tentative smile, while her mouth remained open as she sucked in her breath.

As we lay there I felt an absurd sense of guilt. Absurd because Donna and I had no understanding, there was no commitment, nothing more than a gleam of hope. And yet it was there, so real that for a moment I burned with that curious feeling of betrayal.

Ellen caught my look and squeezed my side. "Don't feel guilty," she said. Her insight caught me out. "This is purely recreational, meaningless. Sex, when you come down to it, is only a sensation that lasts for a short while. It's importance has been blown out of all proportion."

She sat up and ran her fingers across my chest and down. "Let's go upstairs," she said. "Bring the bottle. You had better stay the night. You can use my toothbrush."

I followed her up the stairs. There wasn't a hint of self-consciousness about her as she went up before me. She was quite happy to be scrutinized from any angle. Not that there was anything wrong with what I could see. Her behind was trim, still traced with marks from the sheepskin, her legs still smooth with only the faintest hint of cellulite on her thighs.

She was a wise old bird. Following her up the stairs and the newness of the surroundings inspired me again. By the time I reached her bed, surprised to find navy-blue sheets and pillow cases, I was sparking on six cylinders.

It was about three when she woke me with a gentle shake. The room was warm. Beneath the quilt it was warmer. Her body, still wrapped around mine, felt wonderful. But her shake became more urgent.

"What? What is it?"

It was dark. Nothing got through the heavy curtains.

"Can you smell it?" Her voice was anxious. She lay close; I felt her hot breath on my neck. I turned away from her and took a deep breath. It hit me like a hammer blow to the chest. I suppose the fumes had seeped into the bedroom gradually but now they were unmistakable. I was amazed that I could have slept through them.

Even as I moved from the bed I said, "It's petrol. Jesus, Ellen, move quickly!"

On the way to the window I stubbed my toe. I heard her fiddling with the bedside light. "Don't!" I warned. "Don't turn anything on!"

I pulled the curtains and a dim light flowed into the room. At the door she struggled into a dressing-gown. I opened the window then turned to follow her. I was halfway across the room, heading her way, when she pulled open the door.

The blast came from down stairs. It wasn't an explosion as such; it came more as a roar that burst up the stairs like a shrieking gale. With that violent report the air rushed into the room, hitting Ellen like a hurricane. She was carried backwards as though she had been shot. In that same instant the landing lit up in a blinding flash. It turned into a maelstrom of flame and smoke. Ellen screamed. The flames leapt through thick black smoke toward her, curling fiercely around the door frame, blackening the ceiling as they erupted into the bedroom.

I launched myself at the open door. The heat was unbearable, forcing me back. Each time a giant flame leapt out of the smoke it seemed as though my skin seared. I reached the door on hands and knees and pushed it closed. Flames still licked between door and frame; choking smoke still poured in.

I picked Ellen up and propelled her toward the window. Even as we reached it the carpet near the door was beginning to melt and glow. Wood splintered and cracked. Flames burst from the floor.

Coughing, barely able to see a yard in front of me, I threw open the other window so that we had one each. Cold air swept in. Smoke swirled. The flames flared and flapped in the wind.

We faced the back garden, dark shapes of bushes and trees. Below us flames leapt from the back door and from the broken kitchen window. Ungodly shadows moved across the garden. Smoke and sparks swept upwards towards us. It was about a twelve or thirteen feet drop on to concrete, no ledges. Too far. At the very least it would mean broken legs.

The flames flared up again and lit up the garden. For an instant I saw a dark figure moving between two high bushes perhaps twenty or thirty feet into the garden.

"Help us!" I shouted, "Get a ladder!"

I don't know what it was about the figure, perhaps the crouch, but I dived across to Ellen and pulled her down just as a flame began to climb. It came through the open window in a huge flash, a solid jet of flame, and burst against the wall opposite, completely engulfing the bed.

Ellen shouted out loud as the heat hit us in solid waves.

"Jesus Christ! It's a flame-thrower!" I said.

I heard some shouting going on outside, angry voices. We got to our feet again and peered out. A group of neighbours had gathered, some of them were handling a ladder. In the distance the sirens from police or fire-engines were faint against the roar from the flames.

The ladder thumped against the windowsill. I helped Ellen up. She swung her feet around. I held on to her until she was firmly on the ladder then I made my own exit. Before doing so I grabbed a coat from her wardrobe and buttoned it around my middle. Modesty and all that. I was halfway to the ground when the flames suddenly shot out of our window. We had made it with about thirty seconds to spare.

"Did you see her?"

Wrapped in a blanket, her hair unkempt and singed on one side, Ellen was white and shaky. The stark ambulance light didn't help. Her eyes were dark and sunken, fearful.

"See who?"

"Who else?" she sighed.

"I saw a dark figure, that's all. For Christ sake Ellen, where would Julie get hold of a flame-thrower? That was a flame-thrower! Can you really see her pouring five gallons of petrol through your letter box and then hanging around with a flame-thrower?"

"But who else?"

"Paddy thought it was his Uncle Bob. That's why Paddy did a runner, to sort Uncle Bob out."

"What do you think?"

205

"I thought it was him too. But Uncle Bob's in hospital having his throat stitched back into place. That wasn't him tonight?"

"Who then?"

"There's only one other person it could be, Ellen. Dr Eliot wasn't lying about Paddy's involvement; he was just mistaken."

She frowned.

I went on, "It was a case of mistaken identity. Uncle Bob led him to believe it was Paddy, but really it was another child that looked like Paddy."

She fell in a second later and it left her mouth open, speechless.

I winked at her. "Paddy will confirm it. That's where I'm going as soon as we can get into your front room."

She looked puzzled.

"Car keys," I said. "They were in my jacket pocket."

"But why? Why do this to us?"

"First it was the boyfriend, then Eliot, now us. It's tied in with your discovery Ellen. The abuse. I don't know why but I guess it's about a cover-up. Even Paddy got it wrong."

She shivered. Her eyes strayed to the soot-coated building. "All my things," she said.

"You better come back to my place."

She shook her head. "No. Himanshu lives down the road. I'll move in there for a while." She laughed coldly. "Believe it or not I've still got some of my stuff in his wardrobe."

"Just as well," I muttered and stole a glance back at the house. The fire was out but the water was still being poured into the blackened rooms, upstairs and down. It was all but gutted. Above us a black cloud had spread out across the clear sky.

We had to make statements to the police. The firemen had convinced them that it was arson. Making statements was getting to be a habit. This time we told them the whole truth about Julie's abuse and our suspicions regarding Uncle Bob. When they heard Delaney's name there was some high-powered talking and speedy phone calls. I guessed that it wouldn't be long before Superintendent Scott made his appearance.

"'Ello, 'ello, 'ello!" he said and grinned into the police interview room. They hadn't forced us back; in fact, they drove us to Ellen's husband first so that she could get some clothes. He even loaned me a suit, three sizes too big. It was Ellen who insisted on going to the police station to sort things out. There seemed no point in postponing it any longer.

So, we reached Delaney's name and watched their expressions darken. Then came a twenty-minute interruption while they fed us coffee from a machine while they played for time, and then Scott's arrival.

He had trouble with my writing so he read through Ellen's statement then raised his eyebrows in surprise.

"Haven't we been busy," he said. It wasn't a question.

TWENTY

Superintendent Scott followed me home in his Rover. By the time we reached Bruce Grove a Boxing Day dawn, slippery and grey, just like the previous morning, was easing over Waltham Forest. I had explained that I was well over the limit but he had shrugged his shoulders and said, "Drive slowly, then."

I changed my clothes while he made some coffee. We sat at the breakfast bar to drink it.

"Where do you get this stuff?" he said. "Walker's right, it is a bit pissy."

I grunted, accepted a Benson's and filled the kitchen with smoke.

"Tell me about Paddy," I said. "Have you got everything you need?"

"Not quite. I mean, we've got the local set-up. Whether it comes to court is beside the point. We know enough to close it down and come down like a ton of bricks on some pretty heavyweight names. Believe me when I tell you there'll be a few early retirements from the council and a few empty seats on the back benches." He glanced across and narrowed his eyes before adding, "There'll be a fair few members of the bar hanging up their wigs as well!"

"That isn't before time," I muttered. "Old men are the scourge of this country. If ever there was an argument for euthanasia those spoon-fed sons of bitches are it. Cricket, football, licensing hours, The Lords, you name it. They ruin just about every aspect of life that might spell fun."

He grinned. "My, my."

I asked, "So what are you missing?"

"I think you know that."

I glanced up, more than a little surprised. "Oh?"

"Paddy told me he's given you some names. The sort that can get you into trouble. Serious shit."

"He told you that?"

Scott nodded.

"He's hallucinating," I said.

"Maybe. We'll see. But meanwhile we're going to be just like that." He pressed his thumb and forefinger together. "This isn't a game, Lenny. There's an awful lot at stake. You could end up catching a serious cold. Withholding evidence, that sort of thing."

"That's bollocks and you know it. I've got nothing that you want."

He shrugged and said, "So where are we going?"

"First stop," I said, "is Mill Hill East."

"Paddy Delaney?"

"Yeah. We're looking for a flame-thrower."

Scott smiled. "You're wasting your time. Julie Delaney hasn't been out."

"Fine, but I still want to know why Paddy sliced up his Uncle Bob. He'll tell me if you're not around."

"You think so?"

"We're friends. Didn't he tell you?" I smiled and added, "He even gives me Christmas presents!"

Scott nodded slowly and smiled back.

The security around Delaney's gaff was as tight as it was around Buckingham Palace since the break-in; probably tighter than before.

I counted two police-cars and four kozzers in the front garden. That was beside Nick and Mario who guarded the front door. God knows what there was around the back.

"The uniforms have been drafted in from Devon and Cornwall," Scott told me before we left the car.

"Like you?"

"Like me."

"It's pretty big then? I mean, you're not trusting the local nicks or the Yard?"

"It's pretty big," he agreed. "The last time a task force was set up like this was when Nipper Read went after the Krays. Before my time. C-eight, the Flying Squad, and C-twelve, the Met's Regional Crime Squad, even C-eleven, surveillance, are all running around like headless chickens. The DPP tried for extradition three times but each time he fought it off. The bastard even

209

married a local girl and tried to put one up her, just like Biggsy, so he could stay over there. Paddy couldn't rise to the occasion, though. He's never slept with a woman in his life. But you can imagine the surprise when he said he was coming back?"

"Not much."

"A lot of people who used to be on a bung have worked their way up through the ranks. A lot of them are still on the payroll."

"You must know Paddy pretty well by now?"

Scott grunted. "Know him? I've slept with his file for the last two months, ever since we knew he was coming back. I've dreamt about the bastard. God know's what my wife is going to make of it when I get back to Newquay; if I start shouting out his name in the middle of the night, I mean."

I grinned.

"He started young, in a pretty small way – gangs, drugs, controlling a few toms through local massage parlours, that sort of thing. Then suddenly he took off, became a noise. Violence followed him around. People looked up to violence. Before we knew it he was running a big slice of the West End. Then he made a mistake of joining forces for the bullion robbery. He got out in the nick of time. One of our lot tipped him off just hours before we were ready to move. He surfaced briefly in Mexico and then Rio de Janeiro. He was always messing with dope, on the fringes of importing and distribution. Now he was up to his eyes in it. He was snorting coke long before he left here, but in Mexico he got a taste for mescaline, cactus buttons, in his coffee. In South America it was anything and any combination until he eventually settled on crack. Paddy's share from the robbery financed a drug network. He imported to this country through Heathrow and Gatwick. A lot of people this end were on a substantial bung and that includes a lot of coppers. As soon as Delaney offered to come back people started to panic. That's why we were called in from the sticks. Being naïve country boys we remain untouched by the evils of city life."

"Tell me about it."

"That was the thinking."

"So Paddy gets *carte blanche*? He gets away with everything in return for the names? He even gets away with carving his uncle into strips?"

"If he did it, then he'll get away with it. Yes. What's the point in starting a prosecution? We'll go to his funeral instead."

"This isn't a safe place to be. Half of London's gangsters and half the Met are probably looking for a way in."

Scott sniggered. "There's plenty of firepower in the garden, believe me. They'd need a chieftain to get in."

While Superintendent Scott went to check his men I went into the house. The Christmas tree lights were turned off. The massive hall seemed strangely gloomy. Nick gave me a nod of acknowledgement, an unusually serious look, and Mario gave me the usual suspicious once over before letting me into the living room. Delaney lay on the chaise longue in his dressing-gown. His legs and feet were bare and white. He raised a weak hand to acknowledge me.

"Hello, Kid," he said. His voice was hoarse. His smile was slack. "You've come for your Christmas present." He lowered his voice and said slyly, "With all the filth around here I got Nick to put it in the post. Play your cards right and that little book could be worth a fortune."

"You told Scott about it."

"'Course I did. You don't think I'm going to make it that easy for you, do you? I want you to have to think about this, Kid, not just pretend it don't exist."

Beside him, on a round table, were half-a-dozen medicine bottles; some of the pills were already loose, ready for the next stab of pain. Held loosely by his side was a plastic inhaler. A tube ran from it to a small bottle of gas.

"Where's Julie?"

He frowned and glanced at his watch. "She's still in bed. Fuck me, it's only eight."

"How much does she know?"

"Well, Lenny, she's not stupid. But she doesn't know it's a matter of hours. Shall I have her called? You could take her out?"

I shook my head and dragged a chair next to the sofa. Even that wasn't close enough and I leaned forward before whispering, "Tell me about Uncle Bob?"

He gave me a curious look. His eyes glazed, for a moment unfocused. He shook his head and said, "I sorted it. I told you."

"You nearly killed the bastard, I know that much. What did

you get out of him?"

"As soon as I heard your story, it was fuckin' obvious. He must have been playing with her for fuckin' years. My old man must have found out and made some threats. That night Bob went round there and torched the place. No doubt intended to get Julie as well. But she ran off. When he realized that she was no threat, that she'd lost her memory, that she had owned up to starting the fire, he let things ride. All these years he's been sitting pretty. Until . . . "

"Go on?"

"Until the treatment began to work. He was terrified of her regaining her memory. First he tried to pin Linet on to her, then when you told him about Eliot he sorted him out. Well, I fuckin' sorted Uncle Bob out!"

Delaney started to cough. He drew the inhaler up to his mouth and gulped in whatever it was. He relaxed instantly.

"You didn't sort it at all," I said. "You got the wrong man."

He frowned. "Come again?"

"Last night Ellen Zahavi's place went up in flames. I was with her. We were lucky. Someone, and it wasn't Uncle Bob, not unless he was holding a flame-thrower in one hand and his throat together in the other, used a fucking flame-thrower! Her house is gutted. More importantly my Bennie Greens have been incinerated. Now *that* really has pissed me off. I want to know what's going on. Anyway, what about Eliot mentioning that he saw both of you? Did you ask him about that?"

Delaney's slack mouth fell open. Something had hit him like a ton of bricks. His frown turned to consternation.

He said, "Oh fuck it!"

"Yeah," I said. "Easy, isn't it? You almost worked it out all by yourself!"

He swung his feet off the sofa and made to get up but instead cried out in agony and wrapped his arms around his gut. "Oh, Jesus!" he gasped. He reached for some pills. His hand shook so much all he did was nudge them. "The white ones," he said.

I put two into his palm. He swallowed them and sat there for a few moments rocking, waiting for the pain to ease. After a while he settled back. His face had gone very grey; his eyes slipped even more. A single tear rolled across his cheek. He flicked it away, angry with himself for showing emotion.

He tried to smile and whispered, "I ain't going anywhere, am I?"

I shook my head and said quietly, "Only to hell, Paddy."

"There's a nurse comes on in a minute. She'll sort me out." He threw me a wry smile. "You're going to have to do it on your own, Kid."

"Tell me?"

"Go and see Aunty Joyce. Good old Aunty Joyce." His face screwed up again and he bit his bottom lip. He coughed up some evil black phlegm and wiped it away before adding, "She'll tell you what the fuck's going on."

"Yeah," I said.

I stood up and hesitated.

He smiled awkwardly. "Don't worry. I'll still be here when you get back. I ain't going anywhere 'till you've spoken to Julie."

I nodded. "I'll be back for her."

"Be careful," he said shakily. "They've got flame-throwers over there. They used 'em on the council to burn back the weeds. Before they started using weedkillers!"

"Tell me about it," I grunted.

He went into another coughing fit. I left him alone in the room. As I passed through the hall the nurse was being frisked at the door.

"You better get a move on," I said. "He isn't very well."

In the car I told Superintendent Barry Scott all that I knew. He listened thoughtfully without interrupting. By the time I had finished his square features were taut. He flashed me a look. His blue eyes had turned to ice.

Joyce Delaney watched us pull in from her steamed up kitchen windows. When she opened the door she was still wiping her hands on a tea-towel.

"I've been expecting you," she said. The bubbly humour that I had seen at our first meeting had been replaced by a resigned tearful despair. She closed the door behind us. The kitchen was full of steam. The lid of a saucepan rattled on the stove. She hung the towel on a rail and stood before us wringing her pudgy hands.

"How is your husband?" Scott asked gently. He surprised me.

Finding compassion in a policeman always did. The job usually ground it away.

"Still critical," she said bleakly. "But they think he has a good chance now." She shook her head and looked at each of us in turn. "Why? Tell me why? What sort of Christmas has this been?" Tears rolled across her fleshy cheeks and dribbled from her chin.

Scott shook his head.

She sniffed and said, "Come with me."

We followed her down a hall cluttered with boxes, tins of food, cereal, numerous tools and dozens of shoes, some of them holed and caked in dried mud. An old ginger cat moved sluggishly from her path and disappeared beneath a staircase. As we went deeper into the house it became musty, a farmhouse smell, a combination of dust and manure. I felt a mild pull of claustrophobia, a fluttering of nerves. The gloom seemed to deepen as we climbed the stairs behind her. Her movements were arthritic and slow. Eventually we reached the top. The landing ceiling was yellow and patched; damp had crept into the attic. The wallpaper was faded and torn in places.

She opened a door on to a huge bedroom. It was more than that: it was a games room that contained a single bed and bedroom furniture on a square of carpet. The rest of the room was bare floorboards worn down in places. It contained a full size snooker table, a table-tennis table, an eight feet long black mat running to a dart board, a pin-ball machine, a host of games that had been forgotten in the rush of technology: skittles, shovel-board, football table, a race track set up on chipboard. The room was a child's dream.

But maybe not. Not in the age of the computer and the zapping of aliens.

Joyce Delaney stood aside. "I think you'll find everything you want in there," she said. "I'll be downstairs." She shuffled back to the stairs.

"What have we got here?" Scott asked as we moved into the room.

"I'm guessing it's her son's room. Cousin Anthony. He's about Delaney's age. That would make him fifteen when Julie was eight."

Scott shot me a cursory glance and nodded. He moved across

214

to the bed where a shoe-box had been emptied. I wandered to the far end. An old box record player had caught my eye. On it stood a photograph of Anthony Delaney. His sleeves were rolled up. He rested his chin on one hand. On his forearm was a scar. A long red scar, like a burn. I remembered Julie in the hotel. The way in which she had reacted to the sight of the blisters on my arm. Next to the player were a stack of 33s, another of 45s.

"That would make him thirty odd now," Scott said. "This doesn't look like the bedroom of a thirty-year-old."

"Thirty-three," I said. "I first saw him at Paddy's place, the party. It seems a long time ago."

"What have you got there?"

"Old records," I muttered as I flicked through them. "People never throw away old records."

"From what I can see he's never thrown anything away."

I found the one I was searching for and put it on the turntable. Moments later Judy Collins crackled from the worn head.

"Carole King?" Scott offered.

"Judy Collins," I told him.

He nodded. "She's terrific."

We stood listening to the start of 'Buddy, can you spare a dime?'

The record was about two-thirds in when the needle slipped and skidded back to the beginning. It would keep playing over and over, never finishing until the plug was pulled. I left it on.

Scott stood by the bed leafing through some papers. "Take a look at these," he said coldly.

They were photographs, polaroids, black and white. He passed them to me one at a time.

"Holy fuck!" he said.

The room hadn't altered much since they had been taken eighteen or more years earlier. The tables, the games, even the bed, were in the same places.

The record slipped again and began again.

They were photographs of Julie and her cousin Anthony. It was nightmare time. He was in his teens. Julie was eight, or seven, or even six. She was naked. In some of them his trousers were around his knees. Some of them showed close-up fuzzy pictures of penetration, vaginal and anal. In most of them she was in obvious distress and pain. In one his penis had discharged on to her flat chest, in another his fingers were pulling her apart. In others a variety of items were used, penis shaped candles and soaps, even a long stemmed bottle of fizzy drink that had obviously been shaken for the froth and liquid glistened at the top of her legs.

I turned away from the glossy prints, wishing that I'd never seen them, trying to swallow against a blocked throat. There was suddenly a lack of air in the room and my thoughts were cloudy, dizzy. I shook away a stray tear. The room seemed to darken as though the light was being sucked away.

We stood in the place where it had happened. While the men worked on the machinery in the yard outside, and the other kids, Paddy included, splashed happily in the pool, while the record played, the stylus skidding across the track, the music blaring to cover her cries, she was up here being wounded and scarred.

Superintendent Scott saw my anguish. "You all right?"

"No. No I'm not."

"Come on," he said. "Let's get out of here."

He said nothing more but his expression was stony and angry as he collected the photographs together and put them into the shoe box. He carried it down to the kitchen.

Joyce Delaney stood at her sink looking out at the grey yard.

"I knew there had to be something. I didn't want to believe it. I never really accepted Bob's story that the kids had been abused by his brother. Jim was never like that." She turned and stared at us. "It's what I wanted to believe!"

"So you knew from the beginning, from the moment Bob took the kids to see Dr Eliot?" the policeman asked.

She shook her head. "No, I didn't know then, not until much later. They fobbed me off with conjunctivitis."

"But surely," said Scott. "Eliot must have seen the difference between Paddy and Anthony?"

She shrugged weakly and said, "In those days they looked quite similar. In any case, Bob had spoken to the doctor. He wasn't going to ask any questions." She shook her head in dismay. "Bob sorted it out, and I didn't question him. I didn't want to hear the answers!"

That Dr Eliot could have mistaken the two boys, was not really surprising. Even in the photographs that Julie had shown me it was quite difficult to distinguish one from the other. In any case, there had been no reason for Dr Eliot to suspect that he had been misled.

Aunty Joyce sniffed back a tear and went on, "When Paddy came round . . . " She shook her head. "He blamed Bob. Of course he did. I don't blame him for that."

Scott said, "So your husband has kept Anthony's secret from you all these years?"

She nodded.

"You had no idea that Anthony started the fire that killed Paddy's parents, Bob's brother?"

"I couldn't live with that," she wept. I believed her.

"Where is Anthony now, Mrs Delaney?"

"He's in the sheds," she said. "He won't face me. Bob told me everything at the hospital. He thought he was going to die. Anthony tried to cover up . . . " She paused and took a deep breath. ". . Cover up what he'd done to Julie. She was threatening to tell Jim and Beth, her parents. When he got back Bob realized what had happened and has been covering for him ever since. I didn't know anything about it. I didn't know he kept those filthy pictures. I didn't know."

I was pretty sure that Aunty Joyce was telling the truth. She didn't know. But I did. I remembered Julie's words while she was swinging to and fro. "He'll hurt you," she had said. She had, afterall, been talking about Uncle Bob. Like father like son. It was Uncle Bob who had given her the VD and she had passed it on to Anthony. Why else would Bob have gone along with it?

"What about Dr Eliot and Julie's boyfriend?"

"And Ellen's house last night," I added.

"Before I left Bob last night he told me that it was more than a cover-up. Anthony had become obsessed. He thinks the boyfriend was about jealousy." She shook her head and gripped her sweater. "I don't know." She turned to me and said, "After you had left Bob they had a slanging match. He told me about it last night. He told Anthony what Dr Eliot had said to you. Anthony killed Dr Eliot because he was frightened that the truth was coming out. By the time I got back from the hospital he had gone . . . "

"To Ellen's place," I completed it for her.

"I went straight to his room and found the pictures." She nodded toward the shoe-box and shuddered. "When he came in this morning he saw that I knew and just ran out to the sheds. I knew you'd be coming. The police. I've been waiting."

Superintendent Scott took it all in and nodded slowly. He said, "I want you to stay here, Mrs Delaney. Understand?"

Her eyes were wide and bloodshot. She nodded then said, "Please don't hurt him. He's . . . backward." She broke down and slumped against the drainer. Her sobs were uncontrollable.

We could surmise, I suppose, and imagine the fifteen-year-old Anthony Delaney, perhaps unaware that he was following in his father's footsteps, terrified that his secret was going to be blown, creeping to Julie's house, knowing that her parents were pissed out of their heads, creeping up the stairs. What was it that woke Julie? A noise? The fumes from the paraffin or petrol? She came out of the bedroom to find him lighting the fire. She tried to call her parents. They struggled, the paraffin spilt on to Anthony's arm, the flames leapt up at him. While he put them out she ran for the front door. He caught up with her. His blistered arm tried to pull her back. Behind him the fire was raging. Somehow she got away, into the woods. With the fire spreading, he couldn't hang around. The following day, or the day after that, Julie was found in the woods. 'I did it', she said. 'I did it!' she remembered, but remembered the words, not her actions. Yes, she did it; she tipped the paraffin that caught fire on his arm. 'I did it! It was me!' And everyone that counted believed her.

I followed Superintendent Scott out on to the concrete yard and took a deep breath of the fresh air. It tasted good and clean. Agreeable.

We could still hear Joyce Delaney sobbing. From an upstairs window the record still played on. He paused at his car to put the shoe-box on to the front seat. He lifted his radio.

"I'm calling in the local nick. No point in me getting involved any further." He sighed. "What a fucking mess!"

I left him talking and wandered past two vans to the corner of the shed. It was a huge corrugated affair, more of a barn that housed machinery, a tractor and tip-up lorry. Some oblong blocks of straw were piled high at one end. By the open door lay the flame-thrower. A simple affair, a jet, a nozzle, the tank for paraffin, the pressure pump at the back. So simple and yet so lethal.

I heard a voice, a man's voice, slightly high-pitched and squeaky. "Don't come any closer!"

Anthony Delaney sat against the shed wall, his head resting back against the rough wooden slats, his legs flat out in front of him. He was no more than twenty feet away from me. He was watching me. His eyes were clear, his skin the colour of the straw about him. He held up a can, perhaps a two-gallon can, and tipped it back on to himself. The liquid flattened his hair and soaked his clothes. I could see the wet stain gathering pace along the legs of his jeans, the little pool gathering around him.

Scott appeared at my side and nudged me. He raised his hands in a pacifying gesture and very slowly edged towards Delaney. His voice was calm. "Anthony, no point in doing anything silly, is there? You need help. We can help you, really. None of it's been your fault. Just stay loose, Anthony."

Anthony Delaney watched his approach for a moment then smiled. It was a simple sad little smile. He held up the cigarette lighter, shrugged his bony shoulders and flicked a spark.

He went up like a Roman candle. The petrol ignited with a whoosh and engulfed him instantly. He screamed and rolled over twice. His arms and legs jerked as the fire raged and then he lay still, a blackened thing beneath the dancing flames. We watched his ears and nose melt as though they were made of plastic, his flesh begin to peel away.

Apart from stopping the fire spreading to the bales of straw, there was nothing we could do. The first burst of heat was too intense for us to get close enough to help. Beside the door a tarpaulin was heaped on the floor. We dragged it across holding it up as a shield. Perhaps only ten seconds had elapsed before we had covered him but in that fierce heat we were probably five or six seconds too late. The flames still licked around the edges. We stamped at them, kicking the fire that clung to our own shoes. The smell of burning clothes and flesh finally got to me and I threw up. I staggered back against the wall trying to stop myself from falling.

Scott grabbed my arm and led me out into daylight. "Sit down," he instructed. "There's nothing we can do."

I did as I was told and slid down the shed wall to the concrete floor. He gave me a Benson's and put one between his own lips. It took him three attempts to light them. As I moved the cigarette from my lips it shook violently, like a kiddie's sparkler.

Out of the window of the house Judy Collins sang on. She was building a tower to the sun, a dream to escape the depression. Begging for a fucking dime.

Tell me about it.

TWENTY-ONE

The vomit still lingered in my throat, along with the smoke and the smell of burning flesh.

It was still only mid-morning when Superintendent Barry Scott drove me back to Mill Hill East. A low sun had appeared; its rays flickered through the bare trees.

The countryside slipping past or the sleepless night had put weights on my eyelids but even when I closed them I could still see the bulging eyes wavering in the heat, and the blackened flesh peeling away from bone.

His voice shook me awake. "Do I get the information?"

"I'll promise you this much: if I get anything I'll give it to you under one condition."

"I'm listening."

"There's one name on the list, someone I know, not a very big fish. I want him thrown back into the water, no questions asked."

"You're talking about your ex-wife's husband? What's his name? Roger Aremetei?"

"How the fuck did you know that?"

He smiled into the rear-view mirror.

"What do you think this is? Jesus, Lenny, you've been closer to Delaney than his nurses have. That had to have my approval. To give it I had to have you checked out. That simple. We know all about Roger; have done for weeks."

He paused before adding, "I'm not really interested in little shits like him. Nor would you be if it wasn't for your kids."

He had me there. I nodded to myself.

We turned from the Ridgeway and cut through the fields. Even before we pulled up in Delaney's drive, Scott was looking very concerned.

"There's something wrong," he said, his voice edgy. "Very wrong."

I glanced about. Everything seemed quiet to me. But that was just it. Too quiet.

"The cars are gone. My people have gone!"

The car came to a halt, crunching on gravel. He pulled down the dash and took out a small black handgun.

"Stay here!" he ordered.

"No chance!"

I followed him from the car. He kept low as he ran through the bushes along the drive. I kept lower. My heart began to pound. This wasn't my scene at all. No way. I left all this shit to Humphrey Bogart.

Mario lay on the path that ran down the side of the house to a high ornamental gate. He had been raked by an automatic. Patches of blood stained his clothes, the last one spreading from his knee. A small pool of blood had turned the dust on the concrete slabs into dark sludge.

"Oh fuck!" Scott said and moved on. The same words ran through my mind, only louder.

There was a movement to our right, in the bushes. Scott swivelled his gun and held it two-handed.

"Don't shoot," came Nick's strangled voice.

While Scott covered me I drew back the bushes. Nick was sitting on freshly turned earth leaning against a pile of foliage that was bending under his weight. His jacket was open. His white shirt was coloured red in two serious places. Blood had run down and soaked his trousers.

"Thank fuck," he whispered. "It was Walker," he gasped. "DI fucking Walker. They got to him. The bastard's been paid off. But I got him. He's over there."

We turned to look. Walker lay in a crumpled heap near the line of trees. Even from a distance we could see a neat black hole in the side of his head.

Scott's mouth dropped in disbelief.

Nick drew a tiny breath and flinched. He went on, "He told your guys you'd been on the radio. Wanted them back at HQ. They took off about ten minutes ago."

The policeman pulled himself together. "What's the situation now?" he asked.

"They're inside."

"How many are there?"

"Four. They're good. Two of 'em are kozzers. I recognized 'em."

"How long have they been in there?"

"Four, five minutes at the outside."

Scott looked around, searching for a plan. "I don't believe they just took off, not simply on Walker's say so," he snapped. "My people would need more than that. They aren't amateurs!"

"If they're not, they're bent!"

"I don't believe that either."

"I don't give a monkey's fuck whether you believe it or not. It's still true. These ain't fuckin' love bites on my chest!"

"I've got to get some back-up," Scott said. "The radio."

Nick smiled and coughed. A trickle of blood fell from his lips.

"Back up, yeah," he mocked. "But whose fuckin' side will they be on when they get here?"

"You're right, there's no time anyway." He turned to me. "Stay here, Lenny. No one's to get that information. Understand?"

Crouching low, the policeman hurried off toward the house. A minute went by. I strained to hear what was happening. Nothing. Nick shifted his weight and pressed a gun into my hand.

"He might need some help," he said. "You point the end with the hole in it."

More blood smeared his lips. He wiped his mouth on the back of his hand and examined the skid marks.

"Fuck it," he said. "If you was a reasonable sort, you'd call me an ambulance, from the car."

I nodded. "Nick, boy, I'll do it from here. You're an ambulance."

He smiled and said, "See, I always knew you had a sense of humour." His smile was cut short by another cough and more blood.

"I'm not waiting any longer," I said.

He nodded. "Good luck, Kid."

At a crouch I followed after Scott to the corner of the building. I needn't have bothered crouching. As soon as I got there two men appeared. Both had silenced revolvers and both pointed directly at my head. They had seen my approach and had waited just around the corner.

They were in their forties, slick black hair, tanned faces, craggy

223

worn looks. They looked like bouncers, but well-off bouncers. Their clothes screamed expensive; below the knee overcoats, black, wool, double-breasted, straight out of a forties gangster film.

My gun was taken. I hadn't even touched the trigger. One of the men, they both looked the same anyway, marched me toward the front door. The other made his way over the garden to where Nick lay. I heard two thuds and glanced back to see a tiny cloud of white smoke clinging to the winter foliage.

I was pushed up the steps. The door opened without me touching it. Superintendent Scott lay just inside the hall. I couldn't see a mark on him and his back rose slightly as he breathed. But he was unconscious. I was shoved again and had to step across him. I walked across the parquet to the living room.

A man sat waiting in the winged armchair. Another stood at the door. Delaney lay on the sofa where I had last seen him and his position had not altered much either. His dressing-gown had parted; one side of it draped down to the carpet. It left an expanse of naked flesh. His penis lay across the top of his leg. But modesty wasn't concerning him. Nothing concerned Paddy Delaney anymore. Nothing at all. His eyes were closed. His body that I could see was white. White with a tiny patch of red spreading on his chest.

The man in the armchair crossed his legs and flicked ash from a cigarette into a glass ashtray at his side. He nodded toward Delaney and said, "I've always thought that the circumsized dick never lent itself to the macho image, know what I mean? He doesn't look much does he? When you see a man with his dick hanging out he seems kind of vulnerable, unprotected. It's funny you don't get the same impression with animals, ain't it? On the other hand, not many animals walk around with their dicks hanging out, do they? Even monkeys seem to have 'em tucked away until they want to use 'em. And donkeys, donkeys carry them in a sheath. You noticed that? Funny old fuckin' world, really." His eyes bored into me, waiting for a response. He flicked more ash and said grimly: "He was already dead when we got here. I shot him in the chest just to make certain . . ." He nodded. "But he was dead."

I looked at him and waited. I felt surprisingly calm.

"Lenny? Lenny Webb, isn't it?" The man spoke again. His lips were wide, like rubber. "I've heard your act. You ain't bad, Kid." He waved the air. "Listen, you've got something that belongs to us. Need I spell it out?"

"I haven't got it yet. It was put in the post to me."

He nodded, "Yeah, that's what Nick said. First-class. It should get to you on Wednesday. Monday and Tuesday are bank holidays. We have far too many holidays in this country." He chuckled. "I want you to give it to Roger. Understand?"

I frowned. I think my mouth dropped open. "Why don't you just wait for the postman yourself?"

"Dear boy, you must be joking? After this little party there's going to be people crawling all over the place. Your place too, unless it looks good. I can't take the chance that one of the good apples will get there first, can I?" His smile was mirthless. "Just to make sure you give it to Roger I'm going to hold on to some of your property. Then it will be a fair exchange. I believe in fair play, Lenny."

He smiled. It was an ugly smile without the slightest trace of humour. "I'm going to keep them down in Portsmouth an extra couple of days. They can come home on Wednesday, after the first post. That make sense to you?"

I nodded slowly while my gut twisted into little knots. I felt giddy.

"We better be on our way then, Lenny. I'd hate to outstay my welcome. When Superintendent Scott wakes up you better tell him . . . Tell him that we know where his wife and kids live too. Tell him what the arrangements are. He'll understand. He strikes me as a sensible sort of chap. Oh, and remind him that he doesn't know which faces in his office are on his side. He'll understand. Fuck me, Newquay in the summer is one of our biggest outlets. All those fuckin' spaced-out surfers." He chuckled. "These country kozzers, you've gotta believe them, haven't you?"

He struggled to his feet. The others moved with him. He paused and raised a finger. "I almost forgot," he said. "The girl. Delaney's sister. What is she, on dope or what?"

I shrugged weakly.

"Well she's out of her fuckin' head."

He said to the man behind me, "You better get her." He looked back at me and explained, "Had to lock her in the hall cupboard. She should be locked up, mental case like that. I don't know what this country is coming to, letting people like her loose on the rest of us. I blame the fucking government! I mean, the streets just aren't fucking safe anymore, are they?"

I was reeling. I could hardly believe what I'd heard, or rather, I did, and that was the problem. The thoughts came at me from all directions. I wanted to run and hide and find some time to calm down and marshal my thoughts. Plan. My legs were shaking so much it was difficult to stand up.

"Oh yeah," the man said again. He stopped a few feet in front of me. "We better make it look as though you're an innocent in all this, otherwise someone might decide that you're to blame." He raised his gun.

I felt a terrific thump in my shoulder. It took me back three or four paces until my head cracked against the wall. I glanced down. There was a neat hole in my jacket. It wasn't red or anything like that, nothing like in the films. But I could feel something very warm spreading out beneath my shirt. It wasn't a sharp burning pain; it felt almost numb, the sort of pain you got with a dead leg. But in the shoulder. Michael Caine would have handled it without a problem. Jack Carter would have handled it. But I began to slip. Amoebas began to swim before my eyes, swim and divide and blur my vision. I hit the carpet and stayed there with my back against the wall.

I didn't see them leave. I heard the front door slam. They must have released Julie on the way through the hall.

She came into the room in a trance, moving with cat-like, slow-motion ballet steps. When they arrived she must have been in bed. All she had on was a satin nightshirt that clung to her thin frame like tissue paper. Her face was pale without a hint of make-up. Her eyes were glazed and slipping.

Suddenly, as the room faded on me, I saw it all clearly. She was tripping, perhaps even sharing her brother's dope; not the crack, but any combination of the other shit, speed, uppers, bennies – Ecstasy. New Yorkers, California Sunshine, Mexican Hats. Yeah, that was probably it. Paddy had been to Mexico.

In her tiny hand she held Scott's gun.

I tried to sit up but the carpet kept moving toward me.

226

"Julie," I heard my own voice. It was a whisper, nothing more. The room tilted. The side of my face touched the carpet. "Julie," I tried again but she wasn't listening.

She knelt beside her brother's body and stroked his cheek with her free hand. "You're sleeping," she said. "It's only a game."

I mouthed some more words, "Julie, for Christ sake!" I could hear them. I could feel my lips moving. Yet they made no impression on her.

"It's a game for lovers," she said. She stroked down across his dark unshaven chin, down his neck, through the pool of blood on his chest. "It was a game," she repeated.

I tried to shout at her: "I told you I was never any good at games!"

The pain was spreading from my shoulder, throbbing into every part of my body. I wanted to close my eyes; sleep would take it away.

Her fingers continued on, spreading a trail of blood downward across his body. She lifted his penis and let it fall back, a dead thing, covered now in her red fingerprints.

"Oh my love," she said. "It was me. I did it! It was all my fault!"

"It wasn't!" I heard my own voice screaming. "It wasn't you! Julie! Julie!"

She rose up above him and began to sway. For a moment she held the gun to her face. Her tongue flicked at the cold metal. "Oh no!" she cried. "Oh no! Oh no! Oh no! It's my fault. Entirely my fault!"

She shuddered and ran her free hand up and down her body, raising her nightshirt on the upward stroke. I could hear the satin whisper. It rose up to her waist. She straddled him on the chaise longue and very gently lay down on top of him. His blood squeezed out between them and ran down his side. Some of it smudged her arms and legs.

"It's only a game," I heard again and watched helplessly as she raised the gun again. Her tongue flicked out to the end of the barrel, and then slowly, so slowly, her lips closed over the cold black metal.

I screamed just as the gun exploded. There was no silencer this time, just a loud crash that rattled the windows. The window next to me rattled just as it was splattered with red dots. I felt

227

the warm splashes on my face. Some of them collected together with my tears and ran down and dribbled across my lips. They tasted salty and sweet. A tuft of black hair drifted down on to the carpet just a few inches in front of my eyes. I watched it land, a gossamer thing, a thread of glistening black, one end touched in red.

Go and tell old Ted Lewis it wasn't raining, not on the outside, at least. He was the guy who wrote *Get Carter*, the gangster film starring Michael Caine, the one my old brother ran for me twice over. Before he started breaking into houses and got himself slammed away for six years. Did I mention that he died inside? They said it was suicide. He hanged himself from some window bars. I remembered those days. The 16mm projector used to hum throughout the film. The film used to break at least twice in every show. He used to stick it back together again with little white stickers. But they were good old days. I forced myself to remember them. Think of Britt playing with herself, think of Caine. Zulu. Harry Palmer. The geezer who shagged his daughter's best friend. What was that? Rio? Yeah, Rio, Rio de Janeiro, that rang a bell somewhere. I needed to think of anything to get away from the nightmare in front of me.

TWENTY-TWO

I was in hospital for the best part of two days. They found me a bed after ringing a dozen wards. I was surprised it was that easy. According to the papers most of them had closed down. They took a bullet out of me and did some stitching and let Superintendent Scott in to see me. He was in another ward but he was mobile. He had what they called a hairline fracture of the skull and he was in for observation. I gave him the message and upset him. Finally he said, "We'll have to make some statements. Are you going to mention the postman?"

"No chance," I said. "Sod that for a living. These people mean business. I'm not putting my kids at risk."

He nodded. There was nothing he could offer and, now that his own family had been threatened, nothing that he wanted to offer.

"They let me out to get some air this morning," he said. "I went for a walk. Got on a bus. Ended up I don't know where. A park someplace. There was some kind of castle at the entrance. I walked round and round, trying to get it straight in my mind. I watched the milkmen, then the postmen. Christ, they start work early. Know what I mean? I was just trying to put things into perspective."

He took my front door key out of his pocket and placed it carefully on the small bedside unit.

In Delaney's house he had come round and stumbled over to me. While we waited for the police and ambulance I gave him a brief outline of what had gone down. It was my suggestion that he take the key.

Now he winked and smiled. "We'll get them," he insisted. "Eventually. One day we'll get them. But not until we know who to trust."

He gave me a secret Benson's and lit it, then kept an eye open for the nurse. There were no-smoking signs everywhere.

I drew in the smoke, coughed, and said, "That's good."

He gave me a plastic cup to use as an ashtray.

I asked, "So what happens now? Back to the West Country and the wife?"

"I should be so lucky." He grinned. "I've still got a long list of names to work through. Paddy's memory was pretty good. Scams, bungs, wages, back-handers, we're talking corruption on a pretty big scale, from minor roadworks to full-blown developments. Even one or two of your friendly neighbourhood banks and building societies are going to be looked at pretty closely."

I shrugged and said, "Well, at least it's a start."

He threw me one of his wry smiles. "See you around, Kid," he said, and made for the door. It opened just as he reached for the handle.

Ellen stood in his way. He stood aside for her and flashed me a curious look before closing the door behind him.

"I hope these aren't sour," she said and placed a lumpy brown paper bag on the side table.

"Sour grapes? That sounds ominous."

She saw my cigarette and narrowed her eyes. "How could you, in hospital?"

I flashed her a quick smile and said, "I'm trying to give them up. I've already switched to a more expensive brand."

She looked puzzled.

I explained, "So that I'll be able to save more when I give them up!"

"Oh, Lenny!"

I explained in detail what had happened in Epping. She took it all in, horrified. She already knew about Julie. The police had contacted her but the papers were full of it anyway. I didn't mention the threats or the police involvement. There seemed little point in putting her at risk. By now I knew Ellen Zahavi. If she learned the truth her first stop would be Fleet Street. Right now that wouldn't help any of us.

"Himanshu's staying over here," she said. "He's talking about using some of his capital to extend the Wood."

"Blimey, that sounds good."

"I am surprised." She gazed at me softly. "Looking after me has made him half human again. I think we've actually turned back the clock. Does that sound silly? Anyway, he's asked, and I've decided, to move back in with him, Lenny. Give it another go." Her colour darkened a shade as she smiled awkwardly, mildly embarrassed.

I nodded gently and said, "That sounds like a pretty good idea."

She stood up to leave and hesitated. "I'm still in shock over Julie. It will take me some time."

"You'll be able to write your own prescription," I said jokingly and wished I hadn't.

She leaned across the bed and kissed my cheek. "Thanks for everything, Lenny," she said. "The intro to Bennie Green and all that."

"You're welcome, Ellen."

She stood for a moment, uncomfortable, shifting her weight.

"It's been very . . . " She searched for the word.

"Different?" I suggested.

"Interesting," she said with a little smile.

As she reached the door, I said, "Keep the fight going, you know, don't let the bastards get away with it."

She smiled briefly. "Don't you worry about that. They're already quaking in Whitehall. Can't you hear them even now?"

"I do believe I can," I said.

She went out briskly. That's how I would always remember her. Brisk. Born in the dark days of the forties but very much a nineties woman. A petite, attractive, pain-in-the-arse, how did it go? One-woman-crusade?

They sent me home in a sling with a bottle of pills in my pocket. I couldn't wait to get there. Ever since the threat had been uttered Donna and the twins had never been out of my mind. Even during my conversations with the police the thought of them overshadowed all else. It was there all the time, the cold fear, throbbing away like the pain in my shoulder. That Superintendent Scott had been on hand meant that the interviews went smoothly. I signed my name. That was it. The use of my door key had been my idea but, even so, the thought of his being seen worried me silly.

Roger was waiting for me. We took the lift up in silence. He knew exactly what I was thinking. I didn't ask him in. Instead I opened the door and blocked his way. The buff-coloured envelope lay on the mat where Superintendent Barry Scott had left it after making his copy. I picked it up and turned back to face Roger.

He shrugged. "Don't worry," he said coldly. "I'm off, just in case."

"What do you mean?"

"Spain sounds nice, at least to start with."

"What about Donna and the kids?"

"What about them?" he said blankly.

"If I see you again I'll stick a knife in your face."

He smiled and took the envelope. "You ain't going to see me again."

He turned to go then paused and without looking back he said, "Those people you met, it was their suggestion. That I took a holiday. You don't mess with people like that, man. What they say is law. They're the people who rule. Know what I mean?"

He didn't see me nodding in agreement. Instead he walked away toward the lift.

The next two hours were the longest in my life. When the phone rang I snatched at it and clobbered my ear. Donna's voice came on and I breathed a sigh of relief. It sent a shudder down the line.

"What is it?" She asked.

"Nothing, baby. Where are you?"

"Portsmouth Station, would you believe? With two cases and three kids!"

"I'll come and get you."

"No, man. Don't be silly. Look, the train's at three-ten. Find out what time it pulls in and meet us at the station."

"I'll be there. "

There was a lengthy silence before she said, "I'm running out of money, so just listen and don't interrupt me. We're goin' to stay at my dad's place for a while. Roger's gone. He won't be comin' back. I need some time to work things out." She paused. Just before her money ran out she added, "He was going anyway, but I wanted him to go."

I saw the twins first, Jack and Laura, as they pushed through the glass door, wide eyed and open-mouthed, and then Donna behind them, carrying the baby. Behind her my ex father-in-law, John Gresty, looked happily across the sparkling room. They stood bathed in the scatter-shot light from the glittering ball. Some of the customers saw them and pointed, surprised to see children in the club. The band hit a couple of crazy notes and the number fell away. The silence spread across the wide room and out into the bar area.

"Will you look at that," Mike said. "Ain't that Donna?"

Clarinet turned to me. The spot glinted in his eyes. "Man, ain't that your ex?"

"Yeah," I said. "Yeah."

The twins continued to look around as though the place was Disneyland and Santa's grotto rolled into one. They saw me on the stage and tugged at Donna's coat, pointing excitedly. She smiled and followed the line of their tiny hands.

Donna bent down to speak to the twins. They nodded and their faces lit up even more. She handed the baby to Peter Selvey who had emerged from his office perhaps frightened to death first by the utter silence in his club and then by the kid's voices. He held the baby at arm's length, momentarily horrified. His eyes skidded towards the baby's face and then he smiled. There was something deeply maternal in it. He drew the baby to his chest and began to rock. His staff behind the bar smiled at one another. There was sympathy, but more than that, there was delight.

Donna straightened her dress, looked directly toward us and started to walk with purposeful steps. People in her path stepped aside.

Keith leaned across to Alan and smiled sweetly. Alan nodded, cherishing the moment. And from the drums Mike said, "Cool, man!"

Donna stood below our platform looking up at me. She beckoned me forward. I leaned down toward her.

She hesitated then said, "I told them we'd go and find their old man. That all right with you?" She smiled. I lifted her on to the stage. My shoulder hurt like hell but I didn't even flinch. I almost passed out but I didn't flinch.

"You're pretty good, man," she whispered. "Do you know that?"

Peter Selvey was in another world, rocking and cooing, the children were in a magical place, open-mouthed at their parents' embrace, old Clarinet had tears sparkling on his fat cheeks, and Mike was hitting his drums as though he had discovered a brand new acid.

Cell was looking on quite bemused. Alan and Keith? They had given up the music and were holding hands. Doing their own thing, like they always did. And old John Gresty? He was beaming so brightly his smile lit up the whole room.

The whole wide world was spinning; applause was in my ears, ringing, bursting, turning the festive season into something festive again.

Well, fuck it! Know what I mean?